From

the

Garden

of

Memory

FROM
the
GARDEN
of
MEMORY

A NOVEL

*Dwight
Williams*

G. P. PUTNAM'S SONS
New York

G. P. Putnam's Sons
Publishers Since 1838
a member of
Penguin Putnam Inc.
200 Madison Avenue
New York, NY 10016

Library of Congress Cataloging-in-Publication Data

Williams, Dwight.
From the garden of memory / by Dwight Williams.
p.   cm.
ISBN 0-399-14331-9 (alk. paper)
I. Title.
PS3573.I44853F76   1998   97-52733 CIP
813'.54—dc21

Printed in the United States of America
1   3   5   7   9   10   8   6   4   2

This book is printed on acid-free paper. ∞

Book design and photo by Amanda Dewey

ACKNOWLEDGMENTS

I am indebted to the following for their support and wise counsel: Kim Witherspoon, Gideon Weil, Julie Grau, Laura Yorke, Hanya Yanagihara, Steven Kozler, Elizabeth Wagner, John Brennan, Mitch Globe, Greg Johnson, Peter Michalson, Dick Gottsegen, Amy Williams, Trace Reddell, Rob House, Charlie Gardenhire, Joe and Azar Doyle, and Tessa, Chelsea, and Jennifer Haynes Williams. I would also like to thank my mother, Faith, and J. R. Heikes.

For Jennifer

Romeo, come forth; come forth, thou fearful man.
Affliction is enamour'd of thy parts,
And thou art wedded to calamity.

Romeo and Juliet III, 3

REALM
of
MEMORY

one

The children of Fayette believed the house to be haunted. It stood
at the geographical center of town, built of limestone, with lacquered oak gingerbread cutouts tucked in the summit of each
gable. Through a screen of willow and soft maple they could see
the dark green moss that flourished in the rock crevices and, at
night, the glass-shaded table lamps that lit the front windows in a
subdued yellow glow. Even some adults who had been inside quietly reported to neighbors that the air itself seemed mysteriously
fraught. The chaos of the family's past, they claimed, lurked somewhere within the walls.

But Kate Willoughby, the final descendant of the first Thomas
Willoughby, who built this house in 1859, never thought of herself
as an extension of any distant and menacing legacy. She was not superstitious by nature, so the idea that her home was haunted made
little sense to her. Still, as a child she found the rumor upsetting.
She became self-conscious and reclusive as she approached the delicate years of adolescence, because many of her classmates believed

the rumor, and such children are oftentimes cruel. But in Kate's mind, previous generations stretched back in time in infinite regress, anonymous and harmless. Memory, she believed, could not carry itself very far beyond the grave, nor could it live within the walls of a house. For her there was only the immediate family, void of all history but for a few final mental portraits.

The most vivid of these pictures was a living distillation of a hundred instances in which she saw herself sauntering into the den each night to find her father studying the dull light as it passed through a prism of glass and ice water. Without a word she came scrambling into his big lean lap, in which she knew just how to fit herself. As she lay there, she asked him to read, and he smiled and reached for a storybook. A moment later, her mind was swept away, lost in another place and time. She could recall how he always smelled of coffee and cigarettes, how his black and gray whiskers scratched her tender face. Her body lay impressed within the cove of his arms while he murmured nursery rhymes, *Grimms' Fairy Tales,* then, later in life, *Arabian Nights.* As consciousness faded, she might have felt herself twitching, actually participating, moving about the setting of the story she was listening to. But eventually the land-scape would brighten, and she awoke to find herself inexplicably tucked deep within her feather bed.

There was a fundamental unreality to this brief but happy time when her family was alive. Dread was unknowable. The world that lay outside the stone house was a benevolent and cheerful place, a land to be explored by flying carpet and unicorn. Because her days were so thoroughly intertwined with stories, she grew up thinking that at some level experience itself was but a dream. And in this dream the voices of her mother and father mixed with the image of her older brother twirling her about the living room, the walls slurring, her hands cinched in his solid grip. Then the room slowed and the blurred colors froze.

Kate's brother, Adam, died when she was six, her father when she was nine. After the first death, in 1972, her teachers began to notice a peculiar change in Kate. Not an oppressive sadness or grief, but a premature seriousness, an air of preoccupation not found in girls so young. Most striking was her capacity to concentrate, to focus her mind in such a way that seemed to demand all her attention. Whenever a phrase caught her ear or she read something she thought clever, she would repeat it aloud so that it might stay with her. This might be a verse of Dr. Seuss or, later, a line from Lincoln's house-divided speech, "I do not expect the house to fall—but I do expect it will cease to be divided . . ." Again and again she would repeat the phrase with an immense book parted over her spindly thighs. This was an effort that stood apart from that of the precocious child, as she appeared to be utterly unaware of anyone around her. The habit puzzled her teachers, but Kate's mother, Addy Willoughby, harbored her own theory: her daughter was trying to memorize everything around her for fear that a precious instant might be lost to her forever. After being blindsided by the death of her brother and father, she would do her utmost to preserve what was left of the world.

As an adolescent she was considered plain in appearance and odd in manner, an opinion that would gradually change as she became a delicate-boned young woman. Her hair kept its straw color, her eyes their aqua green. A nervous metabolism burned away all accumulation of flesh from bone. Daily life with her mother grew more peculiar after her father, Cecil Willoughby, died, in 1976. Addy quickly came to depend on her daughter's good sense in practical matters, even as a nine-year-old. Kate drove the family car at age twelve, paid bills, balanced the checkbook, and drove to St. Louis unescorted through her high school years. Neighbors thought it strange but didn't see anything especially harmful in the arrangement other than that Kate was being deprived of a conventional childhood. To her mother and everyone else, Kate seemed an adult, which allowed Addy the luxury of sequestering herself within the walls of her home, away from the curious eyes of a small town. She was forgiven to a limited degree by the community for being touched in this way, having been married to a man whose blood carried dementia and brilliance down through the generations as consistently as other lineages carried Alzheimer's and baldness.

Nevertheless, the townspeople generally didn't socialize with Addy and Kate after Cecil's death. The family's longstanding history seemed a joyless series of years highlighted by extraordinarily hard luck, and it was considered polite to maintain a respectful distance. The men of the Willoughby line tended to die early and abruptly, condemning the women to dull and lonesome lives that gradually ebbed into despair. Inexorable events merely appeared to be playing themselves out. But Kate did have one friend, Martha Duncan, a girl her age whose father had also died suddenly and too young.

It wasn't until well into grammar school that Kate and Martha met. Martha was smart and frumpy, her tiny chin embedded in the top of a short thick neck, her laugh an adenoidal snort. Already at age ten the pink flesh about her waist had begun to marble. Like Martha, Kate seemed out of place in school cliques with her flat blond hair, glimpses of adolescent acne, and mysterious filial demands that kept her from socializing regularly. So every day after school, she and Martha simply vanished within the limestone walls of Kate's home. Here was a young girl perfectly suited to be a friend to Kate Willoughby.

They met in art class. While constructing a papier-mâché piñata with strips of newsprint and flour paste, and smoothing it into the shape of a burro, Kate asked Martha if she was close to her mother. Kate's voice was a quiet mutter issued from behind a sheer curtain of platinum hair. There was a long pause during which Martha tried to meet the question, fix it in the setting of sixth-grade art class. She stared into Kate's eyes defensively, then offered, "Closer than I used to be."

"Your father died," Kate said, petting the saturated newsprint.

Martha nodded, puzzled by the candor.

"Mine died a while ago," Kate went on, not looking up.

Another long silence, filled by the clamor of their classmates.

Minutes later, Kate said, "So now it's just you and your mother?"

"That's right," Martha said.

Somehow they seemed to know each other from that point on.

two

Kate sensed that Martha felt most comfortable when they were outside the walls of her home and its heightened atmosphere of decay. Though Kate didn't know precisely what it was, something about the upstairs in particular seemed to spook her friend.

But this was where the girls came each day after school, as Kate felt she had to be home as much as possible for her mother, and Martha had no other friends to speak of. So Martha sought compromise. As delicately as she could, she indicated to Kate that she liked the baronial setting of the swimming pool, which lay surrounded by flagstone beneath ancient hemlock and oak trees. In place of a privacy fence, the tiny oval pool was sheltered by wild blue-green shrubbery and flora so dense that only splinters of sunlight could penetrate at any angle. There were stone lions with metal pipes sunk into their mouths that once acted as fountains, and the original canvas furniture that had been fashionable in its day. The pool and all the apparatus that went with it had been refurbished again and again but were always in disrepair and conveyed a general sense of abandon. The surface was littered with greasy hemlock needles, twigs, and oak leaves. Algae grew strong and green.

The girls often lay about in this antiquated setting, where one might expect nymphs or cherubs to appear. Kate rehearsed her lines to some play, while Martha made meager efforts at more generic homework. She watched Kate mouthing the dialogue, gesturing on cue, imagining the blocking. The sheer spectrum of Kate's understanding, the ease with which she inhabited other characters, astounded Martha. And Kate was so young. At fourteen, she drove to St. Louis to the Ambrosia Playhouse for class every other weekend. She was the young darling of the troupe, the blond starlet from some nameless farm town that lay somewhere beyond the perimeter of the city. She found she loved the process of complete immersion into another psyche lodged in another world where all events were foretold and nothing was at stake. She spent an hour or so each day that fall on the rote memorization, then worked on how the spoken word would be delivered. The voice had to fit in the character's mouth, she told Martha, the part had to be grounded to her instincts. An actress had to be a human being on stage. Her small lower jaw gaping, Martha nodded in agreement.

The remains of their high school careers occurred in happy little episodes of adolescent drama and melodrama. They grew inseparable. Martha was fascinated by Kate, and Kate found she liked her friend's tacit admiration. So they spent the night together four or five times a week, and Martha's mother didn't seem to care. When Martha thought of Kate, she thought of how she could cross a room with such ease and inhabit a sofa or chair with such languor and economy of motion. Her vertebrae seemed catlike, curving and conforming to whatever she chose to lie upon. Martha thought of Kate's talent, how she could really call herself an actress. If a fortune teller were to predict that Kate would one day become a famous movie star, it would be possible for Martha to believe her.

Together the girls developed a routine. While Addy busied herself in the upstairs—cleaning, constantly cleaning—they would retreat into the living room, where they sprawled on the Oriental rug. In the summertime they drifted to the sleeping porch, where Kate would tell Martha endless stories about her family in alternately serious and happy voices. The hot, damp air cooled as it passed through a rusted mesh of screen that lined the porch. Outside, the sun stood in a salt-colored sky, while inside, the girls lay sheltered within shade, protected from the electric crackle of insects. The wood trim was painted a brilliant white, and the sheets and down pillows on the two beds were white as well. This would be Kate's lingering recollection of this happy time: whiteness. Their brown and red mosquito-bitten skin, their sun-darkened shapes moving through the whiteness of this room, and the gravitation of their spirits toward a wonderful hedonism at age sixteen. Then the world began to tilt.

One hot autumn afternoon of their junior year Kate sat in a canvas chair with a script parted over her thighs. She sighed and stood, then traipsed about the stone edge of the pool, dipping a naked foot into the cool green water. Beyond the silhouette of the house descended a vegetable sun, the sky darkened to a half-light. She slipped out of her clothes and lowered herself into the water wearing her panties and bra. Martha looked on from the edge as Kate eased through the water with smooth, even breaststrokes, her wet blond hair sleekly tapered against her skull and trailing like a painter's brush in the wake of her head. Finally she rose out of the pool, water peeling off her body in clear curtains, and sat beside Martha on the ledge of rounded stone, their legs hanging in the troubled surface. That's when Martha saw something. While admiring the smooth skin, she noticed a faint shape to her friend's shoulder that didn't belong. The line was wrong. She saw it as an imperfection, a blemish. Without thinking, she ran a finger over the taut skin while Kate's feet stirred the water.

"I've never seen that before," Martha said.

"A bump."

"It's new."

"Then a new bump," Kate said. With that she playfully rolled Martha into the pool.

Not for two or three weeks would Kate give it another thought. Not until one evening as she sat at the kitchen table, dawdling through her homework, when her mother noticed it as well. Addy didn't say anything at first. She stood at the kitchen sink, rubber gloves pulled up to her elbows, steam rising from the greasy dishwater, while across the room Kate toyed with a calculator. She saw Kate running her fingers over her shoulder, feeling its shape, its density, her eyes shifting all the while between the calculator and the textbook. Addy said, "What's that on your arm?"

The following afternoon, Kate left school in the middle of her day for a doctor's appointment. Her mother sat in the car before one of the immense brick cupolas that stood above either side of the broad granite staircase leading to the front doors of the high school, having arrived forty-five minutes early. The car silently idled away while Addy kept her fingertips to her mouth, gnawing at the reddened tips, stricken with an agonizing worry that Kate might forget her appointment.

In Addy's mind, the afternoon had to proceed flawlessly. A delicate orderliness had to be applied to the day; no one could be late, things had to go as planned. If the details of Kate's care were handled with precision and grace, then they would somehow conspire to influence the larger process—and ultimately her daughter's health. After the death of a son and a husband, Addy believed that all misfortune was ineffably interconnected. So she sat in tense silence, waiting for her daughter to appear at the summit of the stairs. Not until Kate came carelessly skipping through the doors shortly before one, sunlight running through her yellow hair, did Addy expel a small, deeply reserved breath. The relief she felt was vast. Once Kate was securely buckled into her seat, they made the short drive down a brick street, the rubbery noise of the tires rolling over its surface drowning out Addy's rambling voice.

"I'm sure this is nothing," she announced.

"It's just a bump, Mother."

"This isn't the sort of thing to worry over."

"I'm not worried."

"I'm not worried either," Addy said before lapsing into a silence that extended all the way to the doctor's office.

What was once the back door to an ordinary residence was now the entrance to the cramped waiting room of a doctor's practice. When they came in through the aluminum screen door, they saw that every chair was taken. All around them sat sullen-faced women and their children. There were no men, Kate noted. A room full of women. Addy checked her daughter in with the receptionist, who told them it would be half an hour before the doctor would be available. So they stood in the awkward quiet, Addy's eyes nervously scanning the room for signs of encrypted omens, Kate leaning against the wall, nearly asleep. An hour later, Kate's name was called.

Once they entered the tiny examining room, the doctor had Kate sit on a padded table covered with a sheet of rice paper and asked her questions, most of which Addy answered from a corner of the small room. Meanwhile he arbitrarily inspected Kate's body. Her hands, an ear, a knee, the throat. Whenever Kate looked at the doctor, she felt the need to suppress a rush of giggles. There was a cartoony quality about him. He was a very short and very fat man, his voice ridiculously high in pitch. He was also bald and kept something of a handlebar mustache, like that of a catfish, which he doubtless had to wax into its present shape. Somehow he reminded Kate of Martha. Finally he came to her shoulder and gently poked it with a short, fat finger.

"Does that hurt, Kate?" he asked in his silly voice.

"Maybe a little," she said, staring down at the doctor's opaque fingernail. "It's uncomfortable, I mean."

"And when did you first notice it?"

"Two or three weeks ago."

"Has it changed in size or shape?"

"Yes it has, doctor," Addy answered from across the room. "It's grown."

"Kate?" the doctor said, lifting his brow.

"Yeah. But not very much."

"Hmmm . . ." The doctor appeared faintly concerned. "I'd like to take a needle biopsy, Kate. Just to rule out some of the uglier possibilities."

Kate nodded. She was pretty sure she knew what a biopsy was.

The doctor turned to a set of shallow metal drawers and produced a huge syringe. This too, Kate thought, possessed the bizarre dimensions of a cartoon.

"This looks bigger than it actually is," the doctor said.

Kate didn't understand. Her eyes narrowed.

"It'll be okay, Katie," Addy said, approaching her daughter's side.

The doctor's eyes met Kate's as he turned toward her. Then his cold chubby fingers and thumb fell on either side of the lump. Kate stared about the room as though she could not be sure of the reality of what she was experiencing. She felt her heart throbbing, her palms warming. Time itself seemed queerly plodding. Then the panic heightened once she felt the needle against her skin. With merciless intent it plunged into her sore shoulder, into that tender knot that she had been so protective of. Then she felt the needle tugging at the flesh and saw the plunger fill with a pool of black blood. A moment later the doctor was pressing a cold cotton swab to her shoulder, fumes of denatured alcohol filling her sinuses with sickening swiftness. For a time Kate thought she might vomit. But she wouldn't. Within seconds, the pain and the scent she now associated with pain had dissipated. The ridiculously large needle was put away, the world of familiar shape and proportion returned, and she was okay.

"I'll have to send this to St. Louis," the doctor said, indicating the bloody sample beneath a towel. "We'll know the results in five or six days."

"I'm sure everything's fine," Addy said, maintaining an unnatural smile.

"I'll call," the doctor said.

For the next five days Addy managed to do little other than wait for the phone to ring. Kate, on the other hand, had dismissed the whole experience from her mind almost entirely. All that remained was the residue of unpleasant memory: smell, sound, and image—a composite she could happily put aside, relegate to the survived past.

But the doctor failed to call. This by itself terrified Addy. Before the office had closed on the fifth day, she decided to call, but by the time the doctor came to the phone it was well past regular office hours. He sounded a little put out that she had intruded upon this sacred time of his. Addy apologized, then gently asked whether or not the results of Kate's biopsy were back from St. Louis. The doctor told her to wait, his helium voice strangely cross. Through the connection, Addy could hear him conferring with his nurse, shuffling papers, his feet passing over the linoleum tiles. Then his voice returned to her ear. Addy stood in her kitchen, patiently listening to the doctor's labored breathing as he rummaged through documents. She noted a pause in the rhythm of his breath. The doctor cleared his throat and said quite pleasantly, "Perhaps it would be best to go over the test results here in the office first thing tomorrow morning."

"Is something wrong, doctor?"

"We'll go over the results first thing in the morning," he said in precisely the same neutral tone. Then the receiver in Addy's hand went dead.

Addy didn't sleep that night. At first birdlight she was rousing her daughter, saying in a regular speaking voice that it was time to get up, the doctor was waiting. Kate angrily emerged from a sound sleep. Eventually she stood, dressed in a stupor, then descended the staircase to the kitchen, where her mother stood before the percolator, impatiently sipping a cup of hot coffee, car keys in hand.

When they arrived at the doctor's office, the sun had risen just above the treetops. A faint orange light came through the foliage, throwing half-shadows across the dewy brown lawns.

"We're too early," Kate said as they walked toward the door.

"We'll just have to start the doctor's day a little sooner than usual."

The moment Addy rapped a neatly balled fist against the aluminum screen door, the doctor appeared before them in his bathrobe, smiling, his voice more sanguine than Addy had expected. Her heart lifted upon hearing the friendly tone. This was not the face of bad news.

"Hope we didn't wake you, doctor," Addy said, smiling the same forced smile.

"No, no. Come right on in."

Kate and Addy followed him through the darkened waiting room to a small office he kept deep in the back of the house. He offered Kate and Addy a seat on a short leather sofa while he sat in front of a roll-top desk and sifted through a collection of papers on a clipboard. A small lamp glowed above his rounded shoulder; otherwise the room was dark. From Kate's vantage she could see an arc of soft lamplight where it fell on the doctor's short pink thighs. She thought that if she could lift up that bathrobe she might find a curly tail. She felt a return of the old panic and nausea.

"Well, now," the doctor said proudly, looking at Kate for the first time. "I have the results of the biopsy right here in my hand."

"We see that, doctor," Addy said, impatience ringing in her voice. "And just what are they?"

"Well, I must say, I've never seen anything quite like it. This is something we usually find in adults."

"Yes?" Addy demanded.

"Well, it's a carcinoma. . . ."

"That means it's a malignancy? Is it a cancer, doctor?"

"Oh yes, it's a cancer." His voice was particularly high now.

Addy wiped the sweat pearling along her brow.

"I have *cancer?*" Kate said, bringing a finger to her shoulder. "This is *cancer?*"

"Well, yes. But that's the bad news. There's plenty of good news you haven't heard."

Kate saw the doctor was smiling. Suddenly she couldn't tolerate the sight of this man with his shiny bald head, his dimpled thighs, the absurd mustache—the whole obscene picture he made.

"I have cancer," she said declaratively. Then she turned to her mother. "I have cancer, Mother."

Addy put an arm about her daughter's slender shoulders, careful of the one, and Kate turned into the embrace. She turned into it like a small child, then lifted her eyes to her mother's. "Are you okay, Mother?" she said, brushing away beads of perspiration from Addy's brow as the blood washed out of the older woman's face.

"I want to say something," Addy whispered into the shell of her daughter's ear, "to ask the doctor a question. . . ."

"Go ahead, Mom," Kate murmured in an uneven voice. Her hand trembled as she brought it to her mother's cheek. Addy's only color was that of her garish makeup against impossibly pale skin. "Go ahead and say it."

But Addy's strength was so depleted she could hardly sit upright. She felt as though she were leaving her body, her skin sloughing away. Then something inside her snapped, something thin and dry and brittle. She felt her body lift from the sofa and drift upward like a balloon until her back pressed against the ceiling. As she hovered high above Kate and the doctor, she again tried to speak. But the moment she opened her mouth, her heart began to race.

"I can't believe this is happening," she said in a breathy whisper. "This isn't real. . . . *You* aren't real," she said, pointing to the doctor's Buddhalike belly, her voice growing louder as she lost control. "Your children are supposed to *survive* you. . . ." Then she slumped deep into the sofa's leathery palm, limp and unconscious.

Kate looked back at her mother's helpless figure, the expression of horror frozen on her bloodless face. Then she looked over at the doctor, who, to her amazement, was still smiling. He brought a hand to his mouth to conceal his inexplicable amusement and chuckled, "Oh, my, my!" Then his eyes met Kate's. A moment later, he yanked his hand away like a little boy caught in some mischief. "She'll be fine," he said. "Just give her a moment."

three

Addy doted relentlessly on her daughter in the wake of the news. She didn't want her rushing through doorways and bumping her shoulder, or drinking too much tea because the doctor suggested that it might suppress the body's immune system. Spinach was served every lunch and dinner. One evening Addy called the Ambrosia Playhouse and told the janitor, the only person there at the time, that she did not want her daughter under those blazing stage lights any more than she absolutely had to be. She offered no explanation, and the puzzled janitor simply replied, "Of course not." Within a week Kate had become openly hostile to the suffocating attention. Though Martha was a witness to the peculiar bickering, she had no idea what it was all about and indeed thought little of it. She and Kate were teenagers. Discord between parent and child was to be taken for granted.

Then one day while the girls lay in the living room, not doing anything but loitering in that wonderfully carefree way that only the adolescent can manage, Martha noticed the plastic Band-Aid stretched over the crown of Kate's little shoulder, concealing the purple dot. The taut skin looked as though it had been somehow messed with. Kate lay with her back to the Oriental rug, her eyes following the slow, steady revolutions of the ceiling fan above them.

"You aren't related to Dr. Brianna, are you?" Kate asked.

"How'd you know?" Martha said, pleasantly puzzled.

"Just guessed."

"He's my mother's brother. Funny you could guess that. How did you guess that?"

Kate only shrugged.

They were quiet a while longer, then Martha asked about the Band-Aid.

"What's that?"

"It's a cancer," Kate said. No smile, no silliness. Ordinarily Martha would have thought it a joke, but the grimness of Kate's delivery, the flatness of her eyes conveyed deadly candor. Kate was serious. By reflex Martha said, "You're joking, of course." Then she watched tears pool in Kate's eyes.

No one would ever know. Kate made this very clear. This would be a secret her mother and Martha alone would share. Her fear was partly of the word itself, the grating ugliness, the way the first syllable was born against the back of the mouth. *Can*cer. Kate Willoughby has cancer. There was the queer novelty, the fantastic incongruity. More than all else was the conventional idea that adults were stricken with such diseases, not sixteen-year-old girls. This made Kate unnaturally old, not unlike, say, the first girl in gym class to develop breasts. Better to be lost in a field of identical faces. Blessed conformity at tender ages.

It was then that Martha began to wonder if there really was something wrong with the family, something innately corrupt in the bloodline. She knew how Kate's father had died by his own hand, how her brother had died a decade ago in Vietnam—an utterly incomprehensible war in her mind. She had a clear view of the pattern of family sorrow that extended back through the last century, as she too had grown up with the stories of the Willoughbys and their haunted house. But she took most to be mere folklore. She understood that they centered around the house itself and its inanimate contents, not necessarily the family. Martha was a bright girl. She understood that diseases like depression and cancer were often passed down through bloodlines, not through estates and heirlooms. She also knew the two diseases were in no way related.

At sixteen Martha fancied herself a scientist, a biologist. What she loved most was viewing the intimate cellular pictures of living tissue on a slide that she herself had prepared, being witness to the random life of the amoeba, the pith of an oak tree, the growth of xylem and phloem. But from time to time even she had magical thoughts. Though she knew better intellectually, she somehow believed that if she could excise a sliver of flesh from a Willoughby and observe it under a microscope, magnification would reveal the source and structure of the familial despair. She could do this herself at the school biology lab. Within each cell of a Willoughby she could see how the genes were marred by something that ultimately expressed itself as calamity in the larger organism. Something like tiny black eels corrupting the orderly process of mitosis. The flaw was just there, buried and encoded within the flesh. But this was a very private suspicion, one she never dreamed of sharing.

Meanwhile, her friend missed school and play rehearsal in a haphazard fashion that fall. Kate refused to see Dr. Brianna for the most routine of tests, and instead drove to a Methodist hospital in St. Louis, near the river. After the short drive across the plains, Kate and Addy came to the Mississippi, the car humming over grated steel, the shrunken brown river far below. Kate parked in the maze of painted spaces that fanned out around the hospital, then they walked side by side, mother and daughter, deep into the massive brick building until they came to the office of the oncologist, whose name they recognized on a small gold placard. Dr. Milo, they were told, specialized in rare cancers, and worked in tandem with a pediatrician. Together they were busy men, professionals. Milo was thoroughly typical in appearance: slender, tall, and nearly bald with a crescent of black hair cut like that of a Roman emperor, with long, soft, almost womanly fingers. A doctor who wore an anonymous white coat and a stethoscope draped about his neck, just as his colleagues did. No absurdities—just a busy city doctor in a busy city hospital. Here the world and all the things in it existed in their proper dimension.

On the first of Kate's visits, the oncologist ordered another biopsy and a series of CAT scans to see if the cancer had colonized other areas of her body. To everyone's immense happiness, nothing was found. Only this one malignancy the size of a large peppercorn on the right shoulder just under the skin. It hadn't metastasized to the bone, so on the second visit the doctor simply prepared to cut it out. The procedure, the oncologist said, could be done here in his office; a surgery suite would be overkill, a waste of money. Addy should wait outside. Kate would be a little groggy afterward, but once the sedatives wore off she'd feel fine. Addy kissed Kate, thanked the doctor, then left, soothed and confident that this could be handled so efficiently. The remedy had been reduced to mechanics. No chemical therapy, no secret battles to be waged within the bloodstream.

The procedure itself was magically brief and painless. The doctor clamped his fingers about Kate's shoulder, prodded it with a needle; then a scalpel passed phantomlike through the anaesthetized flesh. After what seemed but a few seconds, he was telling Kate to lie back and relax until she thought she could sit up. When she finally did so, her mind emerging from the initial fear, she saw her shoulder was neatly dressed in white cotton gauze and tape; on the counter sat a bloody mass in a small glass jar. Within a few minutes she was standing. Addy came in, her smile rigid and nervous at first, then simply happy once she saw her daughter was all right. Kate told her mother the procedure had been hardly painful at all and that she was ready to go home. After taking a few careful breaths she repeated herself and simply left the room. In no time, it seemed, she and her mother were racing through the tiers of St. Louis highways, crossing the Mississippi, and watching the Arch as it diminished in the rearview mirror. Kate was silent all the way to Fayette. Though the cancer was gone, traces of anesthesia still lingered in her blood.

When Addy and Kate got home that night, Martha was waiting for them on the front porch steps. Addy was fantastically buoyant as they came up to her.

"It's all gone," she announced from across the darkened lawn.

Kate, by comparison, was still subdued. She was super tired, she explained as she slowly reached for Martha's hand. But Martha shrank away. A shiver passed through her spine with the anticipation of Kate's touch.

"It's all gone?" Martha asked.

Kate reached for her hand again, and this time Martha let her take it.

"All gone," Kate said.

When distraught, the posture of her neck and head pitched her hair forward, tossing the bangs over the eyes. The pale skin pinkened. And this was how Kate was through much of that colorless winter. One evening as she and Martha sat in her father's study listlessly perusing their homework, Kate lapsed into a long silence. Martha watched Kate's eyes passing over the bookshelves, the uneven plaster under a layer of dingy wallpaper. When Martha finally asked what was wrong, Kate rolled her eyes as if her friend had disturbed a current of pleasant thought.

"The wallpaper," she began, gesturing with a lazy finger.

"What about it?"

"It looks human if you stare at it long enough. It's like skin stretched around the house's ribs."

"That's the lath. That's what looks like ribs."

"It's kind of eerie, don't you think?"

"The plaster shrank."

"I think it's eerie."

"Well," Martha said, now deeply spooked, "it's not."

This was Kate's tendency. When she looked at things, she seemed to look through them, as if intent on seeing what lay beyond the world of physical objects. Her former ability to concentrate evaporated. As the year drew to a close, her moods deepened, while her mother's only grew more joyful. And this made for an odd household. With each trip to St. Louis for tests there was a short period of grisly anxiety to be endured while they awaited the results. Blood was collected, then mother and daughter would drive home and wait. A day would go by and the hospital would call, only to tell Addy that everything was as it should be. Kate, however, never seemed to share in the relief and joy, her mind being fixed on final things.

But a year of unbroken peacefulness passed, a reprieve in the wake of the initial diagnosis. The girls spent another summer and fall around the pool in t-shirts and boxer shorts. As time passed, Martha again became more at ease. It was the house, after all, that gave her the creeps, she told herself. Not Kate. Martha realized that she hadn't come to this conclusion by any method of reason, but how could she explain it? She no longer liked being left alone in particular rooms of the house. But at least it wasn't her friend that made her feel this way. So she and Kate got on with their lives. Through the winter, they prepared their applications for the same college in New Hampshire. Kate received her letter of acceptance in February, then two weeks later Martha found that she too had been accepted. The girls were thrilled, especially Martha. The friendship would carry on in another state, another setting. They would know each other as young ladies, in another time and place, free of the unsettling influence of this house, Martha thought. The future, suddenly visible and bright.

But the happiness lasted only a few weeks. Imperceptibly at first, it occurred to Kate that she couldn't go. She simply couldn't leave her mother by herself in the house. She tried to imagine Addy passing through a day by herself—awaking alone, her voice filling the catacombs of stone, dining without company. Her mother had never lived liked this. Kate pictured Addy alone at the kitchen table, and at that moment she decided that her mother needed her, if only as an answering voice. And thus she came to a decision. But she found she didn't have the nerve to tell Martha, and so she waited. Not for five weeks did she tell her. Not until one day as they lay on the Oriental rug in the living room, their trigonometry homework spread out before them.

"I just can't imagine leaving," she said without turning to look Martha in the eye. "Too much has happened."

The room went silent. Finally Kate turned and saw how Martha's small mouth had contorted. "You can't not go," she whispered as tears thickened in her eyes.

Kate could only part her hands.

The tears spilling over her lashes, Martha quietly gathered up her books and ran out of the house.

Martha didn't come over for a time after that. Whenever Kate saw her at school, she seemed strangely subdued, sedated in a way. As she walked alongside her friend, Kate tried to explain why she couldn't go, saying that her mother would be too lonely, that she didn't want to be so far away from her doctor in St. Louis. What would her mother do? How would she get along? And Kate herself couldn't imagine being away from the house for months at a time.

"And I can't imagine going all the way to New Hampshire all by myself," Martha said as tears again rolled over her thick, pale cheeks. "Have you given that any thought?"

Kate's heart throbbed as she observed Martha's profile—the purple chin buried in the trunk of the thick neck, the sloppily applied eyeliner, the teal eye shadow.

"I don't know what to do," Kate said.

"You can't stay here," Martha said, her voice vaguely mocking. "What will you do if you don't go to college? That's what comes next. High school, then college."

"I don't know," Kate said. "I just don't."

"What about acting? I thought you wanted to be an actress."

"I did," Kate mumbled. "I do. But it all seems so *impossible* now."

"*Why?*"

"Because I just can't leave right now."

With that, Martha began to cry convulsively.

She stayed away for a few days more, then one Saturday afternoon she suddenly appeared at the veranda door, where behind her a gleaming coat of rain covered the streets. Her small gray teeth were revealed in a shy smile, her eyes sad, apologetic. In her arms she cradled a stack of literature on sororities at the college. When Kate invited her in, Martha attempted to act as though nothing had happened. Something in the way she pretended struck Kate as agonizingly desperate.

"I'm thinking about pledging a sorority," Martha said. "Wanna go through this stuff and help me choose one?"

"I don't know anything about them," Kate said.

"Me either."

Together they went into the living room and sprawled on the rug as they were so used to doing. Above them, they could hear the familiar hum of the vacuum sweeper and Addy's voice as she talked to herself. After a few minutes of perusing the various brochures, the subtle comfortable habits seemed to take over, and suddenly they were again old friends, laughing and giggling, slipping back into the familiar rhythm of friendship. They worked like this through the afternoon, comparing statistics, mimicking the glossy pictures of goggle-eyed coeds, imagining Martha in the various communal settings. At times, Kate appeared sad and regretful of her decision to stay behind in this mundane town, while Martha tried to contain the mounting thrill she felt, a kind of superiority over Kate that she had never known. Kate's future stood in plain view, direly unremarkable, while Martha's toyed with the imagination. Martha squirmed with delight as she lay beside her home-bound friend. Suddenly, in the midst of this, they heard something upstairs. It was a noise, more felt than heard, a crumpling thump followed by a shift in the vacuum motor's pitch that had been an everpresent hum against their own voices. The girls momentarily looked up from the brochures as though to affirm that they'd heard the same thing.

"Mother?" Kate called out. Not hearing anything, she shrugged.

Then the girls smiled as they stared into each other's eyes, happy to be back in the company they were so used to. After a few silent seconds they returned their attention to their happy work of choosing a sorority for Martha.

Not for another half-hour did it occur to Kate that the vacuum motor was still howling in the same off-key pitch. It was more of a sharp whine than a howl, hovering above them, stationary and constant. Kate stood and stretched, then ascended the hanging staircase. She called for her mother as she rose and, not hearing a response, quickened her pace with Martha right behind her. Then, as they rounded the corner and looked down the long, dimly lit hall, they saw the heap of Addy's figure and the vacuum sweeper silhouetted against the setting sun beyond the curtains.

Kate approached her mother calmly, almost casually, while Martha kept to the far end of the hall with a hand to her small mouth. Kate called her mother's name as she approached the stilled body and the noisy machine that inhaled the home's sour air. But her mother just lay there. Kate bent down beside the body and took the sweeper's handle from the pale bluish hand. When she flicked off the motor switch, the noise died like a jet engine expelling its final breath, diminishing gradually into a terrible quiet. From down the hall Martha began to whimper. Again and again she mumbled Kate's name, every now and then asking if Addy was okay. Kate didn't respond. She simply took up her mother's hand, feeling its thorough coldness, its infinite stillness. Then, as she slumped down alongside her, Martha began to bawl like a infant. A minute later, Kate sat up as though suddenly comprehending that her mother had passed on and began to cry herself. Her mother wasn't merely asleep. Through her bleary vision she saw that Martha was now standing over her, her large head in her hands, her washed-out brown hair contained in her short plump fingers. Her lipstick was smeared into a red circle at the center of her face like the mouth of a crazed clown. Rivulets of tears clogged with tiny chunks of mascara fanned out over either cheek.

"Shouldn't we call an ambulance?" Martha said in a wretched whimper, her voice choked with phlegm.

Kate began to cry harder. "I think it's too late," she whispered. She took up her mother's hand once more, brought it to her cheek, and just sat there. Martha's whimpering suddenly stopped and she said something Kate would not recall for months to come. The words were merely absorbed, lodged deep within the bank of memory without having been comprehended.

"I've gotta get out of here," Martha said, blindly stepping backward, slowly feeling her way with her hands along either wall. "Kate, I'm sorry, but I have to go," she went on, now in a clear speaking voice. "I can't stay here . . . in this house."

At the end of the hall, Martha paused as if to contemplate what she should do next. Her eyes shifted laterally as she strained for the view in each corner of her vision. A moment later, she abruptly spun about as if expecting the presence of a zombie or a ghoul, then, seeing her way was clear, rushed the stairs as if for her life, and staggered down the elegant bend, wheezing and panting.

Kate could do nothing but listen to Martha as she stumbled down the stairs. The timbers of the old stone house shook as she descended, her fettered breath echoing against the aged floral wall-paper. Kate then heard the impact of Martha's body against the floor at the base of the staircase. In her rush to leave, she had fallen. Kate could hear her friend scramble to her feet, and then the hinges of the front door creaked open. A moment later, the broad plane of oak slapped shut. Kate sat, frozen, holding her mother's dead hand. Once the final echoes had died away, the house was again quiet.

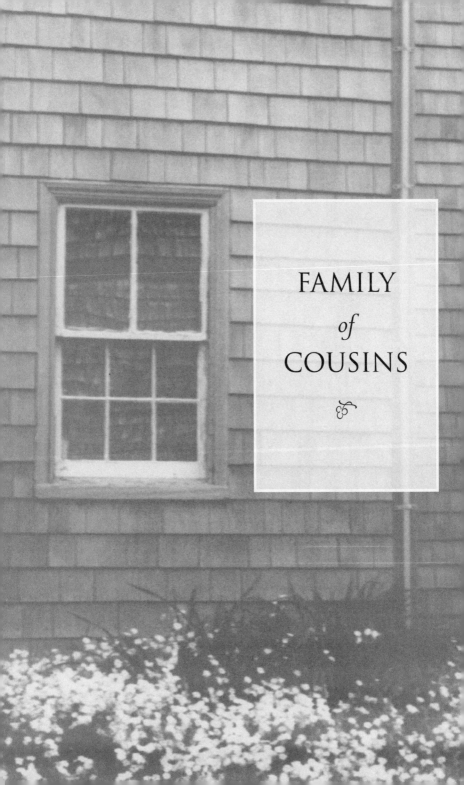

FAMILY
of
COUSINS

❧

four

He was a very large and wealthy man. In certain light he appeared bald, as his fair hair and scalp were of the same pale color. He made his money as a farm implement dealer down in Missouri, and could not only survive but thrive in that uneven economy. What had once been but a single metal building filled with exotic machinery that tilled soil and harvested crops was now the seat of a regional chain. He sold gigantic eight-wheeled tractors equipped with air conditioning, and the sprawling implements that furrowed and shaped the earth in their wakes. His manner was blunt and coarse, always over the top, his voice so steeped in the land from which he came that he could hardly be understood by those of Fayette, this small Illinois town descended from New Englanders. Because of this and his tiny V-shaped mouth, he struck many as stupid and bull-headed. But Uncle Charlie was smart enough.

When Kate was a child, the household was visited every summer by the only other surviving strain of the family, who lived in the boot heel of Missouri. This was the family of Charlie Willoughby, whom everyone, including his two sons, knew as Uncle Charlie. In 1959, his young wife died in a car accident, and for the next sixteen years he raised his son, Gilbert, with the help of an endless stream of Mexican and Haitian nannies and housekeepers, most of whom left the residence after a brief and ugly stint of child rearing under his auspices. Something in the way he treated the hired help, people tended to say. It was widely believed that Uncle Charlie had a good heart but a simple view of the world and its tender nature. In 1965, when one of the Mexican nannies died suddenly, he adopted her young son, whom he named Happy, later contracted to Hap. He did this, he openly claimed, so that his biological son, Gilbert, would grow up with a younger brother, believing as he did that flesh and blood could be manipulated like land.

Two days after Addy's death, Kate was once again among her family's more Southern counterparts, whom she hadn't seen for nine years. Parcels of her mother's clan were scattered throughout the house as well, though they rarely mixed with the Willoughbys. Addy's mother sat next to her aluminum walker in Cecil's study, her mind lost in an Alzheimer's daze. Both of Addy's brothers and her only sister, from Wisconsin, sat smoking cigarettes at the dining room table, looking profoundly out of place in the antique setting, perhaps not unlike Addy herself might have appeared had the spirit of the house not inhabited her skin through the passing of thirty years.

Kate neither looked nor felt well. Martha hadn't called or come by since Addy's death, and Kate secretly didn't expect her to. She had come too thoroughly undone that afternoon, and Kate doubted that her friend was capable of ever entering the house again. From time to time, Kate herself was overcome by a feeling of dislocation, that she was somehow outside her body. Voices tended to meld and become a single dollop of sound. Whenever a relative or a friend of the family approached her with his condolences, it required a heightened level of concentration simply to comprehend what was being said. At times she felt she couldn't trust her faculties of self-control and feared she was embarrassing herself in the midst of all these distorted faces. Panic rose up in her chest and she felt a sudden urge to bolt from the room. But the impulse inevitably faded like a mirage, and she again felt stable.

Eventually she came across her cousins, Gilbert and Hap, and Hap's beautiful Haitian wife, Isabelle, who had gathered in a corner of the living room. Here Kate found a kind of sanctuary. They stood by themselves next to a glass gun cabinet—cool, aloof, and magically detached from the sullen air, together a collection of handsome Southerners, drinks in hand, effortlessly deflecting the attention of complete strangers around them. In a single collective expression her cousins could convey sorrow and humor—they were at once funny and empathetic. And they dressed so well. Thus Kate noted, even in her precarious state of mind, a contrast between the two families: her mother's side appeared to have come to Fayette at the bidding of decorum and obligation, whereas the Willoughbys were here, at the very least, to have a good time while they soothed their unlucky cousin.

The presence of the Willoughbys was also nostalgic for Kate, as there was a greater past shared among them. Gilbert was the same age Kate's brother would have been. They were childhood companions and lived together in her memory as a pair, so seeing Gilbert for the first time since Adam's death brought comfort. They'd been nineteen together, and like Gilbert, Adam would have been thirty-one. The skin about his neck would have been less elastic, his hair thinning, his eyes heavier. Beside Gilbert stood Hap, with his austere gold-rimmed glasses, the lenses of which were so thick they made his eyes appear misshapen, embedded in his plump brown face. He was reserved, as she'd remembered him as a child, though he was now very overweight and not any taller. He was clearly Latino, but somehow seemed Gilbert's true brother. Kate had never met Isabelle, though she and Hap had been married several years. Even in this company, Kate felt an occasional return of the overwhelming sorrow that distorted the world around her. Her cousins seemed to sense this and made jokes at the expense of her other relatives in an effort to put her at ease.

"Your mother's side of the family is fond of hors d'oeuvres," Hap whispered as Kate's fantastically obese aunt floated by, her Chinette plate buckling under a load of paté and candied ham impaled on toothpicks.

Kate brought a hand to her mouth.

Seeing how Hap's comment brightened her mood, Gilbert added, "This isn't a Rotary luncheon. If you want, I'll send the larger ones on their way."

"Gilbert just wants the bourbon all to himself," Isabelle whispered confidentially to Kate.

"They aren't here for the bourbon," Gilbert replied. "They came for the potato salad and angel food cake." He saw that Kate was smiling more broadly, which appeared to please him no end.

Kate felt vaguely flattered that her cousin, handsome as he was, would pay her such close attention. Gilbert had a preening, almost feminine beauty about him. In some oblique way, she felt as though he was here solely to quell her anxiety; she felt safe at his side. Meanwhile, she secretly watched him as he looked about for other targets of amusement. Eventually an obscure uncle of Kate's emerged from the bathroom with his toupee buckled in half, exposing a quarter-cresent of bald head. He looked and was very drunk.

"Um, Kate," Gilbert whispered. "Would you, um, please ask your uncle there to batten down that hair plug?"

Kate didn't want to laugh; she didn't even think the remark that funny. But she suddenly felt a complete loss of control. She turned away from the crowded room, trying to contain the surge of emotion. But it surfaced so violently that a stitch cut at her side. All around them, her mother's family stopped eating and smoking and stared at Kate's glistening red face and doubled-over figure. The room hushed. Isabelle tenderly ran her long brown fingers through Kate's hair.

"I'm all right now," Kate finally said between deep, even breaths. "I'll be okay." And for the time being, she was. She leaned against the gun cabinet and gathered herself. Her eyes cleared, the muscular pain in her stomach faded.

Then, as they stood in silence, Uncle Charlie's brusque voice suddenly filled the room. He wanted to introduce himself and his children, he announced—apparently in order to divert attention from his niece.

"Afternoon, everyone!" he hollered as he threw a thick arm about the neck of each son. "My name's Uncle Charlie, and these here are my two boys. I'm from Missoura. I work for a livin'. Most people I know work for a livin'. That's how our civilization advances itself. But neither of these hooligans has ever held down a regular job. I don't know how you make a livin' without workin', yet they drive around Memphis in new pickups."

Uncle Charlie seemed oblivious to the incredulous eyes upon him. No one could quite comprehend what this outburst was all about, how it was connected to the death of Addy Willoughby. The room appeared to be whirling into chaos.

"This one here's a pianist," Uncle Charlie went on, looking down on the crown of Gilbert's head, "and this one's involved in who-knows-what kinda hanky-panky. They're two of the laziest hillbillies I ever come across. But I'm proud. Gilbert has run through an impressive string of girlfriends lately, while Hap has himself this real sexy wife." He gestured with his tiny forehead toward his daughter-in-law and shouted, *"This here's Isabelle, everybody!"*

Kate was now standing alone in the corner, fully recovered. To her surprise, Uncle Charlie's introduction didn't seem to offend his children in the slightest. Isabelle merely blushed, then toasted her

husband and his brother. The maternal side of Kate's family, however, was horrified. They could only stare and chew their food.
Then, one by one, they slipped out of the room.

In the wake of this episode, Kate lapsed into a hypnotic calm.
The silliness, she understood, broke the vertiginous spells of sadness. She was in control and believed she had her uncle and cousins
to thank. She also recognized the source of her feeling of dislocation. The world seemed to be rearranging itself haphazardly, without regard for her mother's memory. She was just gone. But as the
afternoon passed, Kate felt more and more poised and tranquil. She
realized that she felt best while standing among her cousins, who
magically became childlike in her uncle's presence. She liked the
reassuring influence of Uncle Charlie in particular because he
could be serious as well as jocular. His pink face loomed above
them, spinning tales about the family. Eventually he began to tell
everyone about her own father after he'd returned from law school
and taken over the family law practice.

"You could tell he was a cut above," Uncle Charlie said, ice jin-
gling against crystal as it swirled in a golden pool of scotch. "Had
one of them contemplative minds. Spoke slow, careful. Somehow
you knew it'd be wise to listen."

Kate smiled. Such speech grounded her to the wider family.
At some point, the cool round shape of a full wineglass floated into
her hand, and so the afternoon advanced, Kate's face flushed with
gratitude for these strange relatives whom she hadn't seen since she
was a young girl.

The following morning, Kate awoke with Gilbert, Hap, and
Isabelle on the sleeping porch. They lay curled together on the
massive feather bed, beer bottles and wineglasses scattered about

the room. They rose, slowly and painfully, and in the bathrooms of the house prepared themselves for the funeral.

By early afternoon, the day had turned balmy and overcast. The flat light cast no shadows as the sun stood obscured by swift, low clouds, their frayed bodies occasionally leaking sunlight onto bright green grass. Within the semicircle of mourners, the rosewood coffin descended into black sodden earth borne on maroon ropes, then was covered with fistfuls of soil. Not until the crowd had vanished into a parade of cars did the burial begin in earnest.

Uncle Charlie drove Kate home, followed by the stream of mourners, the jewel-like glint of their halogen beams tossing in the rearview mirror. More hors d'oeuvres, wine, and punch were served in the kitchen and dining room while family and friends lingered throughout the house, discussing in hushed voices what was to be done with Kate and the house and the estate and how they wished only to be so lucky as Addy when their time came. Throwing a massive blood clot to the brain was indeed the way to pass on, so long as it killed you instantly. Kate stood among them trying desperately to make herself small until she found her cousins again. She raised a porcelain teacup to her mouth, holding the saucer to her chest. Then she did her best to make sure that she was always surrounded by them.

Uncle Charlie appeared characteristically boisterous as he circulated through the rooms holding a small glass of scotch sweating through a white lace handkerchief. He told everyone he'd driven up from Missouri, as he always had, in his Suburban. Travel by car or train, he remarked in his Southern grandiloquence, was dignified, whereas airports with their intercoms and congestion simply appalled him. He was a gentleman, a squire from a conquered land, a man who claimed to see the worthiness of those bygone values that held time and space in their proper perspective. The human mind was capable of absorbing only so much stimuli and negating a relatively small constant amount. The car and locomotive had some-how been built with this reality in mind. Though no one seemed to understand his marbled accent, this was what he spoke of as he reintroduced himself to each little old lady, each obscure tendril of this scattered family that seemed so estranged from itself.

After hours of shifting about the house, he finally approached his niece, who appeared to be doing her utmost to manage her anxiety beside Hap and Isabelle. In a sweetly hushed voice, he asked how she was holding up. Without a word she took his thick white hand and led him into her father's study, then closed the door behind her. There in the quiet she simply said, "Addy's dead."

"She was your mother, Miss Kate," Uncle Charlie said. "You shouldn't call her by her name."

"Addy?"

"Yes."

"Why not?"

"Because she was your mother, and she's dead."

"That's right."

"You ain't feeling so well, are you m'honey?"

"I'm feeling better," she said.

Uncle Charlie ran a big gentle hand over her hair as if calming a high-strung pony.

"Oh," he whispered, so softly Kate could hardly hear. "You poor little creature. You poor little thing."

five

By noon the next day, most of Kate's relatives except Uncle Charlie and the cousins had left town. Uncle Charlie would be the one who stayed behind to look after her finances, he announced, to make sure his distant niece would be secure after having entered the adult world with such suddenness. For the next few days, he sat at Cecil's desk and began arranging for Kate a trust fund that would pay for her schooling if she chose to go to college, another that would cover living expenses indefinitely, and yet another that she would not have access to until she was twenty-five. He visited the bank, the law firm. He called stockbrokers on his pretty little niece's behalf. Money would never be a problem. He would see to it.

Before his death, Cecil Willoughby had managed to resurrect the law firm that had languished in the family for generations. After returning from law school with Addy in 1956, he worked with an unflagging resolve, drawing new clients to the firm from surrounding counties. Through these years, the Willoughbys had steadily grown wealthy. After his death, the firm that still bore the family name became an auxiliary source of income for Kate and Addy. On the seventh day of each month, a small percentage of the proceeds was delivered to their mailbox, and through the years a number of the partners in the firm had come to resent the ritual set up by their former employer. Now it was all to go to Kate, and Uncle Charlie found his work cut out for him.

After a few days, however, he discovered that he rather enjoyed sitting at Cecil Willoughby's desk, making phone calls from Cecil's phone, beating up on pencil-necked lawyers, watching over his dead cousin's daughter. And he liked the air of the study, the sense of refuge he found there, this place quite unlike any he had ever known. Uncle Charlie had never been a bookish man, but he liked it when people took him for one. And here, within the study's book-lined walls, he experienced a familiar pride. A few days after the funeral, it occurred to him that he wouldn't mind looking after his niece a while longer. The structure of Kate's life had to be rearranged, and this would take some time. He'd have his files sent up, and for the summer he would run his own operations from Cecil's office. Free enterprise by remote control, he called it. The move would be good for both him and Kate. When he asked her if this arrangement might work, she began to cry a little. "I love you, Uncle Charlie," she whispered. "I love you so much."

From that moment, Uncle Charlie saw himself evermore in the image of Cecil Willoughby. Kate began to sense this the following afternoon, when the high school principal appeared at the kitchen door with a potted geranium in one hand and a gleaming black briefcase in the other. As he stepped inside, Kate recognized at once his reaction to the antique setting. He looked around the room warily, like a child entering a dentist's office.

"This is from your classmates," he announced, handing her the clay pot containing the immature plant. "Everyone's heart goes out to you and your family, Kate."

Without thanking him, she took the flower and placed it on the sill over the kitchen sink.

"I know you're quite a student," he said, still gazing about the room. "Quite an actress too. If you don't want to come back until next week, I believe you could still graduate. In your case, anyway, I think we can make an exception. . . ."

While the principal stammered on and on, Uncle Charlie quietly sauntered into the kitchen. His pale face contorted as he looked down on the bald head from behind, his nose crimped with vague disapproval as though a foul odor emanated from the tiny man.

"You should take your time in this period of transition," the principal continued, unaware of Uncle Charlie's presence. "Come back soon, but not too soon." He laughed with inscrutable insincerity.

At that moment Kate's imagination locked on a mental picture of the school's interior. She saw herself passing Martha in the hallway, neither acknowledging the presence of the other. A sudden panic struck.

"I won't be going back to school," she said decisively. "I'm not going to act anymore either."

"Not right away or not at all?"

"Not at all."

"You might want to think about it before making a decis—"

"*Sweet* mother of God . . ." Uncle Charlie interrupted, his voice bellowing through the room. "You can drop her diploma off anytam!"

The principal jumped. With a hand to his heart, he turned around to see the giant Uncle Charlie glaring down on him.

"You may find a structured class schedule is just what you need," the principal said to Kate as he gazed up at her uncle.

"See here, little fella," Uncle Charlie said, "there can't be so much as a month of school left. So why are you bein' such a ninny?"

The principal's eyes compressed beneath his shiny forehead. "And who might you be?" he asked.

Uncle Charlie's tiny mouth smiled.

"I might be her parent," he said proudly.

"But her father died several years ago."

"Thanks for stoppin' by," Uncle Charlie said.

"I'm not sure I understand. . . . You're her legal guardian?" He paused and held up his briefcase, as if it demanded an explanation. "See, this is something we need to clear up."

Kate took the principal's shoulders in her hands and steered him toward the door. "We'll clear it up some other time," she said. He walked off under her direction, visibly puzzled by this orphan and her oversized uncle.

Once the door had closed behind the principal, Uncle Charlie's sons and daughter-in-law casually wandered into the kitchen.

"What did he want?" Gilbert asked.

"For her to go back to school," Uncle Charlie said. "Can you *imagine?*"

Hap's gaze slowly shifted to Kate. "That principal of yours takes himself pretty seriously."

"Way too seriously," Uncle Charlie added.

And from that moment on, Kate fell into the company of her cousins and uncle as a traveler might fall in with a roving band of carnival workers. Entertaining her seemed like a conspiracy among them. The weather had turned from springtime to summer overnight, so every day was now a fiesta, with parties out by the pool and picnics along the banks of creeks throughout the county. In the aftermath of her mother's death, Kate discovered that such carrying on was not only possible but necessary. Though she understood her cousins' presence to be a mere distraction from the pall of sadness at the center of her world, it provided a kind of structure for a new life. Structure and ballast. Uncle Charlie's family was a society that was kin to her, blood of her blood. She would be walking into a new world from this moment, which she recognized as the present, the infinite now, a present that extended seamlessly into an unknowable future. So she came into her cousins' sphere of living as though they represented a kind of retreat in the face of some great unknown. Her last memory of Martha was tangled up with that of her mother's crumpled body. And both were just gone. The people who had made up her previous life were all just gone.

That Gilbert, Hap, and Isabelle could afford such time away from work didn't strike Kate as strange. She hadn't been around working people since her father had died. For her there was little connection between work and money, or work and independence. These people simply did not hold regular jobs, as nearly everyone she knew did not. Money came from the bank. That was where it was kept. Before you ran out, it was a good idea to go there and inquire about getting some more. They unfailingly gave you whatever you asked for.

But Kate was not so naive in other matters. So long as there was a reserve of cash available to her, she could conduct her life rather adroitly, having run a household since age nine. Everyone knew this about her, so they more or less left her alone—everyone but these four peculiar relatives who had made themselves so at home here. Together they formed their own society, a circle they kept closed to the rest of the town. The summer deepened with their coming and going, sometimes one at a time, sometimes together. But one or all would generally stay behind. In time, Kate's days settled into a reassuring pattern. She was generally the first to rise; an hour or so later came Uncle Charlie. Not until deep into the day would they see his children.

One morning, Uncle Charlie's tall, thick body appeared in the kitchen door frame. A squeal came from his tiny mouth, a release of tension. As if still asleep, he approached the refrigerator and poured himself a glass of tomato juice. Kate sat at the kitchen table in her bathrobe with a yellow pencil in her hand, the morning paper spread out before her. She watched as the pepper grinder showered black and gray flakes into her uncle's glass. He carried it to the table and sat.

"Scotch an' sleep. They don't mix," he said. "Sons a mine still unconscious?"

"Pardon?"

"Still asleep. My sons . . ."

"Hap and Gilbert? Are they asleep?"

"No. M'other sons."

Kate's neck extended, her mouth opened.

"I'm kiddin', young lady. They're the only sons I got. I know they're asleep. Didn't expect 'em up buildin' an empire."

"It's still early."

"Yer up."

"I'm always up."

"Family trait."

"We always got up early."

"That's part a what makes you different, special. Gilbert, well . . . I ain't turning blue over no Grammy."

Kate thought: We have the same family, speak the same language. Why can't I understand him? Then she said, "Uncle Charlie, where did our family come from? How are we related?"

He sipped his juice, then inspected its viscosity, as though it were a rare wine.

"Genealogy an' history's my thing. Know all sorts of minutiae."

"There's a painting of Thomas Willoughby in the cellar. He was the first Willoughby, right?"

"Course not. He's just the first anybody knows anything 'bout."

"He lived here, didn't he? In this house?"

"Goddamn right. But he came from Miss'ippi."

Uncle Charlie paused to chug the tomato juice, then began to speak in his laconic, tour-guide staccato. Kate saw that history was sacred to this large, pale man.

"Ancestry sprung from Thomas and his stepsister, Corbett. Married her in Natchez in 1854. Age thirty-two he decided to bring his seventeen-year-old wife north. Probably not so much out of any moral prescience, as everyone'd like to believe. Had to be a sense of impending doom. Slave owner, after all. Sprawling estate, plantation home with the gaudiest goddamn decor imaginable. In 'fifty-six Corbett bore a daughter, two years later a son. Named the son Cecil. That's my great-great-grandaddy, your great-great-great. Couple a generations later the family tree grows a branch, and you and I part company."

Uncle Charlie's tiny eyes narrowed as they focused on the glass again.

"Probably moved north to evacuate his young family from the anticipated battlefields of a war of conquest. And of course to raise his children as citizens of a victorious land. Coulda juss grown weary of the goddamn heat down there. Sold his slaves, estate. Loaded the family's earthly belongin's onto a north-bound steamboat in Natchez that wouldn't dock till it was north of the confluence of the Ohio. Come St. Louis, he headed overland due north till he found a wooded town in the lower belly of Illinois, not unlike the one he'd left behind. Land a Lincoln. Re-created his home here, only this time by his own sweat and that of hired hands."

Uncle Charlie gestured toward the kitchen window, as if to confirm the evident truth of what he was saying.

"On the town square, built of limestone. Juss like what he had before, with a wraparound porch. Plenty of hired white help. Mighta been a nigger or two, which he now had to pay. Eventually opened a law practice, a small-scale facsimile of what he once had. Spring of 'sixty-one came news from Charleston Harbor, then four years of night. Must've felt they'd escaped something by migrating where they did at juss that time. But nobody coulda known what. Wars ain't like that anymore, Miss Kate. Wholesale carnage. Massive attrition. We cain't comprehend. We juss cain't."

Kate stared across the table, the yellow pencil still clutched in her hand.

"People considered 'em somethin' of a novelty at first. Southern manners, warm-blooded disposition. All that. Accent's faded, though. You don't got it; I spent some formative years in Galveston. You talk like a Yankee, me like an oilman. Back then the family accent was more pear-shaped."

Uncle Charlie parted his hands, palms up, as if to ask if he'd answered her question adequately.

"How d'you know all this?" Kate asked, slowly twirling the pencil in her fingers, feeling its coolness.

He leaned forward on his elbows and looked her in the eyes. "Gotta know where you come from, Miss Kate," he whispered, as though passing along some hard-won knowledge. "Save humans, morphic nature don't have no record a where it's been. We're better than that. In my book, if you ain't got a story to tell, you ain't human."

Kate nodded. This seemed to make perfect sense. Something to remember.

So began a ritual. Every morning Uncle Charlie would stretch within the door frame, then stagger toward the refrigerator. A complaint about cheap scotch, a glass of tomato juice chugged, an anecdote about her grandfather, her father, her mother. As Kate listened, she held her shoulder in her palm and slowly passed a fingertip over the little scar in ever-diminishing circles. One morning Uncle Charlie went on to tell her his comprehensive theory of how history lent coherence to the chaos of experience, that this was its purpose, why our forefathers invented it at all. When assailed by the universal forces of trouble one could look only backward, not forward, and discern the structure of that which came before. All history is but a constellation of stories, he claimed. An elaborate myth, not so different from a dream. It is a malleable thing. All stories eventually run together and become a thing, a single line, just as all rivers run to the sea. "This is who you are," he concluded, taking her chin in his thick fingers. "This is who *we* are. Ultimately, Miss Kate, we become the stories other people tell of us."

six

Fayette was not a town accustomed to strangers. It was a town of white people, most of whom belonged to any one of twenty-three Protestant churches or the Catholic parish. So the sight of Kate Willoughby traipsing through the local taverns and pool hall with a young black woman and her Latino husband was met with silent bewilderment. When the rumor circulated that they were somehow related to the Willoughbys, it created utter incredulity. Because the Willoughbys were a respected family about town, the scuttlebutt was hushed. Nothing, however, could stop the talk. The topic propelled itself, quietly thrived on its own. But this was not an especially intolerant town. It was more like a gathering of kind-spirited gossips.

To many of her neighbors, the relationship Kate shared with her cousins seemed to possess a rather peculiar dynamic. To others, it actually seemed quite normal and proper. But those who thought it strange thought so because of Kate's relationship with Isabelle. They often held hands and embraced in public, and in small towns such displays of affection between young women are seen as more mysterious than they really are. The strangeness, if there was any, lay in their closeness, the uninhibited proximity by which they came to know each other. And when alone, they were closer still.

One night early in June, as they lay in the sunroom, a thunderstorm approached from the southwest. While Gilbert and Hap slept on the floor before the blue flicker of the television, Isabelle silently motioned for Kate to follow her outside. Kate took her hand and walked out into the long grass, smiling as she followed the vague figure through the darkness. When they came to the center of the ragged lawn, they sat together, shoulder to shoulder, their eyes on the silent flashes of approaching lightning. All the while, Kate wondered what they were doing. Eventually the storm broke in cold heavy drops. It was then, with the impact of the first rain, that Isabelle stood and casually pulled her top and shorts off. Then she sat and smiled up at Kate with playful wickedness. Kate stared, quietly amazed. *"Isabelle,"* she whispered before realizing she didn't know what she was about to say. She understood—intuitively. A moment later, she undressed herself, tentatively at first, and they sat naked like that as invisible black clouds pushed the stars and moon into the horizon. In an instant of lightning, Kate saw Isabelle's hands running through her black hair, the wetness of the storm beading on the purple nipples. Kate looked up into the sky and closed her eyes. She listened to the rain all around her. She felt the rain on her skin as she had never felt rain before.

Once the storm passed, they strolled across the darkened lawn toward the pool, where they laid themselves down on the wet sheets of flagstone, their cold naked backs flat against the rock. After a while, Isabelle crawled to the pool's edge, where she slipped into the cool green water headfirst as a salamander might. Kate followed in the same fashion, and for an hour or so they swam underwater, surfacing from time to time like sea mammals, gasping for air. Not until late in the evening did they climb out of the dark water and come back into the house through the doors of the sun-room, where Gilbert and Hap lay just as they had before the storm. They tip-toed over the sleeping bodies, ascended the hanging staircase, and went into Kate's room. Chilled and shivering, they changed into clean cotton t-shirts, then collapsed in the bed on the sleeping porch, swaddled in the sheets and comforter.

A new moon crossed on its belly through clear black sky. A few hours later, a yellow triangle of sunlight formed high on the wall. It swung slowly and precisely across the bed and eventually struck Kate's eyes, waking her. Across hills and valleys of white, she observed Isabelle's brown face, lost in sleep, until the eyes opened. At first they spoke in hushed voices. The night before was mixed up in dream and memory, a shadow in the brilliant clarity of morning. Then Isabelle began to speak soberly, her mind having settled on something.

"Hap isn't what he appears," she said. She'd never met anyone like him, she explained, and now she didn't even look at other men. She felt she was in some holy union with him. *Holy.* It might sound silly, but that was precisely how she felt. Some rare love . . . Physically he never made her, well, swoon—this was true. But women do not live by that alone. She was a woman with a broad imagination, yet she couldn't imagine loving anyone else.

Kate just lay there, quietly listening and learning.

By midmorning they had dressed and wandered down the steep, narrow back staircase to the kitchen. Kate ground coffee and prepared the stainless steel percolator. She hopped up on the counter while Isabelle brought in the morning paper from the porch steps. Finally, Hap and Gilbert came in from the sunroom, dazed with sleepiness. Gilbert quickly grew alert after pouring himself a cup of black coffee. A little later he offered to fix breakfast. Ham and eggs, hash browns, grapefruit. Then Uncle Charlie's voice entered the room. Kate smiled at nothing in particular. The house was filled with human sounds, alive with distinctly human smells. She sat apart from the others, thoroughly astonished. Her new family had arrived.

In June came the funnel clouds. Young row crops were torn from the earth. Later that month, a conical early-nineteenth-century barn was scattered about the county. Sirens filled the night sky. Then came July, August. The summer grew old and hot. The peppermint garden withered, the tea roses shed their petals. After three rainless weeks, the lawns around town began to burn.

Through the hot afternoons and evenings, there was the steady trickle of alcohol. The four cousins would rise late, prepare a picnic basket, drive in a caravan of two trucks and a car beyond the outskirts of town, and lie beside a stagnant muddied creek within the shade of an immense walnut tree. There they would prepare champagne screwdrivers, carve up cantaloupe or musk melon, and become quietly drunk through the afternoon. This was a kind of laziness new to Kate, this genteel ease. In the early evening they returned, only to fall asleep in the sunroom, lying together like a family of cats, the ceiling fan pushing the soft cool air down upon them. Uncle Charlie would wander into the room, smiling but wagging his head with amused disapproval. He would then quietly return to his work in the study.

One morning at the breakfast table, Uncle Charlie explained to Kate how he was at once tolerant of and disgusted by the behavior of his sons. He was of another time, he claimed. When he was a boy, hard work and frugality were seen as vital components of one's moral character. Somehow he hadn't succeeded in passing this idea along to his sons, perhaps because he didn't entirely buy it himself. He'd met some pretty rough-living folks in his time who'd be the first to lay down their lives for their loved ones. Oftentimes the diligent were the most ruthless. By way of an elliptical pattern of logic, this was meant to explain how absolutely he adored Isabelle. And she was so beautiful. Her mother had been an employee of his, a nanny. She had died. Uncle Charlie appeared to mourn her death for a moment, then he continued his narrative. The three of them made an amusing set, he thought: two sons and a daughter-in-law—all seemingly allergic to real work. It was the novelty of their decadence that appealed to him. He loved his kids—not despite their faults but because of them. Inappropriate, even lewd behavior made an otherwise intolerably dull world interesting.

Kate smiled at her uncle with unabashed affection. These meetings in the early daylight hours were becoming very dear to her, taking on as they did an instructive role in her young life. She now believed that the only people who really understood her, who really knew what she was going through, were this very peculiar family of hers.

That afternoon Kate and her cousins wandered by foot down to the pool hall, where they mixed with the townspeople, all of whom knew Kate. She was still a minor in the state's eyes, but this didn't count for much in such a small town. Gilbert in particular liked the pool hall, as it was a place of his youth. He felt a wonderful nostalgia in this room with the intricate design pressed into the tin ceiling that hovered sixteen feet over the floor. He liked the metal standing fans, the smell of cigars and pipe smoke and leather, the snooker and pool tables, the dark green felt. This was a place that existed outside of time, a living fossil from another epoch. Little or nothing had changed in the fourteen years since he and Kate's brother had come here to escape the midday heat. Little had changed through the last century. Time, it seemed, operated at a different velocity in such places.

Kate and her cousins had come to play a lazy game of snooker and to drink. It was boys against girls, and the boys were losing very badly. Kate knew the game—how to send the diminutive red ball into the mouths of the narrowed pockets—and for this she appeared to have earned Gilbert's deep and abiding admiration. Neither Hap nor Isabelle was very much interested; they made it clear that they were here for the sanctuary of cool air and the drinks. Certainly not for the game.

As the afternoon deepened, two women came into the otherwise empty pool hall. Each carried several shopping bags, and they sat at a table near the front of the building. Kate watched the two silhouettes, dark against the brightness of the windows. They seemed somehow familiar. A moment later, Kate heard the clotted voice, the nasal-toned pronunciation. While she pretended to study the pattern of balls scattered across the table, she tried to determine whether it really was Martha and a friend who had walked into the pool hall.

From Kate's vantage they were merely shapes against the bright plate-glass windows at the front of the building, visually anonymous but for the outline of their profiles. Kate could make out Martha's thick neck and recognized the whooping laughter. Once Kate had played through her turn at the table, she saw that Martha had noticed her as well. At that moment, all sound seemed to fall from the air around Kate. She propped her cue against a table and walked toward her friend. When they met, somewhere in the middle of the bar, Martha emerged into full view. Kate could see at once that she had lost a lot of weight. She had also become more adept at applying her makeup. As they stood facing each other, Kate could smell cigarettes on Martha's breath.

"Hi, Kate," she mumbled almost in a whisper.

"About to leave for school?"

"Day after tomorrow," Martha said. "That's Lindsay Thompson. I found out a few weeks ago that she's going to the same school." Lindsay Thompson gave a sort of noncommittal wave to Kate.

"You've been shopping," Kate said, pointing to the collection of bags around the foot of the table.

"Last-minute school things," Martha said quietly, as if caught in an act of betrayal. "We'll be pledging the same sorority." Martha paused and looked down at the sandals on Kate's tan feet. Her lips pursed like an infant's. "I'm sorry about your mom," she whispered.

"I know."

"I'm sorry I didn't go to the funeral. But I couldn't. I was kind of freaked out. I've never seen someone, you know, *dead* like that."

Martha blinked as if in apology for her frank language. Kate said nothing and smiled. Her eyes drifted beyond Martha to her new friend sitting in front of the plate-glass windows, reading a brochure of some kind.

"Lindsay's pretty smart," Martha said, following Kate's eyes.

"I guess I don't know her all that well," Kate said. She could hear a pause in the sharp click of snooker balls and sensed it was her turn.

"Who are they?" Martha asked, gesturing toward Kate's family.

"Cousins. They're from Missouri."

"I've never met them."

"They came for the funeral."

"And they're still here?"

"They decided to stay," Kate said as she stared warmly upon the picture of Hap kissing Isabelle's forehead and stroking the underside of her chin with his fingertips.

"They look like they're a lot of fun," Martha said.

Kate nodded. For a moment both girls stared in silence at their easy, languid movements.

"Lindsay and I are taking the same organic chemistry class," Martha said. "She wants to study sociology and anthropology. Organic chemistry's just a requirement, a core class. I'll probably be helping her get through it."

"Chemistry's going to be your major?" Kate asked.

"Well, botany. I think I want to become a professor someday. I think I'll really like college."

"Oh," Kate whispered. She felt her face warm with blood. Behind her, she heard Gilbert softly call her name. It was her turn. "Well, hope everything works out," she mumbled, not knowing what to say nor how to bring the awkward conversation to a close.

"I'll see you, Kate," Martha said, her voice trembling slightly. Her eyes moistened until Kate thought she was surely going to cry. But she didn't.

When Kate turned and walked toward the snooker table, she saw that Gilbert was holding out the pool cue for her and smiling. She took a moment to study the table, shot, and missed. Across the room she could see that Martha's eyes were still on her. The ancient bartender hobbled toward her old friend's table and delivered two bottles of Coke. Kate felt her embarrassment diminish now that she had found refuge with her cousins, surrounded by their voices. Nevertheless, she felt that she too should be doing her last-minute shopping before leaving for school. She should be preparing to study at a distant campus, but instead was shooting pool with her cousins—though she loved them dearly, she reminded herself—while she quietly and pleasantly idled away her life. As she stood at the snooker table, her fingertips stained with blue chalk, she realized she had no ambitions, no plans that required more than an afternoon to fulfill. Her family was gone, and with it her former capacity to dream of a life very far beyond the limestone walls of her haunted home. She feared that Martha could see this, that it was clear from where she sat.

That evening Kate and Gilbert sat on the gray paint of Kate's porch, a thick stone pillar at each of their sides, watching dry waves of sheet lightning silently rush from west to east. They could hear Hap and Isabelle inside playing strip poker on the living room floor. Isabelle was screaming while Hap laughed with deep satisfaction. Kate buried her thin shoulder in Gilbert's chest as they witnessed the steady progression of weather and the play of fireflies over the lawn. A stream of cars continuously rounded the square, most of them refurbished American models driven by high school students. They witnessed the activity of any Midwestern town, what had been done for decades and would continue for decades to come. Kate had come to love these moments when she could be alone with Gilbert.

"I remember that old bartender from when I was a kid," Gilbert said. "I like that place."

"I haven't been in there for years," Kate said. "I forgot he was still alive."

"Funny how you can recall smells, isn't it? That apple-butter tobacco from his pipe, that aroma. I swear it's locked in my brain."

Neither spoke. The evening was quiet for a while.

"Was that girl at the pool hall a friend of yours?" Gilbert asked, finally breaking the silence.

"She was," Kate said, her voice blank.

"Was?"

"It's kind of a strange situation," Kate said, her voice suddenly taking on some inflection.

"Ex-friends in small towns. I can imagine."

"She was here when I found my mother," Kate said, her voice softer.

Kate could feel Gilbert's eyes on her. "I didn't see her at the funeral," he said.

"The whole thing freaked her out. I think it made her think our family . . . or the house—well, that there was something wrong with one or the other. Or both."

"Something wrong?" Gilbert asked.

"I can't explain it."

"But she stopped coming by after that?"

"Yeah. The day after tomorrow she'll be leaving for school in New Hampshire," Kate said. "We had plans to go together."

"Well, you've got us now," Gilbert said, pulling Kate into him.

"That's the thing about family; you've got them whether you like it or not."

"I guess that's true."

"You can always surround yourself with family," Gilbert said contemplatively.

As night drew on, the breeze cooled, the air pressure abruptly dropped. At precisely the same moment, they noticed the difference in their ears. Soon the sidewalk began to crackle with rain, then without a word Kate took Gilbert's wrist and led him around the house to slanting cellar doors. She parted the wooden halves and descended into a musty blackness. Once they were standing on an invisible brick floor she tugged on a cotton string shiny with use, which fired a naked lightbulb in a porcelain socket screwed into a joist. The sudden flood of light startled their eyes. But the room was revealed, the walls of ancient portraits, the dusty oils, the baroque gold-leaf frames, the dark furniture that stood in shadows, piled haphazardly as though intended to be forgotten. Though he was not fond of such words, Gilbert felt the room possessed an aura, an unmanageable sense of presence. Perhaps it was merely the dark wood of the furniture, the rows of brass and iron beds, intricately tooled dressers and jelly cabinets that clearly belonged to another age. Or more likely it was the trajectory of the dozens of eyes of ancestors, immobile on the walls, the faces frozen in oil. Whatever it was, it unnerved him, but quietly so.

"What is all this?" he asked.

"Heirlooms."

"Why are they down here?"

"Who knows. We never get rid of anything."

Again she took his wrist and led him down a path of parted chairs and trunks and rugs to the far wall, where she pointed out a portrait of the very first Thomas Willoughby. They stood before it in reverent silence. His ancient eyes appeared tired, his face and neck lean. In his slender hands he held a stovepipe hat.

"He built this house," Kate said, casually extending an arm. "And he owned slaves once, down in Mississippi. Can you imagine? *Slaves.* Owning another human being."

Gilbert said he looked ill and asked how he died, though he'd doubtless heard the stories at some point in his life. Kate said she knew two versions: a suicide or a duel with mother-of-pearl-handled pistols. Gilbert found the latter implausible. The antique image of two men in capes taking so many strides, turning, then firing at each other in the shadowy blue light of dawn seemed ridiculously romantic to him, so over the top.

"He doesn't look the type to duel. The eyes are too meek. Looks more like a syphilitic poet." Gilbert paused to consider the evidence of his great ancestor's character. "Yeah. It had to be a suicide."

"Uncle Charlie says the family produced more history than it could forget," Kate said.

"Judging from this cellar, I'd say he has a point."

They wandered through the maze of artifacts a while longer, then once again they were beneath the light; Kate tugged on the string and led Gilbert back through the murky darkness. When she parted the overhead doors, they gave way to a sharp pattern of stars. They walked through the sodden spears of bluegrass back to the porch steps, where they curled into each other against the cold. Gilbert lit a cigarette. For a moment neither spoke against the hiss of cars passing over wet pavement.

"Why'd you take me down there?" he asked.

Kate turned away, her self-conscious gaze trailing in the corners of her eyes. She looked out at the glistening black street and contemplated an answer.

"Because that's our family."

"Well, that *was* our family."

Kate lightly drew her fingernails over her windpipe.

"Sometimes you seem like you're in love with the past," she said. "Kind of like your dad."

"You think I'm sentimental."

"Uncle Charlie's sentimental. Not you. You're only intrigued by the olden days. Uncle Charlie *longs* for them."

Gilbert nodded. He could buy that.

"In some ways you seem kind of, I don't know—old-fashioned," Kate continued.

"How's that?"

"You don't listen to rock and roll, you play the piano for a living. You spend all of your time with your brother and his wife. . . ."

"That's old-fashioned?"

"Well, you just don't seem completely *modern*."

Gilbert turned away from Kate, smiling. He expelled a long plume of cigarette smoke into the night.

"I'll accept that as praise, Miss Kate."

Kate blushed in the darkness. She felt the weight of a privately complicated moment. With a disciplined effort, she put a tangled thought out of mind and replaced it with something else. . . . She was coming to see the family and her place in it as though from a distance, she told herself. She felt capable of viewing the world around her and perceiving it with detachment, the way it really was.

As Kate thought about this, she saw that Gilbert was getting ready to go to bed. Her heart sank. She reached for his hand as he ground the ember of his cigarette into the sidewalk with the heel of his boot. He said he was exhausted and put his arm around her shoulders. "Good night, Miss Kate," he groaned. Then he stood.

"Good night," she whispered. She turned back to the street and listened as he walked up the stairs of the house.

seven

One morning the following week Kate found a pink Post-it note
in Uncle Charlie's hand reminding him to call his secretary to tell
her of his impending return. A few days later, she overheard Isabelle on the phone, telling someone that she and Hap would be in
Memphis any day. The revelations made Kate nervous, so much so
that she began sleeping late. What made it particularly difficult was
that no one would openly share these plans with her, and she was
too afraid to ask. Of course she understood that they must dread
breaking the news. Then it finally came.

An orange sun stood in the kitchen window. Insects hovered
over the lawn in the evening air, sunlight refracting through their
translucent wings. Uncle Charlie came into the kitchen, where
Kate was finishing the last of the dirty dishes. He touched her little
brown shoulder. "It's time for me to get back to matters down
South, Miss Kate," he said.

The dishrag hung limp from Kate's pruned hand. She could
hear him breathing.

"I don't wanna go, but I gotta," he went on. "Few things we need to talk 'bout first."

He led her into the study and sat at her father's desk while she took a seat in the corner. For the next hour or so, he explained the three trust funds he had established on her behalf and had her sign various documents. He then delineated his reasoning—all in his extravagant accent and unique grammar. No mortgage. Just property taxes, utilities, odds and ends. Of course, plenty of money for fun and games. He thought twenty-five hundred a month would do. This could easily be raised on the interest of her family's investments alone without cutting into the principal.

A pause.

"I don't want you to go."

"You'll be fine, m'honey. The kids'd like to stay behind. Keep you company."

Kate released a hot breath.

"When you get tired of their antics, ask 'em to get the hell out. I know they can be too much. Just hand 'em their walkin' papers."

"You can't all leave."

"If somebody leaves, somebody else'll come back. There might be a few days here and there when you're alone. But that's all right. Remember, bein' alone's all right."

Kate put her arms around her uncle's thick waist and cried a little.

Two days later Uncle Charlie came down the hanging staircase and set a bag at either side of his long flat feet. He kissed Kate's forehead. After a long silence, he released her, picked up his bags, and walked out to his Suburban, surrounded by his sons, Kate, and Isabelle. Once his children had said good-bye, they returned to the porch and sat on the steps.

"The grown-up's gone," Gilbert said as they watched the awkward vehicle turn the corner and vanish. "A party's in order."

"Absolutely," Hap said.

That evening Isabelle and Hap bought tiki torches and staked them around the pool and placed the stereo speakers in the windows. Through the night, they danced and swam naked in the tiny pool by torchlight. Liquid yellow flames floated on the water's surface, Elvis's voice carried through the lilacs and soft maples. Hap fixed gin and tonics on a small wire-mesh table next to the pool, an arm's length from the water's edge. Hoisting their drinks overhead, they drifted together within the ring of yellow light.

Late the next morning, Kate awoke next to Isabelle on the sunporch. They lay together beneath an afghan, the imprint of the carpet pressed into their cheeks. They rose and made a simple breakfast of sausage and eggs. As they sat down to eat, Isabelle told Kate she had some news. She and Hap and Gilbert had to get back down to Memphis. There was some business that needed tending to that required the three of them. They planned to leave toward the end of the week. But they would be back, Isabelle insisted. Soon and often. Isabelle put the idea to Kate tentatively, as this would be the first time she was alone in the house since her mother had died. To Isabelle's delight, Kate took the news quite well. She smiled across the table at her cousin and said firmly that she'd be fine.

But Kate felt a terrible dread. She wondered what she would do with herself in this big empty house, though she tried not to worry. She played over in her mind what Uncle Charlie had said about being alone. Through the week she grew more and more used to the idea, and when the day finally arrived, it actually brought with it a sense of relief.

The departure was sudden and casual so as to appear temporary to Kate, which it was, after all, meant to be. After the goodbyes, she sat in her kitchen and watched the two trucks pull away and vanish into the town. Not for some time did she turn from the window. She just sat listening to the empty house, eyes fixed on the wall clock, immobile, utterly still, as though her breath had left her. Then she abruptly went about the house with a feather duster. A little later she turned on the stereo and went to work with the companionable voices of St. Louis talk-show hosts and callers following her from room to room. The house was again alive, she told herself, as it had always been.

For the next few days, Kate fell into a restless routine. In such a large old house there were always things to be done, familiar motions that gave each day a reassuring pace and rhythm, the illusion of purpose. But she couldn't drive away the harrowing loneliness. It seemed to accumulate in the walls of the house, to become a presence unto itself. Then one day while she vacuumed the section of hallway where her mother had passed away, she saw something glittering embedded in the trim of dark wood between the floor and wall. She flicked off the machine and picked up the sparkling object. She caught her breath. She passed her thumb and finger over the clean edges, the soft metal. As she did this a fine quiver rose in her chest and radiated throughout her body. For a moment she felt her mother's nearness, could smell her. Then the feeling was gone. Kate slumped to the floor and held herself. All around her lay nothingness, a vast absence. Addy wasn't coming back, Kate told herself. Nobody was coming back. She lay shaking, certain that a mad loneliness had attached itself to her forever. Then the quiver slowly began to subside, and the terror she had felt was replaced by an eerie calm. She stood up, her mother's wedding ring tight in her fist, then quickly turned on the vacuum. For the rest of the afternoon, she tried to lose herself in its familiar howl.

The memory of this day lingered in Kate's mind. She feared the experience of the terror, the total comprehension of what it meant to be alone in the world. The feeling was no longer an abstraction in her young mind but lived with her from moment to moment. She believed the only way to fend it off was to continue to busy herself with projects she could complete in a day, meaningless unending chores. She kept the house clean and mowed the lawn in brief stints through the remains of the hot Indian summer. In the early morning she would climb out of bed, pull on a pair of cutoffs, and step into the dry air. For twenty minutes the mower could be heard droning across the lawn, then it would suddenly die. She came back inside, her brown skin shiny with sweat. She climbed the stairs to the bathroom and flooded the porcelain tub with cold water, then lowered herself into it, her blond ponytail dipping over its arched back. She might fall asleep like this before washing herself, but she eventually came downstairs, fresh and awake, to fix tea and commence the crossword puzzle.

A short part of her autumn passed in this lazy yet anxious cadence. Then one afternoon she saw Gilbert's blue and gray truck pull up in front of the walkway that led to the veranda. Kate felt her throat tighten when she saw he had returned alone. She watched him from the kitchen window as he came up the steps carrying a large duffel bag.

"The little chatelaine," he said as she stepped out onto the veranda.

"The pianist."

He came to the top of the steps, set his duffel bag down, and took her into his arms. She felt so young. Like a little girl, she thought. As he held her she sensed the relief of an immense ache slowly leaving her chest, an ache much larger than she thought it could possibly contain.

Daily life was mundane enough, as they kept to themselves within the warm honeycomb of the house. Gilbert mended the trellis around the veranda, the guttering along the south wall. Domesticity was new to him, he told Kate, but a realm he wanted to explore. One day they even decided to buy a dog, something they would do together.

That evening they left the house in Gilbert's pickup with the classifieds lying between them on the bench seat. They drove in silence, the windows down, the red and orange sunlight pouring over perfect rows of tassel-less seed corn, to a shabby farmhouse that slumped between a small knoll dense with walnut and oak trees and a sheer plane of ripening corn. Since she was a child, Kate had known this place, this area, as the Penny Farm. They drove up the wash-gravel drive to the barn, where a woman stood expectantly with her hands sunk into the pockets of her filthy apron. She waved them toward the barn with a lazy, expressionless gesture. They stepped out of the truck, both doors slapping shut simultaneously, and strode over the gravel toward the yawning draw of the doorless entryway, where the woman's figure vanished in darkness. They followed her through the punky rich smell of rotting hay to the back of the barn, where alongside the smoothed knotty planks a hutch was constructed of warped and frayed plywood. Without a word, the woman sank her chubby knees into the floor of moldy hay and slipped her hands into the mouth of the hutch, whereupon she drew out a sleeping puppy.

"How much?" Gilbert said into the moist dim light.

"He's the last of the litter," the woman said, not turning to address them. "Daddy thinks he might be retarded from being stuck in the birth canal. Seems kinda slow to everyone. Little clumsy and slow."

"How much?"

"Ten dollars? We sold his brothers and sisters for a hundred each."

Gilbert pulled out his wallet and handed her a neatly folded bill. Kate crouched and took the sleeping dog from the woman. She petted the sleep away from the dull, wandering eyes, then smiled up at Gilbert. They owned a dog. Together.

On the way home neither spoke. From time to time Kate gazed across at Gilbert's profile as the wind swept a lock of his hair.

At the house, Kate fed the dog cubes of chicken breast, then fixed a bed for him in her father's study. While she did this, Gilbert sat at the piano and played "Way Down Upon the Swanee River." Slow and solemn. Kate went to the doorjamb and watched him surreptitiously. His back was to her, his eyes lost on the gleaming black wing of wood that angled up toward the curtains like that of a giant raven. She watched him for fifteen or twenty minutes. This is his reprieve, she thought. At such times she felt she was betraying him in the most intimate way.

Sometimes he reminded her of a small boy who had just had his hair cut, an image of the child she had known years ago superimposed on the man. His eyes were clear and round and self-conscious like a child's. She remembered how his air of boyish innocence had been marred by something dark and potentially vicious. The evolution had been sudden and deft, and it was the abruptness more than what it turned into that was most startling. These spells of madness, she now suspected, were tangled up with the past—with Uncle Charlie, and, in a way, with her dead family. Trouble was magnetic about Gilbert, part of the charged atmosphere surrounding a barroom pianist, a thirty-one-year-old hostage to memory. This was the center of his charm.

There were stories obscured by time and distance, fragments she had cobbled together long after the fact. They lived in her mind as a montage of overlapping memory and narrative told by her parents. She could recall how Uncle Charlie had always held a sense of wonder about her father when he was alive. Uncle Charlie liked to remind Cecil that he was of the same pedigree, that they shared the same blood and mind. Family was dear to Charlie, and they were family, no matter how tenuous the connection. He wanted their sons—Gilbert and Adam, at least—to know each other, to become close. And during the summers Gilbert and Adam shared, they did so in a way neither had ever known, which in turn drew the two families together. Kate could recall how Adam and Gilbert hunted together and carved duck decoys in the basement. In the afternoon heat, they played pool in the cool darkness of the pool hall, and one evening Adam showed Gilbert the easy spatial joy of downers. Gilbert was the only friend Kate could remember her brother ever having. It was during one of these summer visits that the relationship between the two families would forever define itself to Kate's young mind.

The day was late in August. She couldn't remember the afternoon itself, as she was so young, but through the stories she could recall that it all began when her father had come home early from the office. He strolled along with his briefcase swinging from his long arm, then suddenly stopped, puzzled by something he saw and heard. From the sidewalk before the house he could see the steady articulation of a slender black rifle barrel high up in the arms of the maple. He heard the sound of an adult's voice mixed up with a boy's. As cars passed, he swore he could also hear the tiny *ping* of a lead projectile against glass, then the two voices in the tree would giggle. Cars swerved as they warily moved on, the drivers startled and bewildered. Cecil's eyes shifted from the tree to the street, the tree, the street. Then he was struck by an amazing comprehension; he finally realized who it was and what they were doing: Uncle Charlie and Gilbert were shooting an air rifle at passing cars from a bedroom window of Cecil's own home.

He was more amazed than angry. When he came inside that afternoon he didn't go upstairs and confront Uncle Charlie. He wouldn't know how to express to a grown man such unbearable embarrassment. That was the thing about her father: he was a reserved man who saw his way around glaring character flaws if only to simplify relations. Friendly relations demanded less tending, and he was too busy. Never mind that Uncle Charlie was a forty-five-year-old businessman caught up in malicious child's play. Cecil only searched for his own son, whom, to his immense relief, he found in the basement with Hap, quietly packing shells for his twenty-gauge. A few minutes later, Uncle Charlie descended the stairs with Gilbert, blushing like a giant child, talking as he came, feigning innocence with fantastic ease.

Cecil had hoped that the episode would just go away, but he doubted it would. Experience had demonstrated time and again that the world didn't work this way. That night, when the two families were gathered around the dining room table, there was a knock at the back door. When Cecil rose to answer it he knew it would be a policeman, and it was. He invited the young officer, whom he knew, into the kitchen with a smile, and the conversation began calmly, respectfully. Clearly Cecil wanted to be helpful, as he felt it should be a matter of example for Adam, a matter of simple decorum. He listened while the policeman explained with touching shyness that he'd received complaints of two boys shooting at cars with an air rifle from a bedroom window of the house. He personally doubted the claims, he said, but he had to ask. That was his job. In response, Cecil politely denied any knowledge, and explained that it couldn't have been his son, as they had spent the afternoon together. The officer believed him implicitly. But just as he was about to leave, Uncle Charlie came into the kitchen, followed by Adam, Hap, and Gilbert.

As Uncle Charlie came through the door, he asked the officer what was going on. When the officer told him, Uncle Charlie attacked the timid inquiry with a bluster of angry denial. Cecil said nothing. He stood next to his cousin, head down, eyes blinking with checked astonishment and contempt, while the young officer tried to explain the matter in a diminishing voice and Uncle Charlie berated him in an ever louder one. Eventually the officer left, apologizing again and again for the error and intrusion on his way out the door. Once he was gone, Cecil looked up and saw that Uncle Charlie was smiling secretly, smiling with unspeakable pride. Then, as everyone returned to the dining room table, Uncle Charlie manfully patted his son and Cecil on the back simultaneously and pointed out how he would always stand up for family. He would be forever unwavering on this point, he insisted. Cops didn't scare him, and he would stand up for family. Gilbert just listened as his father spoke, his cheeks shot with red, eyes glassy. Kate's father said nothing.

At last the night came to a quiet and peaceful end, and the next morning, Uncle Charlie and his boys prepared to leave. The two families gathered before the house to say their good-byes, then Uncle Charlie and his sons climbed into their Suburban. As they drove away, Cecil did not conceal his relief. "Hope they never invite themselves back," he mumbled to Addy.

Not until later in the day did her father speak of the incident, and then it would be for the last time. When he came home for lunch, he told Adam what his relatives had been up to while he had been packing shells, and why the police had come to the door. This was an example of *hubris* and *horseplay,* Cecil explained. Adam understood the term *horseplay,* but Cecil had to define *hubris.* This, he said, was an overweening pride and vanity that inevitably results in tragedy. Though Kate was puzzled by the terms, she would later attach them to Gilbert and his family. They would always seem to apply.

But now, more than a decade later, as Kate furtively watched Gilbert at the piano, she saw how he had grown into a man very different from his father. Somehow he seemed older than Uncle Charlie, yet he still had that air of boyishness. He seemed more like her vague recollections of Adam, any one of those indelible images she retained of him as a seventeen-year-old. She could recall how both Gilbert and Adam were so skinny and anxious, how they smoked ceaselessly—not to be cool but because they seemed to crave the nicotine and the repetitious motion of the habit. Perhaps it was the product of the generational ties between the cousins, as even in panorama they must have recognized themselves in each other. Their lives ran parallel, though the common direction was at times difficult to decipher. But both were about to graduate from high school in the spring of 1972, and both were academic failures. Both had the map of Vietnam hanging before them like a reverse image of California. Both developed peculiar relations with their fathers. So they would always see themselves as common blood, no matter how diluted and faint the actual biological connection might be.

But during his senior year of high school, Gilbert prepared to attend Tulane, though he would barely graduate, and then only because the high school administration and faculty wanted to be rid of him. Uncle Charlie knew some of the regents at Tulane, who owed him a favor or two, so the machinery was in place, and Gilbert had agreed to go. This was what Uncle Charlie told Cecil and Addy during a phone call. They had no such influence or network, and a more determined son. So there was nothing anyone could do about Adam's enlistment. Unfortunately, Uncle Charlie explained to Kate's and Adam's parents, his influence quickly petered out once you moved north of the Ohio, and a few weeks later Adam was gone. Kate wouldn't see Uncle Charlie and his family again until Adam's funeral, and then a few years later for her father's. When she saw them next, she would have no other family to speak of.

eight

Early one morning Gilbert found Kate roaming about the kitchen, gathering thick white crockery and lowering it into a lacquered reed basket. A steamer hummed on the stovetop as green beans cooked within its steel belly. Beneath star-shaped iron grates, the oven held chicken legs and thighs. The noise of boiling grease raged.

By late morning they were driving along an asphalt road, from time to time passing through gray arms of smoke that reached out of the ditches where farmers burned the grass along the fencelines. Gourds lay in the browning fields, ripening through the shortening days. The dog they had named Bedford lay between them, his lazy mind adrift between vague sleep and a stunned wakefulness. When they came to the rusted steel-girded bridge Gilbert swerved down the road of dried black mud to a hidden trailhead leading into a forest. He brought the truck to a stop, then they got out and headed down the trail, Kate carrying the limp dog, Gilbert the picnic basket and quilt. They crossed the glade and entered the shade of the trees on the other side. When they came to the creek, Gilbert spread out the checkered quilt and they lay down in quiet luxury. Kate, he noted, had a way of making simple and mundane acts seem so lush. So they lay together with the puppy and basket between them, alongside the foul brown stream that cut through the prairie and woods, carrying away precious topsoil to the Mississippi. After several minutes of silence, Kate felt the desire to speak, to talk about something, so she asked Gilbert how long he had stayed in school. Gilbert turned his head and saw that Kate's eyes were closed.

"I barely finished high school," he said. "It took Uncle Charlie nearly every favor he could call in just to get me into Tulane. Not that that was so difficult."

"How long were you there?"

"Three months. I gravitated to the bars and clubs, you know. You can lose yourself in that town."

"Then you dropped out."

"I was put on academic probation, then I simply quit." Gilbert tapped a cigarette from its pack and rolled over on his side to face Kate. Suddenly he seemed uncharacteristically serious. "You have to remember this was 1972, and if you left school the government had plans of their own for you. It was a shitty time, Kate."

"Then why didn't you have to go to Vietnam?"

"Because my father knows more people than he lets on. I remember talking with your brother and him telling me how he actually wanted to go, how Fayette bored him to tears."

"He wasn't right, was he? You know, in the head?"

Gilbert looked her in the eyes. For a moment he thought he couldn't speak to this, that he couldn't see his way clear of the initial discomfort of candor. But Kate seemed so casual, so objective, and it came to him, everything he wanted to say.

"It's not that he wasn't right. He was smart. *Real* smart. It's that he seemed to live in a world that was all his own, and nobody could penetrate it. Sometimes he just seemed so gloomy. Not many guys wanted to actually go to Vietnam, especially by then." A silence fell over the blanket. Then: "Nobody knew why he wanted to go. It was as if he were programmed. . . ."

"When did you hear he'd died?"

"Why do you ask, Miss Kate?"

She shrugged. She didn't know why.

"You're the only person I know who knew Adam. I mean, who was really close to him."

"It's strange," Gilbert said, his thoughts seemingly lost in the arthritic movement of the walnut branches against the blue. "He still crosses my mind once or twice a day."

"He was hard to get to know, wasn't he?"

"In some ways."

"He liked you, though."

Gilbert didn't respond. He seemed to be turning something over in his mind, something that wasn't altogether pleasant. It was as though an opportunity had presented itself beside this stream, upon this blanket, within this shade, beside this retarded dog and this girl who was his cousin. His eyes pinched a little in contemplation as he gazed through the foliage at the patches of blue.

"You know, Uncle Charlie was pretty upset when Adam died. More upset than you might think."

"Who told him?"

"Your father called. I remember how Uncle Charlie set the phone down and walked straight over to me as I sat on the couch watching television and how he just went up to it and turned the thing off. Then he told me, calculating each gesture, each word, for greatest effect. That's what he's truly great at, you know. Taken together, he was saying, 'Look at my son: comfortable, lazy, safe, stupid, decadent; meanwhile Cecil Willoughby's son is bleeding to death fighting Communists in the jungle.' He can convey a lot without speaking. That's his gift. But he was truly upset. Not so much by Adam's death, perhaps, but by the comparative spectacle I made. People were bound to make comparisons. I'm sure all this occurred to him in a rush of horror. Suddenly I was birdshit on the family's Purple Heart, which is why your family didn't see much of us after that."

"You're too hard on yourself," Kate said. She wanted to reach across the blanket and run her fingers through his fine hair.

"Trust me. I'm not."

"I think you read too much into things sometimes."

"I've thought a lot about this. I mean, a *lot*." Gilbert paused. "It was a shitty time, Miss Kate."

"Were you surprised?"

"That he died?"

Kate nodded.

"I expected it. I mean he was just marked for it. Somehow I knew Adam would never make it out of that place if he went." Gilbert stopped talking. Then something struck him as funny. "Uncle Charlie says Vietnam was America's second Civil War. That immediately qualifies Adam as a hero in his eyes. He lives in Valhalla with Bobby Lee and John Wayne."

"You and your father are melodramatic. You always have been."

Gilbert smiled. Somehow he felt a relief incommensurate with what he had shared.

"I might be in love with some of the past," he mumbled. "But not all of it."

That night they sat out on the veranda in lawn chairs, watching the cars round the square. A six-pack of beer sweated through the brown paper sack between them. Neither spoke much. Kate closed her eyes and held a cool aluminum can to her chest. Heat lightning illuminated the horizon in soft flashes. They sat for an hour or so, awash in the cool air, until a rainy wind kicked up and wetted their bare feet and shins. As they came into the darkened kitchen, the church bells throughout town marked the eleventh hour, and Gilbert said rather meekly that it was probably time for bed.

Kate said something, her voice frayed by thunder and the weight of the rain washing over the house. Gilbert took her in his arms like a lover, feeling her shape. Then he corrected himself. He said goodnight and vanished up the stairs, into the darkness. A few minutes later, Kate went to bed too. She slipped between the soft, damp cotton sheets and lay awake for a while, listening to the sound of rain rolling off the roof, thinking Gilbert had come back for a reason. . . . But is it done? Then another question occurred to her. Who is left to object?

In the morning, Kate came down to the kitchen, where she made herself a cup of tea with water that Gilbert had put on the stove. She wondered where he was, so she carried her cup from room to room. But she couldn't find him. Maybe he had gone to the store for cigarettes and scotch. Finally she came across him in the living room. He was standing before the tall glass doors of the gun cabinet, where six intricately tooled Kentucky rifles and Holland & Holland shotguns stood just as her father had left them nine years earlier. Kate came up to him as he studied the guns through the glass. A soft layer of dust shifted as the door swung freely on its oiled hinges.

"Good morning," she said softly so as not to disturb the calm.

"These are really something," Gilbert said without turning to her. He was entranced.

As he lifted each gun he appeared surprised by its cold weight. In his hands they had the feel of antiquity, that they had been fashioned in a time that preceded all machines other than those that made guns. The metal was vaguely worn, the engraving on the breeches faded by the touch of hands. The tooled scene on one of the gun's chambers was that of a covey of mallards scattering over a swamp as the sun rose behind hills. Something about the tableau was of the last century, he said. The hills were too steep and rolling, the ducks too thick in the sky.

"How long has it been since any of these were fired?" he asked.

"My dad and Adam were the last to shoot them. Nine, ten years, I suppose."

"Should we make sure they still work?"

Kate smiled.

That evening she gathered the old ammo boxes in the cellar while Gilbert carefully wrapped each gun in its own quilted blanket, then stowed them in the bed of the truck. With only an hour or two of sunlight remaining, they drove toward the river, looking for an unmarked dirt road that abruptly strayed into a wild forest. At the foot of a short descent, the trees grew out of water, their roots like pale fingers reaching out of the calm reflective surface. They drove to a small meadow where hunters parked their trucks on the matted brown grass, then unloaded their things.

Gilbert set the guns out in front of the pickup and tenderly unfolded the quilts. He tucked pairs of twelve-gauge shells in his pocket. Then he chose a shotgun, the youngest of the four, with its birthdate cut into the left chamber in an archaic cursive—*Nineteen-hundred-thirty-two*. But now that they were here, ready to shoot, he realized they needed something to shoot at. They had no clay pigeons, and Gilbert insisted he wasn't one to shoot living creatures. Kate found this hard to believe. Nevertheless, she threw sticks and dry clumps of dirt while Gilbert imagined them as ducks against the brass bead that stood between the two barrels. She would throw ten or twelve clods into the air, the charges of shot scattering all around them, and they would fall to the earth unharmed. But every now and then, one erupted as it arced across the pink sky, and Kate would pause and smile toward Gilbert.

When they came home that night they found Bedford lying on the veranda, his head and neck spilling over the top step. Gilbert took his tiny skull into his hands and rolled the fleshy coat. "What a stupid dog," he lovingly mumbled. He carefully draped the living room coffee table in newspaper and brought the guns inside, while Kate prepared drinks in the kitchen. On a tray she carried a decanter of whiskey, a small bucket of crushed ice, and two crystal toasting glasses. As Gilbert passed a cloth saturated with gun oil over the gleaming barrels, Kate placed the tray beside the gun-cleaning kit and poured the whiskey.

"What's the occasion?" Gilbert asked.

"No occasion," Kate said as she poured.

"Just thought a nip was what the night lacked?"

"It was a good day."

"It was."

Later that evening, Kate turned on the stereo and played more of her mother's Elvis records. They danced for a while and drank, then danced some more. The room grew warm as they twirled about, and they became breathless. Finally Gilbert said he was going to step out to the front porch and have a cigarette. Kate simply collapsed on the sofa to let her heart catch up. A few minutes later, she went to the screen door and watched him smoke. She watched the orange ember of his cigarette burning in the night, solitary and anonymous. The smell of rust mixed with that of the feathery plume. Eventually she came out in her sock feet and sat beside him as he watched cars round the square. They sat in silence. Then Gilbert finally spoke.

"I don't want to leave."

"You don't have to."

"I might," he said. "But only for a little while. I have to make a living, you know." He turned and looked at Kate with silly, boyish regret, then drew thoughtfully on his cigarette. "Of course I'll be back."

Kate put her hand to his shoulder.

"I don't want you to go."

They sat there without facing each other, listening to the stereo as it hissed and hissed at the end of its cycle of play.

"Please don't go," she said.

She turned to look him full in the face. When she looked into his eyes, she saw herself reflected.

At first there was the vivid recognition, the common childhood—Gilbert too lean and precocious at sixteen, Kate the anemic younger sister, daddy's girl, a child. The shared memories were clear and cinematic. After a moment of hesitation, Kate kissed his temple. Gilbert flicked his cigarette butt onto the sidewalk and together they watched the incandescent ember shatter against the concrete and extinguish itself. Gilbert rose, turned to Kate, and extended a hand. When she took it, he led her into the darkened house, through the living room, and up the hanging staircase. She could hear the effort of her heart in her ears and felt weak in spite of the adrenaline lining her blood. In Kate's bedroom, he turned in the darkness and took her face in his hands. Then he slipped his hands beneath her blouse and felt the sweat forming along the ridge of her vertebrae. A moment later he lifted her by the thighs and brought her up against the wall. She slung her frail arms about his neck while he held her, her damp back pressed against the plaster, her eyes closed in the darkness, the floor invisible, seemingly miles beneath her.

Eventually Gilbert carried her to the bed, where he held the small of her back in his hand. She felt alive beneath him, like a small animal. Her vertebrae curled over his palm as her stomach lifted and met his. He felt her hand against his naked chest.

"Wait," he heard her say. "I've never—"

"We don't have to," he murmured.

"No, that's not it."

She was still beneath him. He could see the brine of tears in the corners of her eyes rise and subside.

"I had cancer," she said into the blackness. She could make out his figure hovering above her. "More than a year ago. Here—on my shoulder." She reached up and guided his hand. "Here," she said. It occurred to her that she hadn't said the word for almost as long. *Cancer.*

"My doctor described it as a mass of dividing cells. They grow without purpose. Cancer cells in the brain never become brain cells, just as cancer cells in the shoulder never become shoulder cells. There's no design. They just absorb food and take up space. That's what happened to my shoulder."

"Were you scared?" Gilbert asked.

"Sometimes. Late at night."

"What of?"

"That this is the way things are. That this is the way all things are."

For a time they lay quiet in the darkness.

"That's why you can't leave," Kate said.

"I won't leave."

"Promise."

"I promise."

She withdrew her hand from his chest. "Okay," she whispered. "Now I'm ready."

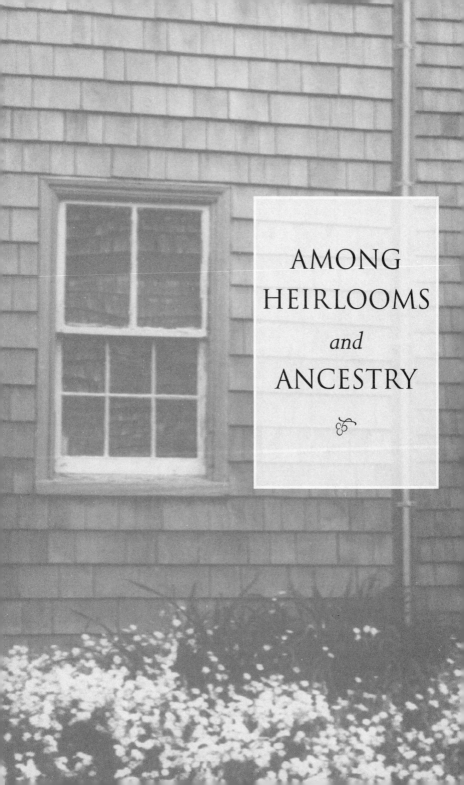

AMONG
HEIRLOOMS
and
ANCESTRY

nine

At thirty-one Gilbert was handsome. Movie-star handsome, Kate thought. His blond hair hovered over his scalp in a way that suggested it was an extension of the whimsical mind beneath it. He was still thin, his voice capable of speaking North or South, a charming versatility that played out of his narrow mouth. He dressed with casual uncaring, and then there was what he did for a living. After dozens of forgettable jobs, he was a pianist, a young man who had drawn a line in the sand and called himself an artist, a musician. He seemed to recognize that he must appear ridiculous to those who knew him well, yet was fully prepared to mock himself as he imagined others did when his back was turned. Kate, however, saw nothing to ridicule. She saw only the debonair artist.

She also saw Gilbert as a living part of her past, a conduit to what she had committed to memory, a moving picture that was now, several months after her mother's death, beginning to fade. Her cousin, her dead brother's friend, her mother's and father's nephew—the fairy dust that brought the past to life.

But there were things she couldn't know. For instance, Gilbert wasn't really a pianist; the piano was an avocation. Gilbert was a thief. For more than a decade he had burglarized homes for a living, stealing other people's heirlooms, jewelry, silver, crystal, furs, sometimes their credit cards. He moved throughout the Midwest, town to town, staying a few nights in a hotel before moving on. Only his brother, to whom he turned over the goods in exchange for cash, and Isabelle knew this about him. Hap sold the goods to a man in Memphis. Isabelle didn't concern herself with the operation's details. So far as she was concerned, Gilbert was a pianist. Her husband a businessman. A wholesaler, she would explain if pressed.

Why he had become a thief was a question Gilbert never could answer to his own satisfaction. Nearly every day of his adult life he'd put a form of the question to himself. But he had no idea. It was just there from the very beginning, waiting for him, like dinner at the end of the day. After he dropped out of college, he spent an entire winter watching television and playing the piano in his father's home. Then his cousin up in Fayette died. Gilbert couldn't make it at school, and Uncle Charlie suddenly seemed so uninterested in his own son's life. None of the tacit uncaring was lost on Gilbert. During this time he found it difficult to pull himself from the sofa, though he someday wanted to be someone who made a living on the scale of his father. Secretly he was ambitious, but the only way he knew how to make money was as a burglar. Eventually he found the wherewithal to go ahead with the plan that had always lived in the back of his mind.

For four years, he addressed his new vocation as a craft. While Hap was away at college, Gilbert grew intimately interested in how locks and hinges worked. He came up with original methods for solving problems unique to cat burglars, and borrowed books from the library for ideas that weren't so original. And it seemed he never could be caught. Something in the way he moved through darkness, how he could memorize the landscape of a kitchen, assume a shadow. This was work he enjoyed, and he was good at it.

By the time Hap graduated from Texas A&M, both brothers knew what they would do with the rest of their lives. Hap was a businessman by nature. At twenty-two, he found he could negotiate deals with other illicit businessmen with uncanny ease. He was calm, deliberate in thought, reliable. In his tweed jacket and blue jeans he would sit in a short chair before the desk of a fat man by the name of Mr. Johnson and tell him about a truckful of odds and ends parked a few blocks away that was worth three or four times what he was willing to sell it for. Mr. Johnson would smile and say, "Five times." Hap's head would bob, and a deal was struck. Nights, he and his wife and Gilbert sat around their kitchen table in Memphis, splitting the pot in two.

Racketeers probably liked Hap for the same reasons Uncle Charlie did, as their ways, their language, were familiar to him. He looked comfortable in clandestine settings. In the midst of cutting a deal, Hap felt as though he were sitting at the dinner table with Uncle Charlie and his business associates—it was all so casual, just business, a game of chess with dimension to it. Every now and then he brought these garish men things Gilbert had stolen that appealed to their higher aspirations, things like crystal chandeliers they could hang in their tawdry offices in downtown Memphis. Gilbert rarely saw this side of the business. What he concerned himself with was the execution of burglary—finding new territory, new strategies by which to plunder working families of their finer possessions. And through the years, his livelihood never changed.

Gilbert now wondered if questions sometimes crossed Kate's mind, if she wondered where his money came from. He told her he played piano for a living, yet he never had to be anywhere. Just hung around the house, read, packed picnics. And as the weeks passed, he began to run short on money. He knew that the move to

Fayette would have to be assimilated into his work, a living had to be made. It began the first night they spent together as lovers.

Long after Kate fell asleep, Gilbert got up and walked naked through the house to the room where he had previously slept. He passed over the wooden floors and rugs with utter quiet and grace, having memorized the black spaces of the house. Such memorization was an unconscious habit, something he did wherever he went. When he reached his former bedroom he removed from the bureau drawers the clothes, the hat. He spread them out carefully over the bed, and dressed in the darkness. A moment later he was gone, lost in the shadows of the old house, then lost into the town.

For him, each evening was choreographed, laid out like a chess board: from the rising of the moon to the manner in which the shadows of a maple standing between him and an electric street-light flowed over a lawn. Always he would try to reduce the evening to mathematics. In this way, everything was there for him to play with; he could manipulate the variables with the utter cool-ness of an old man playing chess with his grandson. His pride wasn't invested, so he never took chances. There was no trace of passion—only humility. He saw this quality in himself as a hallmark of professionalism.

On that first night, he moved from house to house, noting dogs, passageways, things that glittered within the frames of windows. As he stood, invisible and utterly still as a slender shadow, he would see a silver tea set resting on a mahogany end table. Then in his mind's eye he would observe himself moving through the house, taking the object, and passing along a corridor of darkness all the way back to Kate's home, however many lawns and openly lit streets away. He saw the whole of the night as an organism, a sys-tem. The choreography of the hand and the individual fingertip to-gether—the design in both micro- and macro-scale. Much was at stake with each movement, a kind of commitment in every ges-ture. When most exhausted, he would sit within the shadow of a chimney, feeling his heart throbbing in his chest. Then he would stand and carefully move on.

He returned to the house and went through the cellar doors with a black bag over his shoulder. A dark Santa. The gray doors groaned as they parted, the two halves yawning open against the night, and he descended into the musty blackness. Below, he stowed his stolen treasure in a small room beneath the kitchen, in the chest of an extinct dumbwaiter. In that room, in the heavy darkness surrounding him, he undressed and tucked his clothes away. He then moved upward through the house, naked and sweating, moving through the living map he carried in his mind. Darkness was not a difficulty. This was the terrain of his livelihood, of so much of what he did. He would lower a hand after taking so many measured steps, and it would inevitably fall on the wooden knob of the banister at the base of the staircase. He rose further up into the still and silent house. This was the rote procedure from which he would never deviate. His night was complete. He might go to the bathroom to wash up, peel away the veneer of glistening perspiration, or he might return directly to bed where Kate lay in a heavy sleep. But that was all. As he lay next to her, feeling the pattern of his heartbeat settle into the stillness, he would tell himself that all that had changed was the face of the clock. The ineluctable movement of celestial bodies and the world's measurement of those movements. In the darkness, where he lay beside Kate's sleeping body, it was merely fifty-eight minutes later. The glowing face told him so.

Then came morning, far too bright and early.

Gilbert's eyes opened after the extended cinema of dream, and there was Kate, lashes fluttering like butterfly wings, conscious for the first seconds of her day. They had breakfast together, then Kate went to the grocery store and later made a stew while Gilbert wrote letters to friends. He sat out on the sunporch with the stationery resting on his lap, and watched the gray sky strip the trees of their leaves. In the afternoon, he went into the kitchen, sleepy-eyed and yawning, where Kate stood before a cutting board, dicing a white onion. He placed his hands on her hips as he spoke.

"I think I need a job," he said. "Some place I need to be at a certain hour. Structure, you know."

Kate turned in his arms.

"And what will you do?"

"What I've always done," he said hurtfully. "Play the piano."

Kate smiled and kissed his forehead as though he were a little boy.

"There's a bar in town with a piano. An upright."

"That would work."

"It's the kind of piano that needs tuning." Kate laughed, imagining Gilbert at the piano in this bar called the Green Room that she had known all her life.

Gilbert drove there that afternoon and spoke with the proprietor about playing in the evenings. As he came in, he saw that the piano was old, the varnish worn, the ivory keys chipped and split. The proprietor's name was Harold. He was fat, dressed like a mechanic, and smoked cigars. His Brooklyn accent was distorted by a slight speech impediment. He said he knew Gilbert.

"Saw you at Addy Willoughby's wake. Your daddy told everyone how lazy you were. Never forget that."

Gilbert managed his poise. He told Harold that he was staying with Kate, his cousin, making sure she was okay in this period of transition. He kept his voice very formal, respectful. He said he didn't want to play piano for money, only for something to do. Harold nodded his guarded approval and said that that was good because he couldn't pay anything. It would all be for tips. Maybe a drink every now and then if people actually came in for the music. From behind the bar he lifted up a large dingy glass that had once been a fishbowl. Gilbert could collect his tips in this, he said. "But don't expect much from the people around Fayette. This isn't New Orleans."

It was fine with Gilbert. He needed a job. What he was really after was a plausible explanation to answer any questions Kate might have concerning where his money came from. It was a bonus if the job involved Gilbert playing the piano. In her mind, this was who he was.

The following evening Gilbert left for the Green Room just before six and began playing to the empty bar as the sun set. After a few songs, a group of former high school students from the class of 1975 came in. They congregated toward the back and didn't seem to notice the piano or Gilbert. Certainly not the tip jar. They spoke of old times, got drunk. When they laughed, Gilbert couldn't hear himself play. He wondered why he was doing this. Then he thought: I am working; I am a pianist.

But from the beginning, it didn't go well. A few people came in and sat at the bar, then after a few drinks they approached the piano with a random collection of change, maybe a dollar bill. Gilbert always nodded in thanks as the change rattled against the glass, and everyone in the bar turned toward the noise. Whenever this happened he couldn't help but feel a keen edge of embarrassment. His face brightened; his gaze settled on the backs of his white hands as they floated over the keys. Shortly after midnight he would gather up his change from the fishbowl and drive home.

One evening at the dinner table Kate asked if she could come to the bar to watch him play. She had nothing else to do, and it would be fun. Gilbert suddenly stopped chewing his food. He cleared his throat and looked up from his plate of fried chicken. He looked her in the eye and, with all the sincerity he could muster, said, "It would make me nervous."

"What would make you nervous?"

"Your presence."

"I'd just be sitting there," Kate said, smiling at his discomfort.

"I wouldn't be able to play."

Kate poked his shoulder with a rigid forefinger and said, "Oh yes you would. You're a professional. And it's just the Green Room, a little dive bar."

Gilbert pretended to be deeply wounded at Kate's description of his venue. The smile left his face. He pushed his plate away as if his appetite had been cruelly assaulted.

"Come on," she said, almost laughing. "You're too sensitive. Let me come watch you play, Gilbert."

"Fine," he said, wagging his head. "Come on by whenever you want."

Kate curled up against his shoulder. "I just want to hear you play."

But Gilbert was concerned about having her come to the Green Room for another reason, and it had to do with Harold. He always seemed suspicious of Gilbert, prejudiced. It was as though he recognized trouble in him, the germ of all bad luck. Whenever he set his eyes on Gilbert, he conveyed the sense that he could see through him, what lay behind the facade, the musician shtick. Each night when Gilbert came in, Harold asked him what he really did for a living, and Gilbert responded, "You're looking at it," which could never sit well with a working man like Harold.

Late the following night, just before the bar closed, Kate came in through the glass doors, her face flushed with anticipation. Gilbert's heart lifted as the door swung open. But he felt a swelling red wave of embarrassment as well. Though he was doing what a pianist does, he didn't care to have her see him in this setting. Upon the shelf of ragged hardwood sat the opaque tip jar in which a single dollar bill lay crumpled, a bill Gilbert himself had placed there to start things off. He tried to convey serene contentment—a virtuoso slumming it so as to be near his beloved. But he now saw how the charade didn't appear so convincing or so flattering.

"Not much in tips," Kate said as she came up to him. She waved to Harold where he stood behind the bar, and mouthed hello.

"A dollar from a drunk," Gilbert said, smiling at her small red nose.

She brought her hands to his face.

"It's cold out."

"I can leave anytime," Gilbert said. "It's not like I'm on the clock here."

"Let's have a beer in that case. Then we'll go."

She smiled ecstatically and touched her nose to his and kissed him on the mouth. Gilbert looked over to the bar to make sure Harold hadn't seen them. Kate pulled her hands from his cheeks, and Gilbert brought the tune to a silly and abrupt lullaby-like close. He rose from the piano bench and plucked the bill from the jar, and together they went up to the bar, where he bought two cans of beer. To Kate's surprise, Harold took the money.

"It's a hard way to make a living," Harold said.

Kate's eyes widened.

"Doesn't he bring in business?"

"Oh yeah. I run outta beer sometimes. Hope you enjoy playing," Harold said to Gilbert.

"Just an excuse to get out of the house."

"And how are you, Kate? People around town are thinking about you. They ask all the time."

"Fine," she said, her gaze batting between Gilbert and Harold. "I really am."

"Me and your father were good friends, you know," he said.

"I remember."

"He was quite a guy. The kinda guy who coulda run for the Senate or something. I wonder what he woulda thought of this character?"

Kate's smile waned a little, and Harold noticed.

"Well, nobody's gettin' rich tonight," he added.

"We'll get by," Gilbert said quietly, resolutely.

"We will," Kate said. Then she surprised herself by acting on an impulse. She couldn't help herself; without thinking about it, she kissed Gilbert on the mouth again. Gilbert tried to shrink away, but Harold stood in front of them, his eyes suddenly down on the washtub, lost on the cloud of suds.

But Kate wasn't sorry. She told herself that she didn't care what the town thought. She suddenly felt the irrepressible urge to display to everyone that she was in love and proud of the man she loved. He was her cousin, he was a pianist, and she was in love.

"Southern boys are accustomed to a different way of life, aren't they, Kate?" Harold announced after an awkward pause.

"I wouldn't know," she said with real anger in her voice. "Let's sit over there," she whispered to Gilbert.

"You be careful, Kate."

Kate didn't answer. Together she and Gilbert slid off the bar stools and walked to the table next to the plate-glass window, where they could see the wind driving leaves and trash down the street. Between them, a candle burned in a glass holder, the rubbery flame bouncing against the force of their breath as they spoke.

"I forgot," she mumbled.

"No you didn't."

"I swear I did," she said, smiling away.

"You probably shouldn't forget anymore," Gilbert said. "He knows we're cousins."

"I suppose I should be embarrassed. Dating your cousin's taboo, isn't it?"

"I'm fine with it myself. But this isn't my hometown."

"I shouldn't forget anymore."

Gilbert lit a cigarette and smiled.

"I suppose it doesn't matter, Miss Kate."

His voice seemed to clear her mood. After a moment of contemplation, she was the cheerful red-faced girl who had rushed in minutes ago.

"You know, I've been thinking," she said with giggly enthusiasm. "I've never *traveled,* I've never been west of the Mississippi, other than to St. Louis. I've never been out of the *county* practically. And nothing's keeping us here."

Gilbert smiled dourly. He gestured with the fresh coal of his cigarette to the shabby upright piano in the far corner.

"I've got that. I can't just leave." A second after he said this he realized how ridiculous it sounded. Pathetic, he thought.

"A dollar," Kate said, laughing. She smacked her small hand against the lacquered tabletop.

"I was kidding, Kate. Trying to make you laugh." Gilbert said. He drew again on his cigarette. "Where'd you have in mind?"

"Well, I've thought a lot about that too. How about . . . wherever?"

Gilbert took her hand. He wanted to make it clear that he was not mocking her.

"When we pull out of the driveway, we have to go down a particular street, toward a particular highway."

"How about someplace warm. Maybe south, then wherever."

Gilbert gently withdrew his hand from Kate's and looked toward the bar, where Harold was drying glasses. He'd seen them again.

"Maybe we should go home," Gilbert said.

"Maybe we should leave town."

Gilbert waved to Harold as they stood, then they walked, hand-in-hand, for the door.

As they drove home with a cool wind rushing through the leafless trees, Kate couldn't help but smile. They had plans. The future contained the two of them: she could allow herself this small happiness. Gilbert brought his arm about her shoulders.

"I hope everything works out," she said.

"What do you mean?"

"I just hope everything works out. That's all."

ten

Within the course of a week, fall had turned to Indian summer, and so their picnic routine was extended for a few more days. Each afternoon, they packed the reed basket, gathered the dog, climbed into the truck, and headed down to the creekside. Then, without warning, their happy ritual was interrupted.

It happened in the early afternoon, while the air was still. They lay in the cool shade upon the patchwork quilt, mostly quiet, each running a hand through the blue-black coat of Bedford, sprawled between them. Gnawed ears of corn lay crosswise on their plates beside a pile of babyback ribs. Bedford's long white teeth sank into the bone and soft cartilage, his gums red against his teeth.

"What do you imagine goes through a retarded dog's mind?" Gilbert asked.

"The same thing that goes through the minds of all dogs. Wouldn't you think?"

"I suppose." Gilbert rolled over and took Bedford's chubby

face in both hands and rolled his thick soft ears. "Just not as efficiently."

With certain affection, Kate said, "He sure looks dumb."

"Dumb and happy."

Then it began, imperceptibly, dreamlike.

As they chatted, a man appeared on the trail, jogging, his figure bright and glistening in the sun. The three of them lay on the blanket watching his approach. He was an old man, the flesh of his thighs loose and undefined in his effort. As he neared, Bedford rose and galloped toward him, his ears tossing, his big pink tongue hanging from the side of his mouth. Bedford was drawn to the shiny sweat on the old man's legs, so he ran, his head cocked sideways, his tongue askew. In spite of the dog's lazy, happy aspect, the old man froze, visibly terrified, and shouted for Bedford to keep away. But the dog began licking, his long pink tongue curling against the shiny hairless skin. The old man panicked. With the first touch of the tongue he screamed shrilly. When Bedford didn't stop, the old man kicked him in the ribs, the shiny blue-black coat rippling each time the running shoe struck it. Terrified as he was, the man's first wild blows were glancing, so Gilbert just sat up beside Kate, laughing at the spectacle of Bedford happily licking salty brown legs that kicked at him. Then a foot made contact, and they could hear the low thud coming from the thick muscular abdomen. As the dog bawled, Gilbert and Kate stood, then Kate took Gilbert's elbow. She saw his eyes draw back, his nostrils flare and pale. She recognized this as a shadow of the anger that lived in the murky depths of his past. Without taking his eyes off the man, Gilbert removed her small hand from his elbow and said, "We can't allow old men to go around kicking retarded dogs, Miss Kate. Why don't you go back to the truck. I'll take care of everything."

"Let's just get Bedford and go," she said with a hand to her mouth.

"Go back to the truck," he repeated calmly, "and I'll get the dog." Then he walked off.

She called after him one last time, but he simply turned and glowered. So she walked away.

As she headed down the trail, Kate felt a subtle dread, a tiny feeling of impending doom. From time to time, she looked over her shoulder to see what Gilbert was doing, but she had already come to the edge of the meadow. Without another thought, she simply headed into the woods along the narrow clay path that cut through the floor of the forest. Then she reached the truck. She didn't want to know what was going on beyond the curtain of trees, she told herself.

So she waited.

She waited much longer than she thought she would. She grew anxious. He was just going to get Bedford and bring him to the truck. She leaned against the warm grille, arms crossed, gaze fixed on the tiny opening in the woods. All around her were the small living noises of a forest. Finally, she heard Bedford's plodding steps, then he came galloping out of the pattern of green, followed by Gilbert. The picnic basket swung from his hand as he came, smiling, chuckling like a naughty little boy. All he said was, "We'd better be going." Then they climbed into the truck and were gone.

It was the pettiness of the conflict that struck her. So much was an affront to him. Anger governed by whimsy. Kate could recall those things she'd heard about him years ago, but thought such boyish behavior had been shed with adolescence, with his passion for bubble gum and baseball cards. But in a very childish way she also liked it that Gilbert would go so far to protect a creature he loved. She herself felt less vulnerable. She felt safe, like a schoolgirl whose boyfriend is a bully. And she understood that in the end she could only forgive him. There was nothing else to do.

That night they brought the canvas chairs out to the lawn and sat beneath a gigantic soft maple within the scattered shade of the electric streetlight. They sat watching the erratic pattern of small black bats scouring the night air for insects, feeling the warm evening against their faces, through the damp canvas, against their naked legs and arms. There were no words, only a carbonated slurp from time to time and the fluttered exhalation of powdery smoke from Gilbert's mouth. The ember of his cigarette rested at his side in the hand that held his beer. The small orange dot hung in the corner of Kate's vision, every now and then moving through the blackness like the curlicue of a child's stick. Invisible ribbons of smoke rose and whirled downwind as she rested beside him in this splendid silence. As the night deepened, the morning seemed more and more removed. Kate didn't ask what Gilbert had done to that old man, as her father would not have. Like Cecil, she was reserved. The night gradually cooled, and Kate's legs pimpled against the chill. She brusquely ran both hands over her thighs and shins as if to smooth the roughened surfaces, kissed Gilbert's temple, and told him she was going in.

The following morning Kate planted tulip bulbs along the south side of the house; in the afternoon they drove out to a pond near the Penny Farm. They rolled over the dirt road in Gilbert's truck with a cooler of beer in the back, and spent the early afternoon swimming and lying on the floating dock in the weak autumn sun. Gilbert drank and smoked while his skin pinkened. The sky gently rocked as the anchor cable clanked, tethering them in place against the warm breeze.

When they returned, in the early evening, they roasted ears of corn and pork chops on the barbecue grill, then settled in for another night of drinking on the front porch. As Kate sat next to Gilbert in the canvas chair, her mind consumed itself with wonderful details. She wanted to polish her mother's silver, dust the mahogany legs of the dining room table. She wanted to find the checkbook and balance it. Things had gone adrift for a while now, and she needed to know where they stood. Without a word, she leaned over and kissed Gilbert's forehead, then sauntered into house.

She stood between the huge doors to the dining room and gazed at the scene before her. Moths swimming in cones of yellow light, purple veins running through the bloody-red grain of the table. Portraits of dead relatives tilting on the walls, the backs of their necks suspended by hanging wire, knickknacks here and there. Dust fell through the yellow light, covering everything, making a fossil of the home. The ancient Oriental rug shone like streams of molten pewter running through the passageways between the cluttered walls and table.

Late that night, Gilbert found Kate with a giant feather duster in one hand and the trunk of the vacuum in the other. He stood in the doorway, watching, as the vacuum howled around her. Happily lost in mindless work. Then he turned away and climbed the stairs and finally fell asleep to the constant noise humming below.

In the early morning, he found her at the kitchen table with a cup of tea. The countertops gleamed in the predawn light. He saw at once that she hadn't slept. The rims of her eyes were reddened with sleeplessness, her hair still hung neatly over her shoulders. She sat before the cup, the cotton string of a teabag wound about her slender forefinger, stirring the pool with the thick brown pouch.

"You worked all night," he said as he approached her.

"Who knows what came over me," she said. "I like it that we can live this way together."

Gilbert took her into his arms.

"You like playing house."

"I think I do."

"Well, I'm going to slip back into bed."

"I'll join you in a little while."

With that, Gilbert kissed her forehead. He sauntered upstairs and climbed back into the warm sheets.

As Kate sat at the table the sun rose over town. She heard the morning paper strike the porch, then the paper boy's squeaky bicycle ride away. She slowly stood and staggered to the door to pick up the tightly wrapped baton. Inside, she dismantled it and found the crossword puzzle in its usual section. Soon she was immersed in the arrangement of the alphabet, her mind happily lost in a sea of words. Then, as she tapped at the newsprint with the yellow wooden pencil, her thoughts easy and lucid, she saw a headline alongside the puzzle: Man found bound in ditch.

Beneath a head-and-shoulders shot of the old man was his name, Robert P. Lester—a retired chemist at an unnamed St. Louis tire manufacturing plant. It was a miracle for a man of his age to have survived the cold night at all, the story began. Lester was suffering from exposure, a collapsed lung, a broken clavicle, a broken cheekbone, and a dislocated jaw. Presently he was in intensive care at an unnamed St. Louis hospital.

The story the elderly man had to tell police was a bizarre tale of random violence. While jogging through the forested hills on the outskirts of Fayette, he was savagely accosted by a party of rogue picnickers. Nothing on his person had been taken, so the motive was not believed to be robbery. He was merely hunted down like an animal and beaten senseless. At some point the blunt end of a corncob was shoved down his throat with such force that his jaw was dislocated. As Lester lay helpless on the forest floor, he was beaten so badly his cheekbone was crushed, his sternum fractured. He was hog-tied with cloth napkins. Wooden napkin rings were pushed into his eye sockets, bruising both eyes. Through the night, he crawled on his belly to the road, only to topple into a ditch. By morning, he was nearly dead with the corncob still lodged in his jaw. Of course the community was horrified. People thought such savagery occurred only across the river.

Kate's throat hardened, her face tingled. One of the suspects, the story said, was a young man with blond hair and a black Labrador.

Kate looked up from the paper, then slowly went to the window over the kitchen sink to see what was outside, quite certain someone would be there waiting for her. But the town was just as it always had been: cars, building, trees, people, lawn, and sky. All seemed very usual, very real.

After gazing at the familiar scene for some time, she turned from the window and stared at the portion of the kitchen ceiling that served as the floor to their room. She took a few deep breaths and slowly strode up the staircase and into the stillness of the room, where he lay sleeping beneath flannel sheets. She sat on the bed next to his head and said his name. He awoke as though he had never been asleep.

"Something's wrong," she said, her voice level, grave.

He took her hand in his.

"And what's that?"

She unfolded the paper and handed it to him, then went to the wall and turned on the overhead light. After reading a few lines he sat up. She observed his expression momentarily display real concern.

"We made the paper," he mumbled as he read.

"We shouldn't be laughing at ourselves right now."

Gilbert looked up from the newsprint and put a hand on her shoulder.

"It would take a better detective than any they got," he said with kindly, knowing condescension.

Kate held her eyes on his. When Gilbert brought the back of his hand to her cheek, she pulled away and gazed at him with suspicion. His casual air frightened her.

"I'm scared," she said in the same level voice.

Gilbert took a moment to read her mood.

"I screwed up, Miss Kate."

"We're in trouble."

Gilbert took her head into his arms. His face pinkened, his eyes gazed over with worry.

"You nearly killed the man."

The silence of the house stood in the air.

"I lost it," he whispered. "The guy swung at me and I lost it. All I can say is I'm sorry."

"They know what we look like. They know Bedford."

He looked at Kate and saw she was about to cry. He drew her forehead to his cheek, as though resting her head.

"What if they figure something out?"

"God, Kate. Maybe I should leave town," he said.

Kate's body shook beneath his arm.

"No, no, no, no, no . . ."

"I screwed up."

"Don't leave," she said wearily, as though irritated by the sound of his voice. Gilbert felt her wet face against his neck. "Maybe this will go away."

"I could leave and come back. After everything's blown over."

"We'll go together. We'll take that trip."

"I'll be back."

"You can't leave. You just can't. Not without me."

eleven

Kate thought of herself as fundamentally naive when it came to judging the character of others. At some level she believed that anyone was capable of anything, that the spectrum of human behavior was complete in every individual. Psychoanalysis and philosophy were the hobbies of fools. This was Uncle Charlie's phrase. However, she did understand the differences between Gilbert and herself. For instance, she understood her own misfortune as being the result of unknown forces. But Gilbert's misfortune appeared more or less self-inflicted. So who could feel sorry for him? She sometimes questioned judgment that was so limited in scope. Yet part of his trouble seemed a shadow cast on him by his father, an overgrown little boy, and she wondered how responsible Gilbert actually was for his own unlucky life. That Gilbert might leave without her was her greatest fear. In fact, it was her only fear. When she imagined life in her house without Gilbert, she felt her skin chill.

But there were things she could not know. For instance, she could not know how fond Gilbert had become of his life in Fayette or of the practical reasons for his staying. His thievery had become profitable, and he felt his nature was elusive enough and this setting so unlikely that no one would ever find him in this house, the home of Cecil Willoughby, war hero, hometown attorney. Couldn't imagine the police strolling up the walkway, a warrant for his arrest flapping from the blue arm of the law. As the days passed, this confidence only confirmed itself.

All Kate knew of the story concerning the old man came through the newspaper. It seemed to live only as a fiction, a story dreamed by a faceless author. Each morning Kate searched the paper for anything related to the case, yet found nothing. Nevertheless, she and Gilbert sequestered themselves in the stone house, with Kate driving to a neighboring town for necessities like groceries, beer, and cigarettes.

Kate didn't want to leave right away either. She wanted to see how things would unfold, she wanted to read the newspaper. Their situation was worrisome but not as frightening as she thought it might be. As the days passed, she likened it to being on the lam. They couldn't wander about as they used to; they were afraid of going to the pool hall or taverns, and Gilbert stopped playing at the Green Room altogether. Though the town seemed unaware of it, they were essentially fugitives. One evening she shared this thought with Gilbert at the kitchen table.

"You shouldn't think of yourself as a fugitive, Kate. I'm the fugitive." His voice was sharp and abrupt. "Robert P. Lester will get better, the world will go on with its business."

Kate sat quietly before her bowl of tomato soup and saltine crackers. Her eyes followed him as he walked to the door, where he paused and drew a cigarette from the breast pocket of his shirt. She smiled weakly at nothing. She saw that he was tired of the subject, and it frightened her. He had already apologized for what he had done, and he silently made it clear that he wasn't going to apologize again.

"I'm gonna have a cigarette out on the front porch. It's an act of defiance," he said in the same severe tone.

Kate stared at him over the bowl of red soup. She would let him alone for the rest of the evening and turn in early. When she finished her soup, that's exactly what she did. Not for another two hours did she hear the kitchen door slap shut and Gilbert's feet softly mounting the stairs. When Gilbert finally joined her in bed, he gazed down at her sleepy face and murmured, "I'm too old to be losing my temper over things that don't matter."

"Just don't leave," she said, looking into his tired eyes. "Don't ever leave."

"No need to worry about that, Miss Kate."

Very late that night, long after Kate had fallen asleep, Gilbert arose from bed and glided down the stairs. He moved through the night and returned in precisely the same fashion. Whenever he deviated from the routine, he did so very conscientiously. Routine was what he loved.

Whenever possible, he walked down sidewalks, so as to appear to be a pedestrian from a distance. When cars occasionally passed on the otherwise deserted streets, he shifted laterally into shadows until the hemisphere of white light had passed and he was again on his way. No dogs, no husbands taking out the midnight garbage to the alleyway. Down the sidewalk he could move quickly in spite of his unconventional dress. And it made him feel better, less criminal. He believed vigilance should meld into an easy manner. This had always been central to his ever-evolving credo. The tense finished last, yet discretion was mandatory. He let such thoughts pass through his mind as he walked because he didn't want to forget anything. The thought process had to move from large to small, from general to specific, so by the time he arrived at the home he was about to plunder, his mind was lucid, relaxed, and fixed on particulars.

That evening he went to the large stucco home he'd cased a few nights before. The neighborhood was quiet, and dense with trees. He came directly up to the house, lost in the shifting wind-driven shadows. He stopped at the trellis, where dried flowers hung, then moved through an opening, curled petals rattling about his shoulders.

The night was cold and moonless. Gilbert had felt himself warming beneath the wool union suit he wore under the thin layer of black, and he now felt a slender column of perspiration cooling along his spine. As he approached the house through the wall of flowers, he felt the return of the familiar thrill. In small ways he loved all of this—the air around him full of the noises of brittle leaves crumbling under his shoes, skeletal branches groaning in the wind. He squatted and contemplated strategy. Not until he had the shape and detail of the plan clear in his mind would he leave the refuge of the shadow. It always came to him.

He mounted the broad blocks of limestone that formed the trunk of the chimney. The rubbery soles of his shoes fit cleanly in the thick mortared grooves between the yellow stones. Within seconds he was on the roof of cedar shakes, resting within the shadow formed by the eaves of a dormer. He moved carefully over the uneven surface, vigilant for any moss or moisture, until he was above a window, where he lowered himself onto his belly and dipped a leg over the eaves, keeping a gloved hand on the aluminum gutter. When his toe touched a ledge, he eased himself down and balanced his weight on the ball of his foot until his balance had shifted from roof to ledge. He was calm, surrounded as he was by avenues of escape.

A rectangle of white light slid from the gray of his cheek to the black of his hat. Squatting, his knees folded and jutting, he faced the window with his fingers cupped under the trim to keep from falling away. He saw the windows were lockless. He slipped a hand into his hip pocket and produced a tiny lockblade. With his teeth he pried out the stunted blade and lodged it between the panes. They swung freely open and he was lowering himself into the relative warmth and quiet. His toe came down on an oak end table between two picture frames. He felt about for stability with the ball of his foot, testing the play of the table's glued joints. All his weight rested upon its top, and he turned and closed the halves of the window.

He thought, moved, thought, and moved again. In the uppermost compartment of an armoire he found a small chest of silver. On the dining room table he saw two small candlestick holders he suspected to be made of either twelve- or fourteen-karat gold. Gilbert believed that by putting his tongue to a particular metal he could decipher its kind and purity. He moved through the dimly lit rooms, taking this or that and stowing it neatly in his bag, or leaving something where it lay, having judged it not worthwhile. For six or seven minutes he moved along, satisfied with what he had collected, before working his way toward the back door. As he passed through the dining room once more, he saw a small silver globe the size of a baseball on an end table. He lifted it into the dull light, feeling its weight, its gravity, and decided to keep it. He put it in his bag and left through the kitchen.

Then he was moving through the lawns, beneath the swaying trees, all the way to his cousin's house, where he came in through the cellar and stored his collection in the dumbwaiter as he always did. Moments later, he was coming into Kate's bedroom and easing himself beside her where she slept, deeply lost in dream. The clock read three-twelve he noted before joining her.

Fayette was proving to be what Gilbert called "a good town."

It was a small wealthy community fearful of publicizing its own misfortunes. Long ago, Gilbert had observed that farms and businesses in such places often did not report robberies, so long as they were small in scale, as it would increase the owners' insurance premiums. They quietly replaced what had been taken, believing that over time this was the less expensive of two solutions. Even the local newspaper balked at publishing word of any increase in crime for fear that it would detract from the reputation of the town and local law enforcement. Negative publicity, it was believed by the more prosperous citizens, was a threat to property values. Quaint little towns like Fayette had the reputation of being safely tucked away from the problems of modern American cities. In this day and age they were rare enough, and as communities they were proud of themselves. For years Gilbert had anticipated and capitalized on the discreet nature of such places. In return—almost with the air of having struck a silent bargain with the town—he resolved to steal only small objects that they did not see or use every day, things their owners often might suspect themselves of having misplaced. So he conducted his burglaries in such a way that they would not cumulatively draw attention.

With this thought in mind, he slipped out of bed around midnight the following evening and drove down a side street toward the highway. When he came to the abandoned Steak and Shake, he drove down another side street that was really a lane, and cut his lights. He quietly stepped out of the truck, pressed his door shut, then turned to the bed, where he unfolded a canvas tarpaulin beneath which lay the black cotton sack of collectibles. With all the nonchalance he could summon, he lifted it from the truck and started across the darkened parking lot toward the single yellow light burning in the night. Beneath it, a figure could be made out. As he approached the light, he felt a return of a familiar nervous energy. A condition of the profession, he told himself again and again as he walked. He came right up to the figure, and together they eased into a shadow as if it were a telephone booth. Then they embraced.

"Isabelle's going to wake up tomorrow a little disheartened," Hap said as they released each other in the darkness.

"The fund will be promptly replenished."

"Kate isn't broke, is she?"

"She tells me we're going on vacation."

"I thought that's what you've been on all along—vacation.

"This time we're leaving the house."

"You're lovers."

"She wants to travel. Says she hasn't wandered a hundred miles from her own front porch."

"You're lovers. I get it." Hap wanted to laugh pretty hard, but didn't.

Without another word, Gilbert handed his brother the black sack and squatted to the pavement. Hap held the bag with one hand and dipped the other into its mouth. One by one, he laid the collectibles out between them. Before the sack was empty, Hap reached around to his hip pocket and produced a thick roll of bills.

"Thanks for making yourself liquid," Gilbert said.

"This wasn't easy."

Gilbert smiled in the faint yellow light and took the bag from Hap. "Let me show you something real neat."

His hand roamed around in the sack for a moment, then he pulled out a small felt bag. He untied the cotton strings that bound the soft fabric and withdrew the small, shiny sphere.

"What's that?" Hap asked.

"A map of the world, little brother."

Hap took the orb into his hands and held it up to the electric light. He felt its weight on the tripod of his fingers and thumb.

"So it is," he mumbled. "Maybe I'll give it to Isabelle. Smooth things out."

Hap lifted the tiny globe into the yellow light again. They both looked at its perfect shape, the fine etchings of continents and oceans, the gentle ridges of mountain ranges. Hap rotated it so that North America was shining down on them.

"The world made of silver."

"So it is, little brother. So it is."

twelve

ↂ

She liked the feel of him in the morning. Somehow his temples were always powdered with what tasted like salt crystals whenever she drew her tongue along the dark yellow line of his brow. She would do this by way of waking him as he lay asleep on his side. Instinctively he would roll over, toward the soft wetness. Then she would bring a naked leg, as smooth and polished as the leg of an antique chair, over his tummy, her shin easing over his flaccid penis, and she would hover. His eyes would not open; he would pretend to be caught in a dream. An ache would slowly form in his brow, crimping his forehead into waves.

She liked beginning his day like this. He would typically fall back to sleep, and she would descend the stairs to the kitchen. This was time she needed for herself. She loved this small portion of the day when she was alone, yet at any moment could climb the stairs, crawl into bed, and be alone no more. She liked fixing his coffee in the mornings, preparing the percolator, filling the columnar steel container with water, and having it waiting there for him. She liked the smell and the chugging sound, though she drank only tea herself. The smell of coffee meant Gilbert was upstairs asleep in her bed. This part of the day had become precious to her, as it accommodated her need to feel that she could be at once happy and alone. She needed this confidence, because it tended to simplify the complex feelings she still held for Gilbert. It also eased the acute sense of loss she felt for her mother, softening the absence. These confident mornings grounded the days and nights that followed. And they worked well for her until one day late in the autumn.

The day broke without warning. Wind whipped through her bathrobe as she lifted the newspaper from the cold gray paint of the porch. When she came inside she poured herself a cup of tea, sat at the kitchen table, and began unfurling the sections in search of the crossword puzzle. There at the top of the page was a headline: Local Couple Missing Two-Karat Engagement Ring. She thought nothing of it. Then she saw the picture, the grainy snapshot. As her eyes swept down the column of print, it occurred to her slowly, imperceptibly, that she was reading an obituary, though she had no idea that the entire page had been devoted to the actions of her cousin. The second story gave the statistics of a life, its movement, its greater arc, the various settings. Then it disclosed that the man had been assaulted a few months ago. The police had no suspects. But now it was murder.

The world swam in Kate's vision. She felt faint. For most of the next hour, she sat at the table. At times she couldn't breathe; panic seemed to attack her throat. Then, in tiny increments, her breath returned. Once she felt settled, she tried to answer a question again and again in the most reductive terms: why was this happening?

Eventually Gilbert came ambling down the staircase. He staggered to the percolator, as though it would provide relief from some obscure agony. He sat beside her. Kate folded the paper as he poured a tablespoon of sugar into his coffee and watched it melt. Then he noticed the bloodless look of her face.

"Anything wrong?"

She shook her head, her eyes lost on the view in the window. "No," she mumbled. "Nothing."

"We should plot our little trip," he said.

This focused Kate's mind.

"We should," she whispered. "We really should."

Now Gilbert was sure something was wrong. But just as he was about to ask, Kate raised a hand against any further questions and insisted she was fine. So it was left at that.

Kate spent the better part of the morning packing in her room while Gilbert charted their trip on a map downstairs. She could hardly think. She had a conversation with her mother, asking her what was going on. Was Gilbert really a murderer? He was family; what should she do? If he left or was taken away, she would be alone. Kate's voice was breathy and uneven, a reflection of the exhaustion she felt. Eventually she managed to leave the house and drop Bedford off at the Penny Farm. When she returned she went directly back to her room. In the afternoon, Gilbert came up and announced he had made a few decisions. They could leave by the weekend so long as the money from his mutual fund had been wired to the Western Union office and he had the cash in hand. Kate insisted this was unnecessary. She just wanted to go. She had money, and lots of it, and she wanted to go now. Gilbert politely declined. He was thirty-one; she was eighteen and on a fixed income. Even if it was a very large fixed income, it was nonetheless fixed and she should be prudent.

As he spoke, she stared into his green eyes. She felt fantastically tired. It was as though a cell of energy at the core of her person had suddenly died. Then she felt his hand on her shoulder. An idea had struck him. He could call his broker and have the money wired while they were on the road.

Kate took his hand and put it against her cheek. "Okay," she murmured. "Let's get going."

Within the hour they were on the highway. Kate had the sensation that they were floating over the surface of the earth. The plains fled by in the windows as they sped along just a few inches above the crowned continent. Kate felt she wasn't really experiencing what was going on around her, that she was watching the landscape unfold within the frame of the windshield as if it were projected on a screen in a movie theater. Once they were out in the countryside, she felt a sensation of relief coupled with dread. Tired as she was, relief eclipsed some of the unpleasantness.

Gilbert's truck had become a getaway truck, and he didn't even know it. They took roads that wove alongside rivers and creeks, roads that crumbled along the edges, then abruptly narrowed to a single lane. Every now and then, ragged cornfields bound by new fence lines sprawled in all directions. By noon they were in the southwestern-most portion of Lincoln Land, that domain of the Eighth Judicial Circuit that the young lawyer had traveled on horseback before becoming president, and continued south through Little Egypt. Just before dusk they came into Cairo, where they spent the night at a twenty-dollar motel built of cinder blocks, surrounded by city sounds of squalor and small-time bedlam—the Doppler howl of passing police sirens, the proprietor screaming at his wife and smacking his daughter. Kate lay awake next to Gilbert through most of the night, listening to the world outside the panelled door and the low, rhythmic whistling of breath passing through her cousin's elegant nostrils. She felt an irresistible urge to awaken him and inform him that he was a murderer. But she just watched him sleeping beside her in this terrible darkness. For the first time since Gilbert had come into her life, she felt anger toward him. What kind of person fatally assaults an old man for kicking his dog? She wanted to tell her mother about her nephew, how he had ruined what was left of her daughter's life. It had come apart and an old man's had ended as a result of a barroom pianist's brutal whim.

Without having rested at all, she woke him at dawn. They dressed in the half-light, then drove to a small diner in what they judged to be the nicer part of town. Then they were on their way to Memphis with the sun rising over the bare trees and harvested cornfields. But as they moved south, the grassy ditches greened, slowly growing chromatic to Kate's eye that was now, in November, accustomed to colorless landscapes. As she rode beside Gilbert, feeling at her feet and face the soft issue of warmth from the truck's heater, she appeared gravely dour.

"Somehow road trips never quite live up to what they promised," Gilbert said, looking away from the road.

"It's been grayer than I thought it would be."

"That why you've been so quiet?"

"I guess so," she whispered.

"You thought we'd leave the city limits of Fayette and the world would turn green and sunny: Vacationland."

"It's greener here."

"Maybe we should keep heading south?"

"Yeah, south."

They took their time, pausing over covered bridges and bright green fields standing against brown forests of hardwoods stripped of their color. The glass insulators of old telephone poles glinted in the angled sunlight. They arrived in Memphis in the evening and drove directly to a bar Gilbert frequented on Front Street. An old man played banjo on a stool in a corner, lit by a single cone of light, while scattered about the bar people lazily ate chicken wings from red plastic baskets and drank draft beer. Gilbert led Kate through the layered yellow smoke to a booth toward the back, where a waitress finally came by to take their orders. Kate said she was having whatever Gilbert was having. Gilbert was having wings and beer.

They passed the evening drinking, not saying much. At times, the bar seemed to whirl in Kate's field of vision, making her feel dizzy. For two days, nothing had seemed real. Again, she felt as though she were standing outside herself. Across from her, Gilbert admired the ironwork of the balcony surrounding the upper level and the staircase rising up to it. He pointed out how fond he was of the place. He also admired the elemental quality of the banjo. Kate said she was sleepy and lay down in the booth. She heard him ask if he seemed very much older than herself, admiring as he did things like ironwork and banjo music—things that were so much a part of the world that preceded her own. Not that this was the least bit upsetting to him; he was just wondering if it upset her.

"No," she mumbled from under the table. "It doesn't bother me."

"Not feeling well?" he asked.

"My stomach's upset."

"Is it tart? The sauce on these wings is too tart."

She didn't answer. A moment later she heard him ask again.

"Yeah, it's tart," she mumbled.

When they finally left the bar, the sun was down, its orange crest of light shrinking against the violet evening sky. The night was cool and cloudless, and all along Front Street music issued from open doorways onto a more or less empty town. The fresh air seemed to settle Kate's mind.

"Sunday night," Gilbert said as they looked upon the emptiness.

"We have money, and lots of it," Kate said petulantly. "No more motels."

As they walked toward the truck, Gilbert asked how much she had brought. He was just curious.

Kate looked him up and down. Without a word, she opened

her purse. She fussed around in it until she found the white bank envelope. Then she parted the paper and drew a thumb over the roof of bills so that Gilbert might see they all bore the countenance of Benjamin Franklin.

"And how many are there?" he asked, his voice slightly stiff.

"Forty."

"Why so many?" Gilbert possessed a reverence for money in the form of actual currency.

"Because I didn't plan on motels. This means that between us we have six thousand dollars minus maybe fifty," she said.

"I guess we can make some adjustments."

"I think we should."

That night they stayed in a two-hundred-dollar suite. It wasn't the most expensive available, but nearly so. Kate allowed a bellman to carry their luggage, then handed Gilbert three one-hundred-dollar bills to pay for the room. She glided up the broad hanging staircase with the bellman at her side while Gilbert looked on.

They lay before the suite's small balcony, glass doors separating them from the lights of the city. A quarter-moon rose through the night and vanished at the height of the glass, and still neither could sleep. Kate lay in Gilbert's arms, drumming her fingers on his bony sternum.

"Where should we be off to tomorrow?" he asked in the cool darkness.

Kate didn't answer promptly. Her small fingers hammered away. He saw that her eyes were open.

"South. Let's just keep heading south."

"It'll be warmer in New Orleans."

"New Orleans, then," she said in the darkness. "Let's go to New Orleans."

Kate rolled out of Gilbert's arms, brought two fingers to her shoulder, and slowly drew the tips over the grainy scar. As the night deepened, her eyes fixed on the hypnotic glow of sodium lights rising up through the glass doors, the fan of colors rotating as traffic passed below. She felt her cousin beside her, his legs working through a dream. She let her mind run unimpeded in the quiet. . . .

Why was this happening? Was this a part of the pattern, the inherent design of her being that fated her life to endless misfortune? What had struck down Gilbert and her brother, what had touched her shoulder with its poisonous finger—was it all the work of the same ghost? The ghost who had touched her mother and father? It now occurred to her in a complete way that her second parent was dead. The finality of it seemed to settle out of the darkness.

As she stared into the twisted light beyond the glass doors, she longed for the steady presence she had known as a child. She thought of the kitchen table at home, how it was the center of her universe three times each day. She remembered how her father was a ritualist in the meals he took, in the time and manner in which he took them. He believed regularly planned meals were important because they lent structure to one's day, ballast. He needed tranquillity around the table, hushed voices or no voices at all. She could recall how the atmosphere might appear grave or sullen to visitors when the family was really quite happy. Her father rarely spoke, and when spoken to he was curt, protective of the calm. Only with Kate did this change. To her, he spoke in a low, hushed voice as he coaxed her to take food. Yet the spoken word still lay surrounded by vast silences.

She could recall how she wandered into her father's study as a young girl. She sought the same peacefulness he did—and to escape the eerie conversations her mother had begun to have with the dead. She could hear her mother's footsteps over the kitchen, accompanied by the voice. As she lay curled in her father's lap, her eyes would sweep the room, noting artifacts, heirlooms—rifles leaning in the glass case, the shotguns that stood in the corner, their dark, oiled barrels forming a vertex against the bright wall. As a child she imagined them as tipi poles. On the chair beside the shotguns lay his wool hunting shirt, the breast pocket bulging with spent twelve-gauge casings. In the small oval mirror she could see the candle box that was originally an old cedar cigar box of her great grandfather's that had been passed down through generations.

Her father's voice would carry on and on in the quiet of the study in a volitionless monotone while Kate gradually fell asleep in his lap each night. This was her ritual for nearly four years, until one night deep in the fall of 1976. Kate could still recall that night quite clearly. Even as a little girl, she recognized that her father had grown melancholy in the wake of Adam's death. His attention always seemed elsewhere, his manner listless. That night he had come home especially late from his law office, solemnly declined dinner, then retreated to the sanctuary of his study. Her mother had prepared a roast duck, which she and Kate ate in relative silence. Kate meticulously pared away at her dinner, taking small bites, but eating grew difficult as her mother's voice became at once louder and more removed. There was an element of hopelessness in the voice, something like that in her father's.

"Why isn't Daddy eating with us?" Kate asked.

Her mother's voice ceased.

"Why isn't Daddy eating?"

Addy abruptly straightened herself. Her eyes jerked out of their trance and settled on Kate.

"He's on the phone with your uncle Charlie," she said softly, her voice impersonal.

After the dishes were done, her mother vanished upstairs and Kate into her father's study, where he sat, more quiet and melancholy than usual, but smiling as his daughter's figure approached tentatively in the half-light. He began with a fairy tale, one he read in a slower cadence, a quieter tone. After lulling Kate to sleep, Cecil took her frail body into his arms, mounted the staircase, laid her to rest upon the ancient feather mattress, and kissed her thin blond hair. Then he left the room, silently closing the door behind him. As he moved through the shadows of the narrow hall, he could hear his wife's snoring. He descended the stairs, the movements of his legs and arms impassive, and entered the kitchen, where he poured himself a cup of coffee. Then he went into his study, set the hot ceramic cup on the desktop, and took from a drawer a small glass capsule known as an "L" pill, a lethal dose of cyanide carried by American agents and servicemen susceptible to capture during World War II. He crushed the tiny cylinder of glass against the hardwood and dusted its contents into the coffee with his left forefinger. After the bitter taste of almonds and a whisper of pain and fear, there was only darkness and nothing. A whisper of pain, then darkness and nothing. A whisper, then nothing. So his sleeping daughter would forever imagine it.

thirteen

Ole Miss was the alma mater of a Willoughby. Either a Cecil or a Thomas, Gilbert explained. Uncle Charlie had told him a long time ago, but he wasn't sure.

The landscape took on new color as they drove, the trees and kudzu that smothered them had an overripe greenness, a dead green, about them. Still, it wasn't summery, Kate thought. But the colors gradually evolved and grew brighter. As they turned, her mood seemed to lift, to change like weather. The situation was too much to comprehend; her life had taken on a dreamlike quality, which served to quell the anxiety of the day before. She felt physically different. Her breathing had slowed and deepened, her ability to concentrate returned. But she still did not feel at all herself. Something in the way she apprehended the world around her had changed. Then she realized what it was. She simply felt numb.

When they came into Oxford, they found townspeople milling about the square. Gilbert and Kate wandered around for a while themselves before coming to the statue of the Confederate soldier. They had lunch at a restaurant that had once been a livery stable owned by William Faulkner's father, then they toured the campus.

"This is where everyone my age is," Kate said as they paused under a dogwood tree.

"It must feel strange."

"Like I'm playing hooky."

"I feel so goddamn *old,*" Gilbert said, gazing about.

"Not to me."

"They're infants." He turned to her and with a look of startled horror added, "Kate, most of these children are older than you."

"You just realized that?"

Gilbert wagged his head. "I guess I did."

They walked around campus a while longer, visiting a museum of sorts that contained Civil War and Faulkner memorabilia. A class of fifteen or twenty students came in, all of them seemingly freshmen. The teaching assistant pointed out a Confederate rifle, a pistol, an old map of Vicksburg. Their procession was strangely quaint and formal, yet the students seemed so young. Kate saw how Gilbert looked pained by the sight of them. She felt her strength suddenly bleeding away. She took him by the elbow and said, "Let's get going to New Orleans."

By early afternoon they were again on the road. That evening they stayed in an old hotel in Natchez that stood beneath the bluff along the riverfront. Here at least it was warm. Next to the hotel was a bar. The tall, broad doors were kept open during fair weather, and men gathered out on the front stoop with drinks in hand, watching the river traffic drift up and down the invisible watery path. Silhouettes of barges and ships could be seen beneath their incandescent lights. Kate and Gilbert watched the flow from the balcony of their room for a while before deciding to join the voices below.

They spent the evening on one of two long church pews that

straddled the bar's entrance. All the men seemed to know one another. One at a time, as though by sheerest accident, they approached Kate and Gilbert, sat at their side, and asked where they came from. All had fantastic histories themselves, and none seemed connected to the everyday world but by the most casual ties. One was a sculptor, another took a skiff up and down the Mississippi, dragging the river bottom for small treasure. He claimed to have found Civil War cannonballs and ancient perfume bottles, the latter of which could bring considerable money. If he found the right collector, maybe eight hundred, maybe a thousand. After a few minutes of talk, each man would stand, go to the bar, then join the crowd milling about in the street, pausing every so often to gaze out on the river. They all seemed so wonderfully idle, Gilbert thought, so easy among themselves.

"I don't feel as old here," he whispered to Kate once they were alone.

"I feel like a child. I feel like I should be in school back at Oxford."

"You are a child."

Kate turned to him and squinted. She wasn't smiling. Gilbert had no idea what she was going through, she thought. And she couldn't tell him.

"Not that you act like one," Gilbert added, putting his arm about her narrow shoulders. "It's because you don't. That's what's fooled me these past few months."

Kate took another pull on the longneck bottle. She felt her senses gathering about her as she drank.

"They don't seem the type who work," she said, returning her attention to the school of fellows in the street.

"Lazy white men. I like them."

"Where're the wives?"

"They all have that divorced look. That burnt-out look, like they've endured a few too many small-time tragedies."

"They look haggard."

"Exactly. Haggard."

After a few drinks, they returned to their room, where they slept with the doors to the balcony open. The air gradually cooled, and for a time the men down in the bar grew boisterous. In the morning, all was perfectly quiet until the sun rose over the bluff behind the hotel. When Kate and Gilbert finally got on the road they realized it was later than they thought, having awakened in the broad shadow of the bluff. But they were on vacation, Kate said. Soon they were in the flow of interstate traffic through Baton Rouge, heading toward New Orleans, and by dusk they were easing down Decatur Street, near Jackson Square, looking for a room.

Kate announced that she wanted to spend all of her money, and spend it in New Orleans. That night they stayed at a hotel on Esplanade Avenue with a backyard filled with a bizarre array of flora and exotic birds. Trees grew out of the red brick floor of the commons area, creating the sense of living in the trees, high above it all. The room led out onto a balcony that overlooked a bend in the Mississippi. On a cedar branch before their door stood an ancient blue parrot with clipped wings, while peacocks strutted below. Here was the color Kate had been looking for.

And it was here that she learned a new way of dealing with everything that was going on in her head. It was a new way of executing the day, a way that involved the conscious release of the past and future until all that was left was now, the eternal, omnipresent now. You slip into it as you would a tub of water warmed to body temperature, she thought. New Orleans was the tub. Here regret and dread dissolved in the present; time lay in ruins before and behind you. At first she thought the idea incommunicable, but later suspected Gilbert had imparted it to her by some black magic known only to him. All she knew for sure was that she was grateful to someone for something she didn't entirely understand. Night dovetailed into morning and morning into day with astonishing ease. Kate and Gilbert moved about town by foot, into this restaurant, through a thicket of tourists, into another bar where she wolfed scotch. The town was here for them, and they would accept it so long as they were having a good time. And they would always be having a good time.

They spent a lot of money, even by Kate's new standards. Every time they left the hotel room, Kate would unfurl two or three new hundred-dollar bills and return hours later with currency smaller than twenties. But Kate was supremely unconcerned. For five days and nights, she wore the same summer dress without a thought of changing. As the days blended, the dress seemed to become a part of her, to belong to her anatomy like a second skin. She showered irregularly. In some magical way, it was a part of this new mentality of infinite and blissful sangfroid. She was losing herself. This was how she put it to Gilbert one bright morning as they sat across from each other at a breakfast table near the river.

"Is it pleasant?" Gilbert asked. "It looks pleasant."

"That's the word exactly," she said. "*Pleasant*. Like being lost in an amusement park."

The waiter came by and Kate ordered another Bloody Mary.

"So you're enjoying yourself finally."

"I'm enjoying myself finally," she said resolutely.

After breakfast they came across a Turkish bar, in front of which a small, ragged crowd milled about. Everyone looked hazy-eyed. Everyone looked like Kate. Gilbert and Kate walked through the bar's indistinct light, ordered double scotches, then headed back into the bright morning light to drink them. "What a pleasant way to start your day," Gilbert said.

"Pleasant," Kate said, looking into his glassy green eyes. "New Orleans is *pleasant*." She then leaned back against the stucco building. With the sun striking her so directly, Gilbert saw that her face was breaking out in little patches. He brought the back of his hand to her cheek and then tenderly ran his fingers over the shape of her jaw.

"Never imagined you letting yourself go like this," Gilbert said.

Kate kept her eyes closed against the sun and smiled weakly.

"I needed to," she said, taking his hand in hers. "I've needed to for a long while now."

They sat in the sun with Gilbert walking in for fresh drinks every now and then. As the morning warmed, he unbuttoned his short-sleeved shirt, then finally took it off. Meanwhile, the street slowly turned into something of a carnival, with street performers drawing small crowds by eating glass, bending foreign coins between thumb and forefinger, juggling torches. Kate opened her eyes. She wiped her brow with her sweat-beaded plastic cup and stood. A crowd had gathered around a barefoot, shirtless boy twirling four fiery sticks. She watched his sweating brown back arch, his head pitch forward, the fire rush from his mouth every so often. His posture was catlike, slinky. He had a kind of shabby, fey glamour about him, something optimistic and hopeful in spite of difficulties she couldn't possibly fathom, the realm of his experience being so far removed from her own. At least this was what she imagined. She walked right up to his side, the fire and wood twirling just before her eyes, then reached for her pocket and threw a neatly folded twenty-dollar bill into the black bowler hat. This caught his attention.

"You should see me at night," he said with an accent, Cuban maybe. "I'm really something."

Kate thought his silly pride touching.

"I'm sure you really are."

"Come here tonight and you'll see."

Gilbert moved next to her, smiled at the fire juggler, and sipped his scotch.

"The boyfriend?" the fire juggler asked, his eyes on his work.

"The cousin," Kate said.

"Good, good," the fire juggler said before igniting his breath. Once the flaming cloud had vanished, he turned to Kate and added, "See you tonight." Then Kate took Gilbert's hand and walked away.

"You like him," Gilbert said as they strolled down the street.

Kate shrugged as though annoyed. "He looks interesting. Like a gypsy."

Gilbert released his hand from Kate's and let her go into the bar alone. He told her he wanted to sit out in the sun and observe the residents of his former college town.

The sun felt good against his skin. From time to time he closed his eyes and tried to recall what had changed, what had stayed the same. The people certainly had changed. A few, however, he actually recognized from occasional visits through the years, some even from his school days. After a few minutes, he noticed his skin had reddened, and so he stood and went inside. He wandered through the darkness and thickening odors until he found Kate playing pinball at one of three battered machines, a fresh plastic cup resting on the foggy glass. One of the bumpers didn't work, nor did a few of the lights behind the leggy extragalactic queen beneath the scoreboard. Gilbert walked up behind Kate and set his hands on her hips.

"This machine needs a mechanic," he said, his mouth next to her ear.

"I'm cranky." She didn't turn to him but kept playing.

"Why cranky?"

"I don't want to go home."

"We can always come back."

"That's not it."

The silver ball zipped precisely between two bumpers. Kate tried to influence its speedy progress with some body English, but the bumpers fell dead against her fingertips. She lightly rapped the dingy glass with a small and neatly tightened fist, then turned in

Gilbert's arms and thrust her narrow rump upon the machine. The glass felt cool through the thin skirt. Her eyes fell to the grimy floor, then she looked up at Gilbert.

"I can't take the thought of spending a winter alone in a big empty house," she mumbled. "I can't even think about it."

"You don't have to," he said. "We could move to Missouri."

"I could move here."

"You could lose yourself in this town. Besides, the summers are something terrible."

Kate looked around and smiled. Her eyes drifted into the distance.

"That sounds so . . ."

"Pleasant?"

"Yeah, pleasant," Kate whispered. "What a wonderful word."

Gilbert brought a hand to her cheek. "You feeling okay, Miss Kate?"

"I'm fine," she said, hopping off the machine.

Gilbert didn't know what to say or think. He only followed as she strolled to the door.

They drifted from bar to bar, then, in the early evening, had dinner at an upscale restaurant famous for its shrimp gumbo. Neither had eaten since breakfast. The maitre d' led them between small round tables toward the kitchen and seated them beside the swinging door. They ordered impulsively from the appetizer and drink menu before ordering dinner, and devoured each tiny dish as it was lowered to the table. When the main courses finally arrived, they simply asked for the bill and left.

Outside, it was cool and dark. Small bands of people in costume streamed by as though dressed for Mardi Gras, carrying drinks, silly and obnoxious. Martians, drag queens, hookers, robots. Kate now seemed less amused with this part of the old town and the antics that went with it. She smiled glibly as she parted the lazy throng.

"Let's find those street performers," Kate said. "Mingle among the home throng."

"I think you could use a bath and a nap, Miss Kate."

Kate ignored the remark and kept walking. They covered ten or twelve blocks, more or less in silence, then made a final turn and suddenly came upon the fantastic scene: a three-man zydeco band, a tiny black boy tap dancing, a midget throwing darts at a strong-man's belly. At the center of it all was a blaze of fire. Gilbert and Kate paused at the curb to take in the whole of the colorful scene before them.

"It doesn't seem altogether real, does it?" Gilbert mumbled.

"It's all so *dreamy.*"

Gilbert lowered a hand upon Kate's shoulder and turned her to face him. In her eyes he saw the reflection of the twirling colored lights floating upon the glassy lenses.

"You gonna be okay?" he asked.

"I feel fine," she said.

Gilbert followed the swirling lights as they drifted over a dilated pupil. He took her in his arms.

"Let's keep having fun," she said as he held her.

"I've no problem with that."

When Gilbert released her, she headed directly toward the fire juggler where he stood at the center of a ring of admirers. She made her way through the crowd and stopped before him, her eyes glistening, her brown skin shiny in the gusts of thick yellow flame. He'd now brought acrobatics into the act—cartwheels, somersaults, handstands. In the cool of the night, he was shirtless. Sweat gathered in the crevasse of his breastbone and Adam's apple, grit and gravel was embedded in the tattooed skin of his limber back. Kate stood, beautiful and vain against the light, waiting for the fire juggler to notice her. Gilbert watched her in amazement. Never had he seen this aspect of the girl he loved, this angle of her personality that retreated so deeply into abandon, this character so capable of carnal vanity. When the fire juggler saw her, she smiled. At the end of the act, he paused and looked Kate up and down.

"You're back," he said in his Cuban accent.

Kate nodded serenely, her beautiful brown arms folded across her chest.

With that the fire juggler prepared his audience for one last spectacle while Kate watched with a kind of critical care. She noted how he seemed so aware of all that surrounded him. As the wooden torches twirled—so slow at first—he cartwheeled, planting a brown hand against the filthy pavement. Fiery wood and tar vaulted through the night sky, the stars rotated between the slouching buildings. He was aware of everything, Kate thought: the earth beneath his bony veined palm, the blazing torches of wood and tar as they tumbled across the sky. His motions seemed so clear, instinctive, contemplated by flesh and blood. She stood there with her arms crossed before her, feeling an eerie electric tingle move up her spine to the base of her skull and into her scalp.

The show ended with immense applause. Kate looked around to take account of the crowd that had grown, then her gaze swept to the juggler as his lean abdomen bowed, an arm extended in either direction, each holding two torches. A small boy passed aggressively through the crowd with the black bowler hat, which was filled in no time with bills and coins. Twenty dollars of his take came from Kate. Again, the juggler saw this and approached her as the crowd dissipated into the night.

"You brought your cousin?" he asked.

"He's around," she said vaguely, though she knew Gilbert was standing somewhere behind her.

The fire juggler blew out each torch with a single severe breath.

"I wanna buy you a drink." He started toward the opening of the Turkish bar, and Kate followed, smiling lavishly, her arms still folded before her.

Gilbert thought better of joining them uninvited. Once they

were gone, he looked about and saw another bar two doors down. He would pass some time there. Kate would eventually wonder where he was and come out into the street. When she couldn't find him, she might panic, he thought. And she deserved a dose of fear. By such thinking Gilbert either subdued or vented his temper and walked off to the bar. He went directly up to the bartender and ordered a beer in a parfait glass and a double scotch, then took the drinks to a small wooden table by the window, where he could see what was going on in the street. If Kate was looking for him, he could see her from here. He settled into his chair, prepared himself for a long wait, and sipped cold beer. After a thoughtful pause, he sipped at the shot and lit a cigarette. In no time at all, his mind was wandering pleasantly.

For the next two or three hours he watched gay men, lesbians, tourists, prostitutes, bourbon addicts as they eased in and out of the taverns and through the street without direction or purpose. Eventually he grew tired of it all and began to worry about Kate. He walked out to the street and, not finding her, strolled into the Turkish bar.

At night, the place was magically transformed into something primeval. The arched, cavelike walls muted the blue and yellow flames of gas lanterns. The flames wobbled as the patrons sauntered beneath them, moving about with fluid languor, their intentions hushed by narcotics and alcohol. Gilbert made his way through the darkened interior and found the familiar band of characters toward the back of the bar. This was a community. A man dressed up as a yogi. A woman who claimed to be an Egyptian psychic, her face caked with makeup. A terrifically fat man wrapped in a gold sarong like an ancient Asian king, tattooed waiters and waitresses. Then he came to the juggler and Kate.

Gilbert felt clear and cool in his head, fully in control, his mind sharpened by worry. Walking in a loose circle about the perimeter of the table, he saw Kate leaning into the juggler's side, seemingly limp with uncaring, her eyes closed, jaw slack. He realized she was unconscious. He walked just outside this ring of creatures, his eyes on his cousin, discreet and easy, until the juggler saw him, struggling to attach a name to the face.

"The cousin," he said. "You're the cousin."

Gilbert felt a surge of unease in this foreign company, but smiled warmly so as not to betray his concern. These were harlequins, gargoyles, crazy people caught up in some kind of pageantry. So he smiled and came up between Kate and the juggler.

"That's who I am. The cousin."

"Well, have a drink," the juggler said, lowering a hand to the filthy Formica tabletop.

"I need to get my cousin home," Gilbert said.

"I'm sorry," the juggler said apologetically. "She's staying with me tonight."

Kate lay within the cove of the juggler's arm and chest, entirely limp as though her neck were broken. Gilbert lifted the dead weight of her arm and brought it across his back. He was about to lift her when the juggler placed a firm hand on his wrist. The table hushed.

Gilbert looked the juggler in the face, coolly noting the sparse black hairs jutting out of the cheeks and chin, the faint mustache, the jagged little mouth. "A boy," he said. Then the juggler smiled in a way that terrified Gilbert. His finely rotted teeth were revealed, pockmarks distorted the lines of his grimace. With a terrible suddenness, Gilbert saw the night dissolving. In his mind he saw himself returning to the hotel alone, Kate lost in the city. So he now drew on that reserve of anger that lay just below the surface of good manners and grace. In a way coldly calculated for greatest effect he let the smile wash from his face and erode into something that was supposed to convey deadly conviction.

"If you don't let me take my cousin home," Gilbert said in a slow, deliberate cadence, "I'll cut you."

The juggler smiled a wildly silly smile. Gilbert blinked slowly as a display of nonchalance.

The juggler took Kate's head, so limber upon her neck, into his naked, tattooed arms. Gilbert told himself how he had no choices, how he couldn't leave without Kate. And it all came down to this moment in this bar. Here he was, flesh and bone, standing before this angry young man, this boy really, ready to do what was required of him to bring this young girl whom he called his cousin, whom he loved, back to the sanctuary of the hotel. But this boy had a look in his eye—the crushed-glass glitter of the retina, the clear lens that so quietly fell upon nothingness. A young boy who had killed, Gilbert told himself. So he became the elder, the senior of the two who had committed unspeakable acts, the one to whom it was second nature.

"She'll be coming with me," was all Gilbert said.

The juggler laughed lightly.

Gilbert pulled Kate to her feet. The juggler looked about and laughed again, this time mockingly. The crowd gathered around the three of them and froze.

Gilbert kept his eyes on the juggler's. I am not a piano player but a criminal. He felt a warm weight on his shoulder. He turned cautiously, his eyes clinging to the juggler's as long as possible, until he saw the benign, happy face of the fat man wrapped in gold.

"Take your cousin," he said in a warm, drunk British accent. "This one's crazy."

The voice felt good to Gilbert. He turned back to the juggler, who stood rigid, his jaw flexed. The juggler appealed to the crowd, who stared vacantly at him.

"He's not her *cousin.*"

Gilbert looked again at the fat man to study his eyes, the intention behind his blubbery smile.

"I'm her cousin," he said.

"Even if you aren't," the fat man said, "I mean this one's *in-*

sane. . . . Tomorrow we'll find her with the lovely little head missing." He began laughing so hard his eyes teared.

An Englishman, Gilbert thought as he brought Kate's weight up against him, levering her with her sticky brown arm. The juggler placed a hand on the crown of her shoulder, his eyes glassy with shame and hate, then backed away, acknowledging the relinquishment and its corresponding cost in pride. Gilbert thanked no one as he parted the ragged crowd, who clapped him on the back. He singlemindedly moved toward the brightness of the door, applause ringing in his head. Then the noise suddenly died as he came into the cool night air. Without looking back, he hurried Kate down the uneven slabs of concrete beneath the weak electric streetlights that lit the path toward their hotel.

fourteen

The morning light fell on the sash, then died as a thunderstorm brought rain over the town. They slept in the cool humid evening while rainwater muted all sound in the room. Not until the housekeeper knocked at the door did Gilbert awake, and even then Kate lay motionless. Once or twice Gilbert actually ran his fingers along her carotid, searching for a pulse within the neck.

He spent the early afternoon reading beside her, his imagination lost in a dream that seemed more real than what he had experienced the night before. He lay there upon the bed, shirtless and clean, a book on Baroness Pontalba parted in his hands, until he felt the slow stirring of Kate's legs beneath the sheets. He closed the book and set it facedown on the nightstand in order to oversee Kate's introduction to the day. Then the motion ceased. Gilbert pulled a lock of blond hair away from her eyes to see her swollen red face, the folds of the pillowcase impressed in the hot cheeks, the mouth ajar as though frozen in the act of speech. He pulled the sheets up about Kate's shoulders and took a chair out onto the balcony, where he smoked and watched the rain roll off the gray tile roofs and churn through flimsy tin guttering. Somewhere above the seamless layer of clouds, the sun had passed and was descending into the horizon, darkening the world as it sank.

In the morning, perhaps, they would pack and drive north. Whether Kate would be the same person or not when she awoke, he had no idea. He was the cousin, not the lover; there was no future in being the lover. So he thought as he sat with his feet propped up on an iron railing that someone had seen fit to paint green. The cousin, the piano player, burglar, lover, or scalawag. He would take her north, back home, then return to Memphis, hook up with Hap and Isabelle. He would assume another role in another town, secretly doing the only thing he really knew how to do: spirit wealth from one place to another. A carpetbagger. This was not the end of the world. Looking from the curtain of rain beyond the green iron railing to Kate's sleeping figure, he told himself how there was never any end to the world.

Long after the room had darkened, Gilbert was still out on the balcony smoking, his gums sore from too many cigarettes. Kate emerged from the bedroom to the relative brightness of the balcony, where the evening was lit by streetlights, incandescent and contained in the watery atmosphere. Yellow globes hanging against the terrific noise of rainfall. Gilbert was holding the ember of his cigarette to the sky, comparing it to the glow of the streetlights when Kate touched his shoulders. The touch startled him at first, sending an electric tingle through the muscles of his back. A general lumbar pain lingered from the strain of the night before.

"I've been sleeping a long time, haven't I?" she said, her voice hoarse.

"All day."

"Before I fell asleep," she said, "I was pretty bad." Gilbert turned in his chair and saw her looking out at the illuminated town. "Rude," she said. "More than rude. Cruel."

Gilbert took her little waist in his hands. She lowered herself into his lap and slipped her slender arms about his neck. Her fingers played with the cartilage of his ears, bending them gently, running a fingernail against the skin. She kissed him on the mouth. Gilbert thought to himself, Cousin, I am the cousin, until a moment later the thought was vanquished in a surge of forgiveness. From that moment on, there was nothing but what he was sensing now.

"You went to the carnival," he said.

"I got us in trouble," she said.

"We're here, safe and sound."

"I'm scared, Gilbert. I need you."

He felt her body shiver, not with cold but with fear. "Everything's going to be okay," he said, and her tremors began to subside. Her hair fell over his head, forming a sort of canopy. Light from the street refracted through the wild tangle at either corner of her vision.

"It's like being behind a waterfall," Kate mumbled.

Gilbert touched her nose with his and nodded. Cars hummed as they passed on the street below, the sound of feet and voices drifted along the sidewalk. The rain fell harder, impossibly hard, Kate thought, as the noise began to drown out all other sound, heightening the sense of intimacy between them.

"Seems like there's only the two of us in the whole world," she whispered. "Like we're hiding." She could feel the warmth of her own stale breath. She pulled her head away and put a hand around each of his boyish ears. "I did something terrible, didn't I?"

"Everything's fine now. That's all that matters."

"That's not all that matters."

"That's all." He heard the edge in his own voice.

"I need someone to take care of me, Gilbert. I need you."

"Well, I'm here."

"You don't like the way things are anymore," she said. "I spoiled it."

Gilbert paused to collect his thoughts. The rain and the accompanying darkness seemed to gather around them. Somehow this served to focus his mind.

"I don't like thinking of myself as the cousin," he said, his voice more Southern and self-pitying than he usually allowed himself around Kate.

She sat up, puzzled by what he was saying and how he was saying it.

"You're not my cousin. Not really."

"When it's handy, I become the cousin," he said solemnly.

Kate's mind reeled through the clotted vessel of recent memory, continuity fading as it neared the present. She recalled drinking from a plastic cup, a room slowly becoming a kaleidoscope of color. The images rotated, then paused; the universe slurred; voices melted and fused into an incommunicable mass, a frozen swirl of thought. Now all that remained was the dross of images: the twirling fire, a sleek brown back. She took Gilbert's head in her hands and said to the silhouette of his face, "We're lovers, like husband and wife."

The following morning Kate slipped out of bed early and undressed before the full-length mirror. What she saw shocked her for reasons she wasn't altogether aware of. As she pulled off her summer dress, the one she had been wearing all along, she saw how the nap was shiny, polished with wear. And then there was her skin. Her complexion, something she had never paid much attention to, contorted the contours of her face slightly, broken out as it was. One cheek hurt from having been slept upon. She watched herself in the mirror, noting the lines where the skin had been sunburnt about the shoulders, chest, and shins. Never had she seen herself like this. She wondered if she could ever change back.

Shower water never felt so foreign. The hot, pulsing stream struck her skull and spine with a force she wasn't prepared to accept. After several minutes of simply feeling the water running over her body—through her matted hair, into her eye sockets, down the channel of her vertebrae and buttocks—she lifted a thick white bar of soap and began easing it over her skin. She felt the hard mass in her hand cutting away oily filth, the hot water melting and loosening it. Her skin began to breathe again. Something had happened, she said to herself. Something in her had physically shifted. She felt as crazy as a loon; she felt vulnerable and scared. Shower water, she realized, did little to ease the sensation. When she stepped before the mirror again she merely felt crazy and clean.

Eventually she came into the bedroom wearing one towel wrapped under her armpits, and another spun about her head like a turban. Gilbert sat on a corner of the bed and pulled on a pair of high-heeled cowboy boots as he watched the morning news. The drive home should be clear of weather, he said. The storm had moved over Alabama.

They finished dressing and packing in silence, then went out to the truck. Kate lodged herself against the door and watched the city roll by the window while Gilbert drove. The morning was bright and clear, the streets submerged in rainwater as leaves clogged the drains at intersections. Vast lakes reflected clear blue sky. The drive north was of a very different sort from the drive down, as Kate's mood had evolved into a kind of placid serenity. She wasn't the same girl, Gilbert thought. When he told her so somewhere around Vicksburg, she leaned over and cast her dainty arms about his neck, and they rode along like that, her head against his shoulder, his arm struggling when he had to shift. They took a highway that ran against the oxbows of the Mississippi. When it grew dark, Kate held the atlas under a soft yellow dome light, every now and then indicating directions with a finger. Gilbert silently obeyed.

That night they stayed in the same hotel in Memphis, and early the next morning were on the road again. Kate's energy and some of her color had returned. The poison had passed, she said, the hemoglobin was again carrying oxygen. What she did not say but thought was that she at least felt more stable in her mind. Sitting beside Gilbert in the confines of the truck for hours on end had served to disperse the overwhelming anxiety, the sense of impending doom. That most of the alcohol had left her body had doubtless helped as well.

By noon they were moving into landscapes that were familiar to her. During the last leg of the trip, Gilbert told her the story of the Juggler and the King, how the Juggler was intent on taking her home, how the King finally saved the day. A living parable of some sort, Gilbert said. He was absolutely certain the fat man had saved her life and likely his own. The Juggler, he was certain, wasn't above murder.

Murder.

Kate caught her breath. Somehow she had managed to tuck the thought in a darkened apse of memory. Murder. She mouthed the word, and for the next few minutes she contemplated its sound and meaning. Doing so seemed to make the word pale, lose its finality. This was the nature of the world, she thought, and there was nothing to be done about it. She could only tend to the moment, see herself through the crisis at hand. It was a selfish thought, she told herself, but she was helpless. The moment she attempted to view the scope of her situation, the immensity of her moral dilemma, she felt overwhelmed. She couldn't afford to do the right thing. And what exactly was that? Doing the right thing meant turning Gilbert in to the authorities—an utterly unfathomable thought. She had no choice but to think of herself, which meant protecting Gilbert. He simply couldn't be taken away. Gilbert did what he did in order to protect what he loved, however cruel and misguided the action was. And besides, she told herself, she couldn't change the past.

After dwelling on the thought for a while she became aware of Gilbert's voice. He was still telling her the story of that night. Once she understood what he was saying, once her thoughts had shifted, she was dumbstruck. It couldn't be. She brought a hand to her mouth as she listened, then cried out in disbelief and sorrow. She saw that Gilbert loved her reaction. Most of all he loved hearing the painful regret, which he could see she truly felt. His heart soared with her tortured expressions. Kate swore she could recall only the earliest moments of the evening. Little else. Only smells and patternless sounds.

"You have to know," she said, taking his arm and pressing it against her thigh, "that I have to have you. I need you to take care of me."

"I know," he said happily.

Kate worked herself over onto her back and laid her head in his lap. Looking up between his arms she observed him from this new angle—the shape of his nose and chin, the way his throat rose up into his jaw. As she studied him, she suddenly felt an irrational possessiveness. Before she had felt this only in flashes, but now she wanted to know that they would be together forever. The need was strong and threatening—seemingly connected to her survival.

"We'll always be together, won't we?" she asked.

He smiled down on her face and stroked her throat with his fingertips.

" 'Always' is one of those words, Miss Kate."

She turned this over in her mind. Her eyes shifted to his hands then back to his face.

"We could marry if we ever wanted to."

Gilbert suddenly felt warm all over.

"I'm sure we could legally." Without his knowing it, his mouth had fallen open. "What's going on in that complicated little mind of yours?"

Kate closed her eyes as though sunning her face in his presence.

"I've been thinking, is all." She slowly opened her eyes and let the smile relax. "That's what people do who want to be together forever."

"You can imagine what people would say."

" 'Those insane Willoughbys. Now we know how they got that way.' "

"Nobody would bat an eye if it wasn't for the last name. That's the catch right there."

"Common last names alone don't make for incest."

"They make for a lot of talk."

Kate sat up and looked at him. "I never took you for someone who cared much about what other people said."

"Nothing's unthinkable. I just want to hear you talk about it. I want you to convince me this is something you really want."

Kate climbed into his lap as if it were a nest and made herself small. He brought his arms around her so he could steer the truck with the very tips of his fingers.

"I want to be married," she said in a little girl's voice.

"But to your cousin?"

"We're not cousins."

"Then what are we?"

"We're lovers."

"Lovers."

"That's right," she whispered, her voice barely audible, even as her lips hung there beside his small, soft ear. "And we want to be husband and wife."

"We'll do it in another town. We'll move."

Gilbert looked down upon her face and smiled.

They drove like this, with Kate riding in his lap like a child, until he felt a wetness on his neck. He gently separated her from him and saw she was crying.

"I'm sorry about that night." She cleared her throat and wiped away the rush of tears to make herself understood. "I was out of my mind."

"All is forgiven," he said.

"I want to be married."

"Then you'll be married."

Kate shifted her weight and leaned against Gilbert's shoulder while the tears ebbed. They drove the last hundred miles in a contented quiet, with Kate asking Gilbert questions about his boyhood from time to time. He spoke in the relaxed Southern manner that seemed to fit the shape of his mouth better. At least that was what Kate thought. She would ask a question then sit back and watch him answer while she studied the movement of his jaw and neck, his upper and lower lips, and their relation to one another. From time to time he drew a cigarette from the breast pocket of his shirt, and Kate watched him smoke. Each knew the other was happy. Gilbert felt a calmness, a deep still center in him, a calm that was just with him as they drove and drove. When they reached the outskirts of town he looked down at the crown of Kate's head. He and his fiancée, content and warm, rolling through downtown Fayette on a carpet of victory. Defiant, untouchable. That was how he felt. Gilbert Willoughby, son of a wealthy Missourian, born of a long line of tortured blood, about to claim what he loved despite the ancestry that bound families together or flung them apart. Gilbert was renowned for taking his pleasures where he could find them, but this was different. There would be words with Uncle Charlie, and he didn't care. So he drove through town, the future spread out before him on a plain of defiant virtue. That's when they rolled down the last few blocks. That was when he felt the last sensation of joy, the final pleasantness. That was when he felt all hope leave him.

It was a boxy white car with blackwall tires and two blue globes tucked in the corners of the rear window, parked adjacent to Kate's home. It didn't sit directly before the house, but nearly so. Kate sensed a shift in Gilbert's posture, a nervousness.

"What's the matter?" she asked, still lost in that blissful state Gilbert had shared a moment ago.

Gilbert didn't respond immediately. His heart throbbed against his throat. He drove by Kate's home, by the police car, maintaining his speed while his thoughts raced. At first, he didn't know what he could say, but once they had moved past the white car with its mud-splattered quarter-panels and no-frills trim, he decided to say as little as possible.

"That's a cop back there," Kate said, her voice ringing with certainty.

"That's a cop," he said, measuring his breath.

Kate fixed her eyes on Gilbert's profile. "This is about the man in the ditch."

"I can't think of anything else it could be about," Gilbert lied.

"That's all it could be about though, right?"

"Of course."

Kate brought a hand to her mouth.

As if by instinct, as if prompted by the impulse of flight, Gilbert turned toward the highway, his face fixed and expressionless. Kate watched him as his mind worked in silence. Quite calmly she said, "The truck's registered under Hap's name, right?"

She felt so calm, and she didn't know why. What she needed to do simply came to her. It could be a play script, a part, she thought. After a short pause for contemplation she continued. "Drive out to the Holiday Inn," she said.

This seemed to aggravate Gilbert. He gazed over at Kate with mild suspicion.

"What d'you have in mind?" he asked.

"This doesn't have to be a big deal. Let's drop you off, and I'll go back and talk to the cop."

They drove toward the highway and pulled into the parking lot of the Holiday Inn. As Gilbert brought the truck to a stop, Kate turned to him and said, "They aren't going to touch me. I'm the daughter of Cecil Willoughby the war hero, the lawyer. My mother just died."

"What'll you say if they ask about me?"

"Somebody's mistaken. That's all it'll take. Then they'll go away, sorry they ever bothered me."

The air was silent for a moment.

"Not necessarily."

Kate gave him a look of grave disapproval.

"Take a cab over after dark. It'll be *fine,*" she said, trying to sound infinitely unconcerned.

"Leave a light on in our bedroom if everything's okay," he said, his face shot with pink. Kate noted how shame always lit up his face in the same way, as though conditioned.

"See you in an hour or so."

She edged him out of the truck and kissed him on the mouth. He gently pressed the door shut, took his bags from the back of the truck, and headed toward the hotel office. She watched him as he reluctantly walked away, then took the wheel.

Driving toward her house, Kate felt tiny and childlike. The truck was big, the bench seat pushed too far back. She could enjoy herself, actually anticipate the smoky world of subterfuge and play-acting she was about to enter into. This was something she had to do; Gilbert couldn't be taken away. As she moved through town, her right foot carefully restraining the immense engine beneath it, she experienced a kind of thrill, a shadow of what she had known in New Orleans. In a sense, she didn't care anymore. Again, she somehow felt outside herself, viewing the cab from above, as if participating in a dream. I'm crazy, she thought. She told herself to concentrate, to focus. She had to know who she would be once she stepped from the aluminum running board and turned to the unmarked car. Without knowing precisely what she was going to say, she had to know how she would say it. This was a part she would be playing. So she drove.

When she made the final corner, she saw the officer's silhouette against the metal screen separating the front seat from the back of the squad car. Her heart quickened as she approached, though she remained calm and organized in thought. The only difference lay in her chest, where her heart beat away like a secret insurrectionist. She eased the truck into the driveway, ostensibly unruffled by the presence of the squad car. All was normal and well, all as it should be. Taking a few measured breaths, she stepped out, turned on the running board, and removed her bags from the bed. Then she delicately hopped down to the frozen gravel and mud and strolled toward the house. She would not acknowledge the presence of the officer. As she neared the house, not five or six strides from the gray front steps, she saw a glimpse of the figure and heard the clap of the squad car door. She felt a thrilling rush of adrenaline, but kept walking, casually, happily, innocently.

"Uh-hummm, Ms. Willoughby . . . Kate Willoughby," she heard. She turned to meet the voice and the uniform. When she did, she felt it all come to her—the role, the air of disinterest. What made this easier was that she recognized the officer as one of those familiar albeit anonymous faces patrolling the town's streets for as long as she could remember. So it was more or less natural for him to address her as both Kate and Ms. Willoughby. Neither alone, she could see, would do. She smiled easily, not even showing curiosity, only a natural desire to be helpful, a by-product of proper upbringing. He winced as he approached her, and she knew she was hitting the mark. She would be open and generous, but on her way.

"How are you, Kate?" he stammered. "I hope you don't mind my addressing you by your first name."

"Not at all," she said cheerfully.

He removed a splintered wooden toothpick from between his teeth and abruptly smoothed half of his mustache with a forefinger.

"I knew your father," he said reverently. His face was red. "Cecil was quite a fella. Kind of guy you'd expect could run for president or something."

"He liked the police officers in town," she said, weighing whether or not this was too much. After a split second of contemplation, she decided it was not. Then an image came to her, an ancient memory: the air rifle cop. . . . She felt flushed with confidence. He could go ahead and accuse her cousin of murder, and she would only smile and smile.

"Quite a fella. Yes, quite a fella," he repeated meditatively. He paused and looked around as though he had heard a curious noise among the bare trees.

"Can I help you with something?" she said. She could feel the adrenaline in her blood. It made her stomach hot.

The cop's eyes drifted to the frozen lawn beneath his shiny black shoes.

"Yeah, you know it's about something we want to keep quiet, keep to ourselves," he began. "We don't want people thinking Fayette has a problem."

Kate's eyelashes batted away.

"I was wondering if you've noticed anything missing outta your house in the last few months. Lately there's been a lot of burglaries reported." His voice thinned as he spoke, trailing off into an incomprehensible mumble.

Kate felt a humid perspiration in her ears. Her eyes welled for a moment, then dried. She tried to appear to give his question serious thought.

"Well, no. Not that I've noticed," she whispered.

The cop smiled and exhaled in vast relief.

"Nothing at all?"

"Nothing but the money in my checking account," she said, trying to contrive a smile. "Maybe you could check my banking records."

The cop thought this much funnier than it was. When he laughed, his belly jiggled beneath the blue coat.

"Well, your neighbors around here have been missing some expensive knickknacks. Jewelry, wedding rings, family silver."

"*Oh no.*" Mildly heartfelt.

"You been outta town?"

"New Orleans."

The cop smiled and looked at his feet again.

"It can get pretty strange down there," she added playfully. This seemed to please the officer.

"Your dad was quite a fella, Kate. I didn't know your mother, but I'm sure she was quite a lady."

"She was," Kate said with a precise measure of gratitude.

"You think you're missing anything in there," he said gesturing toward the house, "you just give me a call down at the station. I'm around."

With that the officer set off for his car, shaking his head as he took his first steps. Kate watched him walk off, then turned to the house. She felt she had to suppress an excitement she could scarcely contain. Once inside she ran up the back staircase, three steps at a time, to her bedroom, where she flicked on the lamp before the parted curtains. She sprawled herself over the bed and rocked back and forth on the doughy softness, giggling like a small girl who'd cleverly gotten away with a peccadillo—like a girl who'd gotten away with murder.

The house was dark and cold, full of the stale smell of not having been lived in. Kate spent the next hour and a half pulling frozen steaks and vegetables from the deep freeze in the basement and cutting them into chunks for stew. As she worked, she imagined what she wanted for the night: when Gilbert came into the house she wanted him to know without having to ask that everything was all right. She wanted him to know by the smells and the sounds the house contained. Within the hour, the rooms would be alive with the sounds and smells of celebration, the stereo would play her mother's old Sinatra records while the gas stove browned little chunks of steak and onion. As she stood before the burners it occurred to her that it would be nice to light the candelabra in the dining room, where they could eat, formally, like husband and wife, at either end of the table. All around them the room would glow. So she worked.

Well after dark, however, long after dinner was complete and stewing in the copper-bottomed kettle, Gilbert still hadn't arrived. Kate ran up the stairs to make certain the lamp was on. Then she ran outside to make sure it could be seen. As she stood before the house in the cold night air, she saw there was no mistake to be made. The window glowed warm and yellow in the darkness, the signal beautifully framed by the pattern of the lace curtain and the sash at the summit of the eaves. All was plain enough. She came back inside, sat at the table she'd laid in the dining room, and waited beneath the quivering yellow flames. The house was still but for the soft music, and for a moment she grew sleepy. But it wasn't long before she heard a small noise in the kitchen, and she was instantly alert. A light metallic clatter like that of tumblers in a lock. She crept into the kitchen and saw Gilbert smiling cautiously from the basement door.

"What happened?" he whispered.

"It was a marvel," she said, adopting his language. "Everything's fine." Unable to contain her mounting excitement, she took him by the hand and displayed the stovetop, then led him into the dining room, where they would eat. But Gilbert wouldn't be led.

"What did he want? What'd he say?"

"It wasn't about the man," she said, playfully annoyed. "It was about something entirely different."

"Well, what? Come on."

"A burglary. Some houses in the neighborhood have been robbed and he wanted to know if ours was one of them."

Gilbert didn't respond right away.

"Well, what did you say?"

"Nothing. He wanted to know if our house had been robbed. It hasn't."

Gilbert drew a hand through his thin blond hair and smiled. "How strange," he whispered.

Kate gazed at him with wonder. "You feeling okay?"

"Yeah," he said absently. "Now I am."

That evening they sat at the far ends of the long gleaming surface of mahogany, just as Kate had imagined the setting hours ago. They ate as though playing house, like children, as though the talk was an extension of the role Kate had played earlier. Gilbert lifted his full wineglass and watched the light pass through its purple belly.

"You're a pretty clever girl, Miss Kate. Brave too."

"He knew me," she said triumphantly. "And he knew Dad from years ago."

She lifted her glass and toasted herself. Then she noticed Gilbert wasn't smiling. She recognized the shame in the lines of his face, the network of engorged blood vessels that rose to the surface when he was embarrassed.

"The business with the old man may make it difficult to marry," he said. "Won't exactly be able to publish the wedding announcement in the paper. I can see the FBI following us on our honeymoon to Jamaica: two dark blue suits coming toward us over the sand."

Kate looked down at her stew.

"We should move," she said. "Go someplace sunny."

Gilbert set his spoon beside his steaming bowl. For a few seconds, he gazed at his own reflection in the thinly oiled surface of the table. Kate could see his mind working; she could see him choosing his words. Then he slowly lifted his eyes to hers.

"I'm in love with you, Miss Kate."

"And I'm in love with you."

Gilbert rose and slowly wandered to Kate's end of the table. He stood behind her chair, brought his arms about her shoulders, and tenderly kissed her temple. When she turned in his arms she saw how tired he looked. The weight of the past few days showed in his eyes.

"You should get some sleep," she whispered. "I'm going to clean up down here."

Gilbert didn't say anything. He kissed her hair and languorously strolled up the hanging staircase.

Kate listened to his footsteps passing overhead. She sat at the table, tapping the rim of her wineglass, studying the sonic motion of purple liquid. Eventually she brought the dirty dishes into the kitchen and filled the sink with hot soapy water. After the dishes were washed and dried, she sat at the kitchen table and toyed with a pencil. She couldn't bring herself to open a newspaper, so she just sat there and thought. Everything was going to be all right, she told herself. If they were in any kind of trouble, she wouldn't be sitting here right now. Once she had thoroughly convinced herself of this, her mind slowly began to stray.

Kate thought of Gilbert and how his manner was that of his father, a grown man who played with air rifles. Here was a family in which fun and risk and cruelty were inextricably linked, all tangled up. She thought of her own parents and what of her spoke of them. She thought of the story Uncle Charlie had told concerning her father when he was young. Kate really hadn't known much of her family's past until after her mother's death, as her parents rarely spoke of it. Most of what she knew now had come from Uncle Charlie. He seemed to possess it all—the order of progeny, who begot whom, and how the lives they led seemed to drift into such peculiar desolation. The stories were so much larger than life. He was strangely curatorial about their family's past, yet seemed utterly uninterested in his own. It was as if he saw himself as the proprietor of a memory that was not entirely his. And the memory lived in Kate's mind as told in Uncle Charlie's heightened rhetoric. His voice lent her past its vast scope, its character.

Through the summer that Uncle Charlie had spent in Fayette, he had attempted to characterize for Kate what he called the family's genetic heritage. To know, he believed, was tantamount to seeing her own ineluctable future, prophecy handed down through the oracle of heredity. Kate said she didn't understand, but Uncle Charlie wouldn't explain. Instead he went on about the family, how the first-born males were named alternately Thomas, then Cecil, Thomas, Cecil, and so on down through five generations. He saw it as a never-ending cycle of self-contempt and violence, and it all seemed to culminate in the person of her father. In Uncle Charlie's mind, Cecil was the quintessential Willoughby. Again Kate said she didn't understand, so Uncle Charlie said he would try to explain. It was an amorphous theory, an unwieldy thing, something he had a *feel* for, an idea of the family that lived in his bones. Therefore he wasn't sure he could convey what it was he knew, because something about the family seemed inexpressible, really. But if she wanted him to, he could try.

Kate felt a creepiness in Uncle Charlie's unusually indirect manner. "Give it a shot," she recalled herself saying. Then she watched her uncle settle back in the mule-ear chair and start with melodramatic reluctance.

"Far's I'm concerned, it all can begin with your grandfather," he said. And that was where he began.

Thomas Willoughby was Old Testament in his ways, he said. Someone who could persuade rural juries by quoting Shakespeare, Milton, the Bible, and weave the words into relevance to the case before them—at once a man of the cloth and a man of the world. The word of God appeared to lie heavily upon his heart, and because of this, elderly juries saw him as an improved version of themselves—a rural sophisticate with the special merit accorded a man who had departed for and returned from the city of St. Louis. Back then, folk wisdom counted for something. But Kate's grandfather gradually shunned the family, fell out of love with her grandmother, Dorothy, and took to drinking martinis. Yet this, Uncle Charlie emphasized, could only go so far toward explaining why her father was an only child.

Cecil was born into the hands of a midwife in August of 1925. The Jazz Age. He was a mama's boy—breastfed until age four, then delivered to the grammar school that stood five blocks away with his hand wrapped in hers. Later she taught him to play trombone. When he was in high school, they naturally separated themselves from each other, which proved to be a silent and surprisingly painful process of restraint, yet recognized as necessary by both. He studied hard and graduated salutatorian, expecting absolutely to attend the University of Missouri at Columbia as well as the law school there. For a time, the future presented itself to Cecil in a succession of pleasant vistas. Then, in early December of 1941 came the news from Pearl Harbor.

In July of 1943, Cecil enlisted in the navy instead of waiting to be drafted. Though military service was never thought of as compulsory, it was expected. The men of the family had all served as though at the bidding of some hereditary inclination—all of them but Gilbert, Uncle Charlie said, interrupting himself and laughing self-consciously. . . . And so Cecil left without much ceremony. Only with his beautiful young mother crying into her apron as his father drove him off to catch a west-bound train. At the station in Galesburg, Illinois, as Cecil was about to mount the short stool to his railcar, Thomas, impeccably dressed for court in black seersucker, conveyed one of the few sentiments of kindness or love that he ever uttered to his son. He said simply and remorselessly, "Best keep that head down." They exchanged the most perfunctory of embraces, and Cecil was gone.

The train shrieked through two nights and days across the plains and mountains, along its way gathering young men to counter the Axis threat. When it arrived in San Diego, Cecil was put through boot camp, then later taught how to operate, repair, and paint an amphtrac, a flat-bottomed, ramp-bowed landing vessel with tractor treads. Among the islands of the South Pacific, Uncle Charlie explained, there weren't many harbors, only sharp-toothed coral reefs lying in wait. "Just like that," he said, snapping his clublike thumb and forefinger, "they'll tear the bottom off of your landin' craft." Military life in San Francisco and, later, Hawaii didn't suit Kate's father, as he was both young and a long way from home for the first time in his life. He pined for home, for the familiarity of routine, for the landscape of the Midwest, the fragrant humidity that accompanies heat. And he pined for his mother. He tried to restrain himself from writing home too often, but the cathartic urge to imagine dialogues between himself and Dorothy overtook him several times a week while he sat in his navy-issue underwear in a tin Quonset hut that acted as a barracks for thirty-nine other men.

Uncle Charlie paused for emphasis and took a few deep breaths. He wanted to make it clear he was moving closer to his point, this theory Kate should give grave consideration.

In August, a letter came from home, he continued. It was a preface, really, a lead-in for what lay toward the end in Dorothy's small compact script which grew smaller and smaller as the letter progressed. If she were telling me this, Cecil thought, her voice would be getting quieter and quieter. Then came the words, Your father has died. It was a filthy habit, she wrote, a bloody selfish heritage among the men of the family, some poisonous tradition. She had considered not telling him, or inventing the cause of death, but she knew he would eventually discover the truth, so she was telling him now. But he must promise, *never* . . . if only to thwart the filthy, bloody legacy. She was sure he would never consider such a hideous act, because she was confident the influence of her blood, half of which was his, would somehow spare him.

Kate sat back in her chair, quietly astonished. Until that moment she had not known how her grandfather had died.

Her father didn't cry the night he received that letter nor any night after. He felt numb, as though he had slipped out of his body and was no longer beholden to its pain nor pleasure. Meanwhile, the navy had designs of its own for him. He was denied permission to return home for the funeral, promptly shipped off to a staging base on the island of Éfaté, and sent through more training on the workings of his amphtrac. Then, later in the year, came the classified news of the long-awaited offensive in the central Pacific and plans for the invasion of a small, heavily fortified sandbar called Tarawa Atoll, in the Gilbert Islands. The rumor produced an electric excitement in the outfit for everyone but Cecil. He merely felt disoriented. It was as if the benign forces of nature were mutating all around him. The sensation was surreal at first but later manifested as a pervasive nausea. In the last three months, simply too much had happened.

Kate's father spent the next few weeks in a unsettled daze. He didn't write or receive any letters from his mother, as the stateside mail came in bunches, sometimes not for months at a time. In October he left for the Gilbert Islands with the Second Division on one of sixteen transports, accompanied by battleships, escort carriers, cruisers, destroyers. This was a journey shrouded in military secrecy, laden with the certainty that the eighteen thousand Marines aboard these ships would soon be firing and fired upon in anger. This would be combat. The word assumed mythical proportions for Cecil as the ships steamed through nameless days and nights and empty sea toward an anonymous, well-prepared enemy. At night he would wander onto the deck alone and lean over the railing to watch a gigantic orange sun drop into the sea. How strange, he thought at these times, that somewhere out there was an enemy that wanted nothing so much as to kill him. And three weeks later, they nearly did.

On the eve of the attack, Cecil mentally rehearsed his job of ferrying his Marines onto the shore of the atoll with his amphtrac. He lay on his narrow bunk, hands clasped behind his shaved head, staring at the flat gray paint of a girder inches from his nose. Below him his comrades cleaned and oiled their rifles, wrote letters, polished their boots, some even shaved. Meanwhile, Kate's father imagined the scene: sometime before five A.M. American shells would begin pounding forty-five hundred Japanese and a few hundred Korean laborers on a tiny strip of sand two and a half miles long and a half-mile wide that lay somewhere beyond this hull in an inky blackness. Conquering this sandbar would pave the road to Tokyo. That was what they had been told, *Pave the road to Tokyo.* This atoll was perhaps the most densely fortified strip of land on the planet, and it had to be taken in spite of the fact that it would be fanatically defended by a strange race of savage miniature men. So they were told.

"But a few hours later, a shell hit his amphtrac because of freak low tides," Uncle Charlie said. "Killed nearly every man in it except your daddy. You probably saw how his shoulder always bore the scar of shrapnel wounds. That shoulder always amazed me." Uncle

Charlie shook his head worshipfully. "I'm enthralled by actual battle wounds. Real scars like those are damned rare anymore. Sometimes I'd ask him if I could pass my fingers over the skin, and sometimes he'd unbutton his shirt and let me. It looked so strange. So lustrous and thin and pale . . ."

Kate caught herself shaking her head. From then on, she tried to conceal her bewilderment at Uncle Charlie's queer pride.

"But it was your daddy's mind that never completely healed," Uncle Charlie went on. "This's what made him so quiet, so isolated and monklike. It was that war that turned his mind down and in the way it did."

Her father didn't return home until the spring of 1944, just as news of the war was growing hopeful. The London Blitz had been survived, Americans had finally taken to island warfare. An amphibious assault on continental Europe was expected in a year or so. The commanders who had coordinated the invasion of Tarawa Atoll were under investigation due to the loss of nearly one thousand Marines. But the atoll had been taken. Of the forty-five hundred Japanese troops dug in there, only seventeen had survived.

When her father arrived in Fayette, he was met at the screen door to the veranda by Dorothy. She kept a small hand to her cheek in an attempt to keep her emotions hushed. No visible signs of surprise, no tears. She wasn't expecting him until the day after, and she had gone over and over in her mind how she would behave when this moment finally came. But here he was. All of a sudden, he was home. The mechanism with which she had stifled the expression of agony through the last year was likely the same she now employed to greet her only child. This was Kate's grandmother's restraint, Uncle Charlie claimed, her trademark. But she could only maintain her poise for so long. As they stood on the veranda, she felt something in her flutter, something that governed her metallic composure. Then from an eye slid a hot translucent tear, which she wiped away with a casual adroitness. But there wasn't any stopping these tears.

Cecil and his mother ate dinner in silence that night, and afterward she led him up the hanging staircase to his room. She showed him how his bed had remained made, the quilts smoothed, the pillows buoyant upon the feather mattress. Then she left him alone, pleased as a child. Cecil listened to her footsteps descending the wooden stairs, leaving behind an expansive quiet broken only by bluebottle flies beating against the windowpane. He drew a few deep breaths with his eyes closed and tried to void his head of static. His mind emptied. "Home," he said in a slow, deliberate cadence, again and again.

"It was a simple desire," Uncle Charlie said, closing his own eyes. "Just to hear the sound and attribute it to a familiar environment."

The kitchen, where Kate and Uncle Charlie sat, fell quiet. Kate stared at Uncle Charlie, sitting across from her, his eyes closed, lost in this moving picture in his mind.

"For the next two years, your daddy holed up. Read more books than anyone I ever knew. It was therapy for his brains," Uncle Charlie said, rapping his bald skull with his knuckles.

In the beginning, Cecil would roll out of bed into the noon heat and head downstairs to the kitchen, where Dorothy kept his eggs and toast in the oven and a hemisphere of grapefruit on the counter. He read the paper while she hummed and ironed. She refrained from speaking, sensing he appreciated the quiet. She smiled in his direction as he read and lifted the ruby meat of the grapefruit to his lips.

These were happier times for her father and grandmother than might have been expected. A vague serenity glazed over the days. Thomas's death was meticulously ignored—how he killed himself, why he killed himself, the emotional and financial aftermath of such an abrupt loss of husband, father, and breadwinner. Thomas was once alive, but was no longer. It was left at that. The irreducible reality. Though they understood this to be coarse disregard for his memory, and certainly peculiar, neither could bring themselves to breach the calm they languished in.

In the afternoons Cecil would listlessly ascend the stairs to his room and sit before his music stand. He would carefully lift his trombone from its crimson velvet case and begin with a scale, then songs he learned while in the high school marching band. He sat utterly stiff and erect. The only movements in the room were those of the flies against the windowpane, Cecil's fingers, and his right foot as it tapped like a metronome. After an hour or two of eerily fey melodies echoing through the tall rooms of this grim home, he would place the trombone back upon the impress of crushed velvet, and stretch himself over his bed to nap. Quiet was what he craved.

But he gradually tired of passively watching the progress of days and nights. One evening he stepped into the muted silence of Thomas's study and sat among those book-lined walls. After a while he pulled down an old copy of *Anna Karenina* and lingered a few minutes over the first pages, then left with the dog-eared novel cupped in his hand. He walked outside to the pool's edge, pulled up a canvas chair, and read by the light of an old hurricane lantern. From then on, he often spent his days and evenings beneath the fragrant shade of hemlock, hickory, and oak, beside the leaf- and needle-littered surface of the pool, lost in the continuous fictive dream of an old Russian count. It was an old thrill he experienced, one he hadn't known since boyhood. The landscape of a vast new world. The grand illusion of another cosmos altogether.

Meanwhile, Dorothy tended to the silent, empty house, every now and then gazing out the window above the kitchen sink at her son, with whom she now sensed a veil of separation. Not that she wasn't satisfied, perfectly happy with his indolent and preoccupied ways. He was home. Moreover, he rarely left, shunning old friends and girlfriends. So he was all hers, really. Hers and the old count's, she told herself. When she asked why he was reading such a long work, he said it was because it didn't end. Dorothy decided that if this was the extent of their separation, she could live with it. So she not only condoned but tacitly promoted Cecil's self-imposed exile. When he had finished all the Tolstoy there was, he read Cervantes and Melville, not so much for the writers themselves or even their stories, but for the length of their works.

Uncle Charlie paused at this point, looked Kate in the eye, and said, "He sought relief in their dreams. It was escape, pure and simple."

Then one afternoon in the early fall, Cecil noticed for the first time since his return that the dining room, which adjoined the living room and kitchen, was locked. It had been used rarely in the past, but never closed off like this. He found the rusted skeleton key on the key rack in the kitchen, opened the doors, and gazed about the room he hadn't entered for months. He came up to the table and slowly passed a hand over the dark mahogany, cutting an arc through the dust. Then he passed his hand through it again and again, and pulled out a chair and sat. He looked around, slowly, deliberately, as though expecting a ghost or an angel to appear against the ceiling. All around him the brooding air of his family's past . . .

Dorothy didn't find him until late in the evening, immersed in the vacuum of silence through which the printed word delivered images. She stood between the parted doors, astounded, repeating his name again and again. But he did not answer, so she left him alone, closing the tall cathedral-like doors behind her, and Cecil resumed reading. Each day that fall he brought himself here, as though it provided some mystical psychic sanctuary, some imaginary place for him to hide. He steadily withdrew to the room as the weather sharpened, seldom straying out to the garden or pool. Time passed in this quiet routine, his mother biding her silence and Cecil keeping to himself. His mood grew dour as the days grew shorter. Then, deep in the season, the strange state of equilibrium was mysteriously threatened by Cecil's announcing one evening at dinner that he wished to attend college. In an assured tone, he told his mother of his plans to attend college at Northwestern, then later, law school, and later still, to return to Fayette and take over the family law practice that was his birthright, as it had been passed down through five generations. Since Thomas's death, the other three partners in the practice had assumed control of the firm by default, though it still bore the family name. Cecil said all this with a rancor that puzzled Dorothy. She didn't know why Cecil was suddenly so possessive of the family law practice, something he had felt only indifference toward until now.

When news of imminent Allied victory in Europe came the following spring, it did not interest Cecil except that he might attend school sooner once victory was achieved. The gas lines were shorter around town now, the rationing less severe, and the general self-righteous air of sacrifice had dissipated, giving way to the American demand for convenience. Yet to move to Chicago and attend school at the moment seemed rather presumptuous. The country was still in the midst of a world war, and school seemed too much of a luxury. Cecil was a veteran, and he simply couldn't matriculate until it was over. So he decided to read and spend another spring and summer within the deep violet shade upon the flagstone surrounding the swimming pool. Then one day in August of 1945, he splayed his book facedown, stood up from his canvas chair, went to the pool's edge, and lowered himself into the cool green water. Because the pool was so small, Cecil never actually swam, but merely floated, taking in the muted sounds of the town as he lay on the pool's surface looking skyward. But on this day, as he took such a break, his mother appeared at the pool side with an extension cord trailing behind her and the radio cradled in her arms. She asked Cecil if he had ever heard of an atom bomb. Cecil wiped his eyes with his fists and said, "Nope."

"Well, President Truman just exploded one over a city in Japan," she said. "Destroyed the entire city." Clearly Dorothy didn't know what to make of the news. "One bomb," she said, incredulous. Cecil didn't know what to believe either.

But later that day Cecil learned he could attend class a semester sooner than he'd planned. In the event of an invasion of the Japanese mainland, he wouldn't have left for Chicago until the following fall, at the earliest. Now he could attend in the spring term, which began in January. As far as the war was concerned, it wasn't his anymore. He did not celebrate V-J Day just as he hadn't celebrated V-E Day. The detonation of an atomic bomb in anger was noteworthy only because it was novel. It was merely historic, a grim event that aptly brought a close to an ugly, grim war. So Cecil thought, consciously or unconsciously, that the time was high to bring an end to his exile. Soldiers would be returning home soon, and with them their stories, which he'd never be able to bring himself to share.

"These were complicated matters, Miss Kate," Uncle Charlie said with grave seriousness. He took Kate's hand and continued, "The trauma of warfare was too intricately woven together with the invisible loss of a father. From then on there would always be this jagged little memory of what had happened on that obscene tiny atoll that was to pave the road to Tokyo. Through the two years he spent immersed in the life of his imagination he felt he'd healed himself. He was ready to be reintroduced into the world. He would go to law school, take over the family practice, and build a small fortune. He would start a family. But this would be tragically interrupted the moment the weight of the family curse came to bear, that horrible memory ingrained in the blood.

"It begins and ends with unresolved grief, Miss Kate. And it's a relentless cycle. When a Willoughby dies, the family meets the loss with silence," Uncle Charlie said, still holding her hand. "This is the crux of the family sorrow. The grieving of those left behind is muted by a natural stoicism, which perpetuates troubles down the road, threatening the well-being of the survivors, and then the cycle repeats itself.

"Willoughbys tend to brood later in life. They brood about the past, about their loved ones who have passed on. But the past is as immutable as cold-rolled steel in a kitten's paw, Miss Kate. Willoughbys don't seem to realize that the effort is futile, and they become forlorn because the past does not change. They die far too early, and those left behind again fail to mourn properly. Blood has memory; it is the germ of a family's character. The story our blood tells is carried down through the line, this tradition of quiet nihilism, this understanding that life is to be conducted in silent agony. This is our family's great, self-fulfilling prophecy, Miss Kate. This is its propagating message. Our forefathers became accustomed to the idea that all that can be hoped for is to see the world come to a quiet end. The prophecy has come down the bloodline. And it has nothing to do with that itty-bitty cancer you had on your shoulder."

Kate tried to withdraw her hand from his but couldn't. Uncle and niece stared into each other's eyes for a long moment.

"I see you runnin' your finger over it," he whispered as if accusing her of a crime. "I see your mind workin'. But that ain't it. That's just childish superstition, Miss Kate."

"How do you know all of this?" she finally asked, her voice at once so frank and puzzled that it jarred even her own ears.

"I have a deep and abiding interest in family," Uncle Charlie said, squeezing her hand as if trying to impress his message in Kate's skin by sheer physical force. Kate winced as her knuckles ground together.

"But why did you tell me?"

"'Cause I want you to know what your family has lived through, and that it's a very real threat. I want you to know what it is you face, what it is you must conquer." Uncle Charlie's eyes were steady with conviction. "It's a natural inclination, Miss Kate. You need to mourn. You need to talk about the death of your mother. Even the death of your dear old daddy."

SONS
and
BROTHERS

fifteen

A light snow fell in the night. In the morning they dressed and went down into the kitchen, warily, avoiding windows, watchful out of habit. But the town was the same as it ever was, going about its daily business, only now beneath a thin veneer of snow. As they sat at the kitchen table, Gilbert quietly stirred granulated sugar into his coffee while Kate sifted through the newspaper for the crossword puzzle. Then Gilbert mentioned that they needed to pick up Bedford.

After breakfast Kate drove out to the Penny Farm alone in Gilbert's truck. As she came up the driveway of polished snow, she saw Bedford emerge from the mouth of the barn, slow and sleepy-eyed. She pulled the truck up alongside the dog, got out, and took him into her arms. That she was familiar seemed to occur to him slowly, in faint drifts of recollection. His narrow hips began to wiggle furiously in her arms, then his healthy pink tongue whipped across her cheeks. A few minutes later, she heard the clap of an aluminum screen door and saw the woman walking toward her in new overalls, sharp creases running from thigh to ankle, where they were rolled. The woman held her bare hands in her overall pockets against the cold as she came toward Kate. Her face seemed carved from wood, Kate thought. A woman who kept to herself and her family. The world around her seemed proper and stable.

Kate thanked the woman and offered her fifty dollars, but she wouldn't take it. All he ate was scraps, she said. Kate felt too weary to insist and simply tucked the new bills into the bib pocket of the woman's overalls. Without another word she took Bedford by the collar and hoisted the confused dog into the truck.

She drove home slowly. Everything was going to be fine, she thought. All that was left was the very private knowledge that Gilbert had killed Robert P. Lester. And it had to remain private. The police were not going show up at the door; Gilbert wasn't going to be taken away. Mr. Lester's case would gradually diminish and then vanish altogether. Kate felt the warmth of tears on her face. Once Bedford noticed he began to lick at them madly, and this made her smile.

As she drove, Kate passed a subdivision going up in what had once been a field of sunflowers. Fresh yellow framing lumber gleamed in the winter sunlight. At the far end of the neighborhood, two men were grooming the dirt lawns with rakes, smoothing the soil for the arrival of sod in the spring. Instant lawns for the first of the completed houses, everything so clean and new. She wondered if life was innately easier in such places.

While Kate was away, Gilbert took the opportunity to call his brother down in Memphis. They had to catch up, coordinate their lives. In the beginning, the conversation was natural, casual. Gilbert stood at the window with the receiver lodged between his chin and his shoulder. He peered at the town through the curtains as he told Hap about the old man and the dog. All Hap said was, "You're going to make serious trouble for us someday, Gilbert. You got to control those impulses." Gilbert said he'd learned his lesson. Then he began to tell Hap about New Orleans and the policeman. Hap was silent on the other end of the line. After a few minutes of Gilbert's stilted monologue, Hap interrupted.

A man they both knew as Mr. Johnson had been arrested. Hap had posted his bail, but that was just the beginning of the expenses. Somebody whose name Gilbert didn't recognize had been caught inside a Neiman Marcus at three in the morning and fingered Mr. Johnson in exchange for immunity or a reduced sentence. For now, Hap himself was outside the loop. Wasn't too worried.

Gilbert could hear his own breath against the receiver as his brother spoke. He didn't know what to say, so he didn't say anything. Hap had always been someone who reserved the spoken word for the pithy moment, the poignant phrase. But now his voice was somehow random, struggling to be casual. This alone frightened Gilbert, stunned him into silence.

"But I might need some help," Hap said. "A few items so I can help Mr. Johnson pay for his lawyer."

"Not a problem," Gilbert said. "How much?"

"It'll be several thousand dollars. Maybe ten or twelve."

"You know where to find me." Gilbert's tone was confident and nonchalant.

"I'll be up in a few days, in that case."

When the phone went dead, Gilbert couldn't put it down right away. He didn't know how to worry about his brother. Hap had always been competent. No matter the situation, he could handle it. Hap, the college graduate.

Gilbert finally managed to return the phone to the cradle, then went to the basement and removed the bag from the dumbwaiter. He stood in the sphere of milky light and stared at the black fabric. The brightness that fell on it seemed to be absorbed, he thought, like snow falling on a warm street. A hole in the air, a place into which the material world vanished. All the magnificent, pretty things, even light. Then he neatly folded the bag, laid it back in the dumbwaiter, and closed the warped wooden door. He came back upstairs and sat down at the piano.

When Kate returned with Bedford, she found him there, his fingers tinkering with the keys, a pencil resting crosswise on a music sheet. Bedford followed her, his immense soft pads galloping over the varnished oak floor, addressing Gilbert tentatively, the wet fleshy nose sniffing at his hands and feet.

"You're working," Kate said.

"Composing . . ." he said, making a fluid gesture with his writing hand. Because he seemed so preoccupied, Kate suspected something was wrong.

"You okay?" she asked.

He looked at her and smiled. "Fine."

A silence filled the paneled room.

"Let's hear it."

"It's only eight touches of the keys." He held up the music sheet and played all eight. After a reverent pause, he repeated the riff. "So far it's a jingle, a commercial."

"Very nice."

Kate joined him on the bench and began tinkering with the keys herself. To Gilbert she appeared happy but preoccupied herself.

"Anything wrong?" he asked.

"Nope."

"Bedford looks well taken care of."

"He was."

"Sure nothing's wrong?"

"I'm pretty sure everything's fine," she said.

He held the back of a hand under Kate's nostrils and felt the soft slow rhythm of a sleeping girl. The clock read four-thirty. He drifted downstairs, dressed in long underwear, and over everything stretched his suit of black. Standing in the darkness, the iron radiators clanking all around him, he felt muscle-bound and hot. He descended into the basement, where he took his black sack from the dumbwaiter, then rose up through the cellar doors into the cold, starry night.

He moved from window to window, house to house, block to block, trying to see the town in a new way. He wanted to see everything in a *smaller* way. As the eastern horizon grew flaxen, he crept beneath a wraparound porch then through the front door of a house in which he'd seen a wallet on an end table, the tableau lit by a boudoir lamp. Something easy that would not be there tomorrow. A hand swooped down for the wallet. Parting the soft calf leather he saw it held a twenty, a few singles. Then his gaze arced across the room, where he saw on the mantle what looked like a woman's wedding band and engagement ring. The welded gold, a shimmer of gritty stones glinting in the soft light. With a few paces he had crossed the room and was holding them in his hand, and after a few more he was out the door, strolling down the sidewalk at five or six in the morning. He no longer knew for sure, nor did it matter. Presently he was just a citizen dressed in black. As he approached Kate's home, he watched the sky fade to the color of tarnished brass, a seam of light thickening in the eastern sky, while all around him lingered a strange blue glow. He felt the encroachment of worry as he walked. Twenty or thirty in cash, a thin band of gold, and a collection of worthless diamond chips. Tomorrow would have to be different.

But the following night was very much the same. He came up against locked doors and windows. Whenever he made it inside a house, there was little worth taking. Silver Christmas-tree ornaments, a small clock. He felt the energy leave his body. In one house he found himself perusing a family's record collection, and in the end came away with two Sam Cooke albums. On the way home the worry came again, followed by a mild fright. It wasn't fear so much as anxiety, and it was still with him as he drove his truck through the vacant streets the following night. During the day it dissolved, seemingly, in sunlight. But at night, it arose like a specter, haunting him as he rode to meet his brother. He parked as he always did, fetched his bag, and approached the same figure within the same shadow. He felt a weariness, a sickness. They greeted each other with a pretense of ease. Hap simply said, "What do you have for me?" Without shaking hands with his brother, Gilbert lowered the sack to the pavement.

"I thought this was supposed to be a good town?"

"It is. And it's cold at night."

"It's kind of like a chain of extortion we're caught up in here. First there's Mr. Johnson, then me, then you."

Gilbert could see Hap's eyes, glassy with desperation, in the shadow. "I'll come through."

"This might seem like a miserable situation we're in," Hap went on, "but it beats prison."

"I'll come through."

"Well, if you don't, the whole show is over. Mr. Johnson's in an uncomfortable position, and he's no hero. He says he's plenty willing to make it uncomfortable for everybody if they don't come through."

They stood facing each other in the darkness, listening to the passing of the other's breath, watching pale plumes of steam arc into the night.

"Think of this as the price of doing business, Gilbert," Hap said.

"Okay."

"Next time, okay?"

"Next time."

And so Gilbert was motivated. At night he made love to his cousin and plundered the homes of this small town's wealthy. During daylight hours, he confined himself more or less to the upstairs, reading, contemplating new strategy. He catnapped and scanned the newspaper for evidence of what he had done a few nights before. Finally, more stories began to appear as the town sensed a need to overcome its precious aversion to bad publicity. Nonetheless, the accounts were still brief and often inconclusive: Lewis Family Missing Original Brady. Leeland Family Reports Theft.

But as the weeks passed, the clarity of Gilbert's work began to fade. Necessity came to guide his actions. Before there had been only a cool pragmatism; now there was this necessity. It blunted what was once clean and sharp, and all that remained was this demanding imaginary voice. He took to driving his truck out to the new subdivisions and filling the bed with television sets and stereo equipment, something he'd never had the inclination to do. It was graceless work, but whenever Hap came to town he seemed so pleased. He could sell televisions and computers. Silver tea sets and gilded candlestick holders were difficult. That night Hap cheerfully welcomed him to the twentieth century, where electricity was king. At such times, Gilbert wondered whether there was anything in this world he appreciated as much as Hap's approval. Years ago he had become a thief because it was the only work he was both good at and enjoyed. Since then, he had come to find that he also loved making his little brother happy.

But Gilbert wasn't so comfortable with this line of work for practical reasons. He didn't like driving his truck through town in the early morning with a bed full of stolen electronics equipment, nor did he care for the heavy lifting. The work was no longer fun, and it made him vulnerable in a way he normally wouldn't allow. When he left a house with a giant television or microwave in his arms, carrying it through the darkness to his truck several blocks away, he was utterly terrified. He could feel his heart against the metal and plastic. And once he reached the truck, where it was parked in some shadow, the danger was only amplified. He had yet to drive through the vacant streets to the house and haul everything down through the cellar doors. He'd prepared a room for the booty—an extinct coal room with a door made of ancient, rough-cut timber, which every night he blocked with a huge, dusty trunk full of old books. The whole operation left him feeling nervous and physically drained. Once his night was complete and the door closed and barred with the dusty trunk, his muscles ached. He removed his clothes, went to the bedroom, and laid himself beside Kate in the darkness only to find he couldn't sleep. Because he could never be sure. Here he had just driven through the empty streets of this small town with a cargo of stolen property in a truck that was now parked in the driveway for all to see. He would lie awake, turning this thought over in his mind, listening to the sounds of the town beyond the stone walls of the house. Not until dawn would his mind finally exhaust itself. When he awoke in the early afternoon, his body still ached and a terrible dread hung in the bell of his mind. This wasn't how he wanted to conduct his life. He understood that it was but a matter of chance, and therefore time, before all this came to an abrupt and ugly end.

But through the cold winter, the life Gilbert and Kate shared seemed to jell, become more settled. When they tired of the same setting, he and Kate simply drove to St. Louis and took a hotel suite overlooking the river for a few days. Here they were anonymous. They shopped, went to the movies, dined at nice restaurants. And Kate paid for it all. When they returned to Fayette, Gilbert resumed his work of filling the coal room with electronics equipment. Though Gilbert felt he was somehow slumming it, he consistently reminded himself that he was helping a younger brother through hard times. He chose, of course, to ignore the fact that if he did not do this, there was the likelihood that Mr. Johnson would soon make him a wanted man.

On one late-night rendezvous, he and Hap counted eight television sets, three complete stereo systems, four microwave ovens, and a well-jeweled woman's watch. This was real headway. Hap could hardly manage his joy in the darkened parking lot. This pickup alone would amount to two or three thousand dollars of Mr. Johnson's defense fund. They transferred the cargo from one truck to the other, then battened it down with an oil-cloth tarpaulin. Before driving off, Hap told his older brother that the case wouldn't likely make it past the grand jury. Mr. Johnson had an absolutely rabid lawyer. He was insane, really. Something to see. But he was also expensive, and Hap needed more; another four or five exchanges like this one, and he could see his way clear of the woods. Through the open window of his truck, Hap hugged his brother. Then Gilbert watched the red taillights diminishing in the darkness. For a moment he felt a wonderful warmth, proud of himself in some brotherly kind of way. Then the feeling mysteriously left him.

For several weeks, Gilbert maintained the same schedule, or nearly so, and Hap left town supremely pleased with each pickup. One night as they transferred the cargo, their bodies sweating beneath their coats in the cold, dark air, Hap mentioned that Isabelle wanted to see Kate.

"She misses her," Hap said. "It's like they're sisters."

"So you're coming up to stay a while?"

"When it gets a little warmer."

"We aren't going anywhere," Gilbert said, straining beneath the weight of stereo speakers. "Kate'll love it."

"So she still has no idea about any of this?"

"She's one of those people who take a while to fall asleep," Gilbert said, enjoying this moment of chitchat. "But once she does, it's as if she's dead." Gilbert felt good working like this, sweating in the darkness alongside his brother. The world was clean and new, built on the solid shoulders of hard work.

"It would be bad if she ever found out," Hap said.

"It would be very bad."

Early the following afternoon, when Gilbert started his day, he told Kate the news of Hap and Isabelle coming to town. Without a word, she went to the phone and called Isabelle in Memphis and spoke in a whisper, a conspirator's voice. Gilbert watched her from the doorway of Cecil's study, where she sat curled into the thick-armed chair, wholly immersed in conversation with his brother's wife. He stood there for a long while, noting how she seemed so removed, so engaged by this electronic voice that fell against her ear as to have left the room entirely.

When Gilbert read the paper that winter, evidence of his presence continued to appear here and there. In the beginning, he'd felt a thrill when he read the reports—the satisfaction anyone who knows an inside story experiences. But silly pride gradually ebbed into worry. As he went out at night, he began to wonder whether there would be anything left of the town by the time Mr. Johnson's legal bills were paid. When he was finished, the county would be a shell, a community of barren homes. This wasn't guilt he felt, but mere concern, an utterly detached business concern. As the weeks passed, the stories proliferated, eventually becoming a single story. By early spring, he began to see how all the thefts were attributed to an anonymous "they." Yet the idea of branching out to other towns gave Gilbert pause, as the early-morning dash home would simply be too risky. One curious sheriff's deputy, and all would be lost. Meanwhile, theories arose and converged throughout town. It was a ring, most likely based in St. Louis, the police chief declared in the paper. One morning, Kate herself mentioned the story. She speculated aloud that this had something to do with the policeman they'd met on their return from New Orleans. Gilbert shrugged. Probably so.

As the date of Hap's and Isabelle's arrival neared, Kate grew anxious, like a small child enduring the passage of days until Christmas. She told Gilbert what she and Isabelle were going to do—how they would go out to bars, how she would ready the pool if the weather was warm enough. The vividness of the scenes she described startled him, how she saw Isabelle and herself omnisciently through each act of an afternoon. They would wake up together on the sleeping porch and go out to the pool, if the sun was shining, to have tea. Isabelle loved tea, Kate said. They would swim in the cold green water, then warm themselves in the sun as they lay on the canvas chaise lounges. They might drink ginger ale as they lay beneath the sun in their swimming suits. But she didn't know for sure. Of course, the weather would dictate much of what they did.

This strangeness, this desperate imagination, prompted Gilbert to think Kate was slightly out of her mind. He didn't say anything as he listened to her. He just sat, mute and astounded. Meanwhile, he kept up the same schedule, though he had to work harder for less and less. Still more doors were locked, more backyards lit. His brother came every week, each time to pick up a smaller and smaller collection. And each time, Gilbert wore the familiar look of sad apology. Hap indicated that so long as Gilbert kept at it, focusing on things like stereos and televisions, everything would work out. But he couldn't go back to his old ways. Romance and convenience had to give way to economic reality, to demand, to bare-knuckled capitalism.

In early May, Hap arrived with Isabelle. From the living room Kate saw the truck pull up alongside the curb, whereupon she bolted out the front door barefoot, her hair wet. She flung herself into Isabelle's arms with the abandon of a lover, and they swung round and round, Kate twirling about Isabelle's slender brown body like a ribbon about a May pole, mad with joy. When they finally separated, they sprawled upon the lawn, feeling the rich cool grass through their clothes. They lay side by side, smiling wildly, holding hands. Gilbert watched from the porch, waving to his brother before listlessly descending the steps to the truck, where he greeted

Hap as though he had not seen him in months. They stood next to the truck, luggage at their feet, staring down in baffled silence at the two women in their lives.

"What is it with them?" Hap finally said.

"Never seen anything like it."

While Isabelle and Kate lay on the lawn, the brothers went inside to discuss business. With his hands placed carefully before him, Gilbert mumbled, "Told you this would be a good town."

"But is anything left?"

"Entire neighborhoods haven't been touched. Of course, others have had their teeth cleaned."

"Kate still has no idea?"

"None."

"Isn't even suspicious?"

"Nope."

"Isabelle and I are going to Jackson Hole to celebrate."

"You know, I was never terribly concerned, Hap. If anybody could've seen his way clear of this, it was you."

Hap blinked away tears.

"Well, you took care of me, Gilbert."

They went into the dining room, where Gilbert poured two glasses of bourbon from a crystal decanter. They toasted Gilbert's recent hard work, their mutual success, their bond, then Hap apologized for his behavior. He was sorry if he'd been edgy. Gilbert smiled warmly down on his little brother and put an arm around his thick brown neck. Hap added that he had some money for Gilbert, proceeds from the sale of the goods.

"Mr. Johnson's lawyer doesn't get all our money," Hap said, handing Gilbert a tight roll of bills.

"He's an expensive fellow," Gilbert said, shoving it into his pants pocket. "I mean, who are the real thieves in all this?"

After another toast, they strolled back out to the front porch, where they watched the two grown women lying in the purple shadows on the lawn. Gilbert and Hap watched them and sipped their drinks in silence. "What is it with them?" Hap said. "Never seen anything like it."

Nearly every night, Kate and Isabelle shared a bed on the sleeping porch. The air was cold and still above the down comforter; beneath it they shared each other's warmth through the night. In the morning they lay together talking until the smell of percolating coffee rose up within the house. When they finally joined Hap and Gilbert in the kitchen, they still seemed lost in their own private world. Gilbert recalled that it had been a year since Kate and Isabelle had first met, how their personalities seemed to have melded, become one. But this was something different. At first he thought it was a matter of degree, that they had naturally grown closer through time. Now he saw how Kate herself had changed. She was no longer the same person. Her identity had dissolved and gelled into something more like Isabelle's—something blissful and eerily serene. Gilbert began to feel alien in this house that had been his home for nearly a year. He slept alone in the room he and Kate had shared, while Hap slept in the guest bedroom down the hall. Hap seemed to view the relationship between his wife and Kate with amused indifference, but Gilbert saw it as somehow threatening. Eventually he wanted Kate back, the way she was. He wanted his brother and his wife to leave and for his quiet former life with Kate to resume.

sixteen

A glass pitcher of iced tea rested on the tiny metal table as they lay beside the pool in the chaise lounges. A faint breeze rippled the water.

"You and Gilbert seem awfully serious," Isabelle said, smiling, her eyes closed against the sun. "I mean—well, you live together."

Kate turned to face Isabelle. "We're in love," she said with mock pride. "Like you and Hap." She rolled onto her back and closed her eyes. For a moment they lay there in the sunny quiet.

"Do you know what it is Gilbert does for a living, how he makes his money?" Isabelle asked.

"He's a pianist . . . sometimes," Kate said, realizing how tentative and absurd her words sounded.

Isabelle laughed; the chuckle was short and sharp, with an edge to it.

Kate looked at Isabelle again. "I'm sure Uncle Charlie helps him out once in a while," she said with more conviction.

"That's what he told you?" Isabelle asked.

"No," Kate said, smiling knowingly. "I'm sure it's a little embarrassing for him. Playing the piano for a living isn't as lucrative as selling farm equipment."

Isabelle laughed again. Kate smiled as if by instinct. Uncle Charlie must be helping them out as well, she thought. A moment later, Isabelle stood, the laughter lingering in her voice. Then she dove into the cold bright green. Kate continued to smile, momentarily puzzled before the thought moved on and the words withered into a faint memory, a wisp of scattered smoke.

In the afternoons they kept to the living room, drinking bourbon and scotch, playing Addy's Elvis records on the stereo, dancing, smoking. At night, sometimes after midnight, they went for a swim. This was how they entertained themselves. One afternoon they made a departure from their routine and drove to St. Louis, where they took the elevator to the summit of the Arch, the four of them curled into the tiny luminescent pod of the elevator car. At the top they gazed through the windows over the city, over the river, over the green prairie of new grass and fields of freshly turned soil to the northeast. The city crawled beneath them. Beyond the sprawling railyards, nascent green plants sprouted from the black earth. Hap indicated the course of the river as it wound south as far as Caruthersville and Cape Girardeau, in the vast distance. They gazed out at the scene before them for a few minutes, then descended within the arced column of stainless steel, the tiny car lurching as it corrected its position. Gilbert watched the girders, cables, and oversized nuts and bolts through the window as they sank to the ground. From the Arch they drove down Broadway and had dinner at an Italian restaurant. Hap and Gilbert sat across from the women, quietly watching them as they toyed with each other's food and giggled like children.

"It's weird," Hap said to Gilbert.

Gilbert poured everyone a fresh glass of Chianti. "In their own little world," he said.

"It bothers you, doesn't it?"

"It shouldn't."

"But it does."

"Ever feel like they don't even know we're here?"

"Sometimes," Hap said. "But I can't say it bothers me."

Gilbert lit himself a cigarette. His eyes hung on that imaginary space between the two women's eyes where communication would live if it were a tangible thing, if it were something he could reach out and touch. Hap, meanwhile, watched his big brother. He shouldn't look so serious about something like this. So sorrowful, Hap thought. He knew never to bring the subject up again.

When it rained, the two couples sat on the front porch and watched the thunderous pummeling of the earth. The storms were brief and severe and, at night, wonderfully somnolent in effect. The time they shared together was restful. Even Gilbert appeared to enjoy these evenings when they sat on the porch, sipping scotch, as he imagined Kate's predecessors once had. Beside him was the living embodiment of that lineage. Being with Kate made him feel as though he were a part of something exceedingly rare in an age of tract housing and franchise restaurants. He found her presence ennobling. Thinking this, Gilbert grew drunk, every now and then reaching for that slender warm hand at his side, while a heavy spring rain fell all around them.

But as the day that Hap and Isabelle would be going home neared, Kate grew increasingly anxious. She seemed to cling to Isabelle, follow her from room to room, as though she offered some form of protection. The night before Isabelle left, they lay awake on the sleeping porch, watching the hemlocks sway beyond the mesh of wire. They stared at the scene contained within the rectangle of painted trim: Venus burning in a clear patch of sky. When Kate turned on her side she could see Isabelle's eyes blinking in her black face. This was the first time she had seen her as a black woman, here in the darkness, upon the broad white sheets. In the silvery moonglow, there was only black and white. Kate ran a hand over the dark skin—a cheek, the chin—as if to affirm its physicality, that it was not a mere shadow on the sheets.

"I look black in this light," Isabelle said.

"You're invisible."

"I'm white during the day."

Isabelle giggled in the darkness as Kate felt her smooth, rounded shoulder.

"When are you coming back?"

"Summertime," Isabelle whispered.

They lay there, facing each other, neither speaking. A thick, cool wind pressed through the screened windows. A prelude to rain.

"Gilbert's a burglar," Isabelle's voice said.

Kate blinked. She couldn't fix the thought properly, couldn't identify it.

"A cat burglar. He swipes things from people's homes, then sells them to a man in Memphis by the name of Mr. Johnson. Hap's what you'd call a middleman."

The wind beyond the room quickened. They could hear it moving through the trees, through the screen, feel it against their skin.

"I thought he would've told you."

"I don't believe it," Kate whispered—not in denial, but as an expression of startled apprehension.

"You've seen the stories in the paper. That's our Gilbert. At least, most of it's him."

Kate slowly rolled over onto her back. Tiny raindrops began to fall against the roof. Gradually the noise grew and the wind thrust the rain through the screens, sending a fine mist across the sleeping porch.

"He works at night," Kate said, her mind tumbling.

"At night he's invisible like me."

"And he sleeps during the day."

"I can't believe he still tells people he plays the piano for a living," Isabelle said, laughing. "Naughty Gilbert."

"He doesn't actually say that."

Kate immersed herself in thought, culling the cinema of memory for evidence of Gilbert's secret life. She saw him waking in the early afternoon, salt crystals powdered on his temples. His theory of panic, his subtle knowledge concerning the habits of police. When she looked at Isabelle, she saw she was smiling.

"And Hap's involved?" Kate asked.

"For years and years. A family business. A partnership."

"And Uncle Charlie?"

"Oh no. He suspects Hap is involved in some unsavory business, but not much more than that. He still thinks Gilbert's a pianist too. Pristine Gilbert, dirty Hap."

"It doesn't bother you?"

"About Hap? Sure. But I'm a woman in love."

Kate turned all of this over in her mind. "Why did you tell me this?" she asked.

"Because you'll find out sooner or later. And because Gilbert's so in love with you. Hap says he's never seen him like this. Can't say I have either."

"Does he know you've told me?"

"No, and you can't tell him I did," Isabelle said. "He'd be crushed. But when he does break the news—and someday he'll have to—tell him how it doesn't matter, how you can't help but love him." And then Isabelle added in a laughing whisper, "Because you're a woman in love."

"So you told me for Gilbert's sake?" Kate said. "So I wouldn't leave him in case I found out on my own?"

"I told you for his sake *and* yours," Isabelle said with a firmness meant to reassure Kate. "We both know there's no one else in the world for you."

Kate felt her face warming in the night. She turned away from Isabelle and gazed into the wild black sky beyond the screen. Her throat tightened as she lay there, and so she began taking deep even breaths. She must have forgotten herself, as seemingly a moment later Isabelle was petting the perspiration from her forehead, and saying in a soft, soothing voice, "Kate, are you feeling okay, honey? You okay?"

"I'm fine," she responded in a breathy whisper. "I really am."

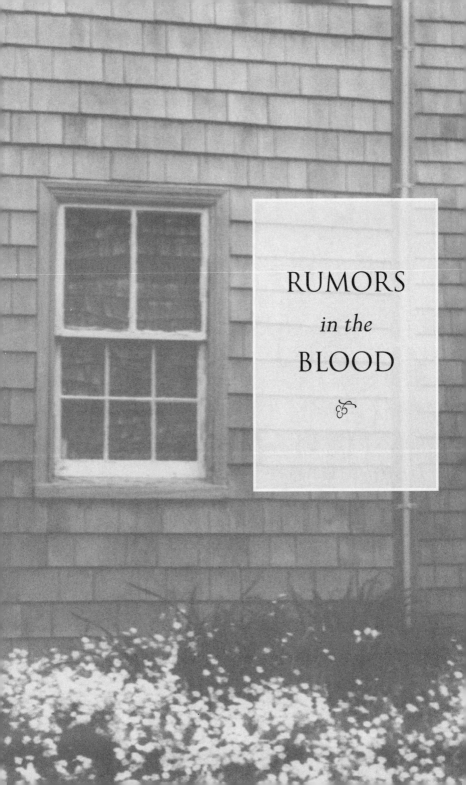

RUMORS

in the

BLOOD

seventeen

In the spring the rains came. Gilbert wouldn't go out at night if the weather wasn't clear, so for nearly two weeks he stayed indoors, reading, writing letters, watching the progression of seamless rain clouds float over town. All the while, Kate studied Gilbert. She wanted to learn how he carried out this clandestine life. After Isabelle and Hap left, she tended to sleep more lightly. She tried to awaken herself in the middle of the night, feeling with a naked foot for his body lying next to hers, and every night she came up against the warm heavy leg. She began to question whether Isabelle was right. Perhaps he had quit, gone straight. Maybe Uncle Charlie supported him entirely. She considered these possibilities for the two weeks that it rained, as it never occurred to her that weather might affect his habits.

But late one night, after the rains had moved on, she felt for the leg and found only the warm impression where it had been a while earlier. She sat up in the darkness and listened to the sounds, the voice of the house. But there was nothing. She stepped out of bed and walked through the darkness, alert for any noises that stood apart from those she knew so well. She drifted from room to room, hearing nothing of Gilbert. After exploring the entire downstairs, she went back to bed, quite certain he wasn't home.

For nearly an hour she sat up in bed, reading one of Gilbert's novels by the light of the streetlamp that poured through the window. She began reading where he had left the bookmark. Then, deep within the stream of the drama, she heard something—a foot upon wood, a tiny unnatural squawk in the night. She quickly replaced the bookmark, set the novel down, and covered herself. And she lay there, waiting for Gilbert to appear in the doorway and rejoin her in bed. Every few seconds came another cry of the house's ancient timber, then he appeared like a ghost, naked and sweating in the silvery half-light. She lay on her side, watching his supple movements, the masculine shape of his hips. When he slipped into bed, she took his waist in her hands and threw a leg over his clammy body.

"You're awake," he said.

She felt him beneath her, his body warming against her skin.

"Where've you been?"

He paused a moment. She thought she could actually feel his mind working.

"A tune came to mind. I thought I might write it down."

Kate didn't say anything. She felt his hands on the small of her naked back.

"You were working," she said.

Gilbert looked up at her. A rectangle of light fell across her cheek and breasts. Her eyes were closed; she was lost in tactile sensation, colorful imaginary feelings. "I was working," she heard him say.

Kate now believed that everyone must come with a fantastic secret, a cryptic history they would reveal only in an intimate moment. The arc of a life was described mostly by the sorrow it endured. This was how people recognized one another—by the shape of their tales. Human beings tended to harbor the trouble they knew as secrets, which those around them guessed at, fashioned into stories, tiny histories. To really know an individual you had to first reveal this unspoken past. What Kate had come to learn of her parents fascinated her most. The incessant calamity seemed so inevitable as her uncle told it. Yet trouble was universal, something to be lived through, a part of everyday life. Trouble. Common as water.

Trouble was something Gilbert believed he could smell, for he alone possessed some unique faculty of detecting, an extra sense. For twelve years, he had avoided it. At times he'd walked right up to its invisible presence, then turned away, just as he came within its sphere of influence. It had the smell of a lake, a scent Gilbert thought he could recognize. Perhaps he employed instinct, perhaps intuition. Whatever it was, he had always trusted the mysterious faculty in his secret professional life as he trusted his own eyes. Then one night in the spring, all that changed.

The earth was soft and moist under Gilbert's feet. He had risen through the cellar doors that evening and walked around the house to his truck. He drove four miles along winding asphalt to a lush spread of bottomland, where he parked in a patch of raspberry bushes that lined the narrow road. When he climbed from his truck, he was surprised by the thorny branches that swarmed around him, and spent the next twenty minutes clearing a path for his return. With a Barlow knife he kept in his glove compartment, he cut the green and maroon branches away from the truck's door so that if he had to leave in a hurry, he could. Perhaps this was the beginning of it, Gilbert would later consider. The first scent.

He approached the darkened house from a soybean field. When

he was within a few dozen yards of it, he climbed a barbed-wire fence strung on ragged oak branches, the loose wire swinging, the plane of fence itself swaying under the sole of his shoe. That's what he would remember—how everything had felt so clumsy up to this point. Once he had crossed the fence, he crouched within the dull moonshadow of a China willow and just stared. The house squatted against the silhouette of a newly leafed hardwood forest, its dormers glinting with clean glass. Hap would approve, he told himself. It had all the hallmarks of having been built by new money. No rooms filled with gilded heirlooms and arcane collections here. Just another new home, four miles from town, shrouded in forest and fields of row crops, probably clamped shut with deadbolts and thermal-pane windows. A house of the new Midwest.

He was entirely prepared to simply walk away. The job would be done either with ease or not at all. Thinking this, he approached the hollow wooden pillars and the pendulum of an extinguished lamp suspended before the front door. He walked through the shadows, directly up to the sharp corner of brick as though he lived there, then slipped behind the stunted hedges, peering through the thermal panes as he moved laterally, each window framing a different setting. A filmstrip. Lava rock crunched under his feet; his fingers slid against the sharp grated surface of new firebrick as he moved.

That the house wasn't locked was a surprise. Only an aluminum door, a wedge of weather stripping to keep out the wind. Inside, it was strangely humid, the heavy air pungent with the smell of soap. A working farm, he thought. Heavy perfumes to cloak the smell of shit, livestock, young children perhaps. The carpet lay silent and plush beneath his feet. Dull gray light from an outside lamp fell through the windows in trapezoids, barely illuminating a room full of cheap sofas and picture frames. Gilbert moved directly through the carpeted dining room into the family room, where he saw a television, a beautiful convex pane of glass wired into a vast stereo system. He knew these people absolutely, how they glided through the years, the weight of their comfortable lives coming down equally on the memory of their forefathers and on their grandchildren. A home that sat on an acre of what was once a thousand. On weekends, they took the motorboat to the reservoir; in the winter, the motor home sped for Phoenix.

Gilbert disconnected the television in the darkness, and within seconds was passing through the front door. He struggled toward the refuge of the willow and its shade. From there he staggered over the smoothly grooved rows of the field, every now and then dropping the black mass of metal and plastic and glass to the earth. His lungs burned as he slumped against the television. He looked up at the glitter of stars, the contour of the horizon beneath it all. A nausea came over him. His heart felt slow, inadequate in his chest. For a moment he thought he might vomit, as his stomach rose up, pressed against his windpipe. Then his breath returned in whispers, the cool air freshening and refreshening the blood. He rose and stretched his long arms into the night, as if to inflate his lungs, before wrapping them around the set and stumbling through the budding crops.

Raspberry thorns cut at his forearms. He shoved the set over the lowered tailgate, then crawled into the bed and pushed it snugly against the cab. He leaned against the set, trying to recover his breath again, contemplating whether or not the stereo with its immense receiver and equalizer was worth going back for. Perhaps just the VCR, he thought. That would be a compromise, something he could allow himself. In a moment of decisiveness he staggered from the bed of the truck toward the house. By the time he came to the fence, his legs felt supple and rested. He carefully placed a hand between the barbs, pressed the wire down, and hopped over the fence. He paused, squatting beneath the same willow to observe the house before him, mumbling to himself. Here stood a home he had just plundered. But all was as he had left it: dark, still and quiet. He stood and scampered across the lawn to the front door.

That night he made three more forays into the house, each beginning with the same studied observation and strategy beneath the willow. Mr. Johnson's lawyer would be paid in full, Mr. Johnson's life would be redeemed. This was the happy prospect that drove Gilbert. Then a strangeness seemed to come over the night.

At first it was a figure, a ghost floating across the short span of lawn, a black shape. Tired as Gilbert was, he thought it did not live in the world he was moving about—it was an apparition dreamed by an exhausted mind. He knew the mind altered what it saw and heard in nocturnal landscapes. As he left the front door for the last time, a wild tangle of speaker wires in his hand, proud and happy as he was, he saw the shape moving through the twin shadows of two walnut trees flowing over the lawn. But it was only a shape, a darkness in the periphery of his vision. He pulled the door tight behind him and crossed the lawn to the willow, into the glittery darkness beneath the iridescent reflection of its waxy oval leaves. Then he felt something.

First came the warmth of a presence against his back; a moment later it was an arm across his throat. For a brief second Gilbert had magical thoughts—that this was a branch around his neck, an apple tree along the Yellow Brick Road. The moment would live in memory as that last flash of hope, the future's final moment. His new life stood just outside the glittering shadows, just past that sagging fence, a hundred yards beyond which sat his truck. Then the arm tightened about his neck, and what followed wasn't real. A cold hard mass pressed against his face, an impact of metal against his cheek. A faceless voice asked his name, but Gilbert wouldn't answer. He felt a gun in his mouth, the metal chipping his teeth, clacking against the enamel. He imagined it discharging, feeling the back of his head erupt, or the bullet passing through his cheek, leaving a perfect little hole in that mysterious pouch of flesh. He dropped the nest of wires in his hands and gagged and fell to his knees while the gun roamed about his mouth.

"Bedford," Gilbert said, the gun still in his mouth.

The man seemed to consider the answer.

"I don't think so," was all he said before yanking Gilbert to his feet.

"Bedford Forest," Gilbert added. Then he went limp, his arms slack with exhaustion. For a moment he couldn't touch the ground. Gilbert thought, This is a big angry soybean farmer holding me. When his feet were once again touching the earth, the man pulled the gun from Gilbert's mouth and pressed it to his nose. Gilbert could smell the strange, rich odor of gun oil. For the first time, he saw the night occurring completely outside the domain of dream. This was real. This black gun against his nose felt and smelled so authentic.

The man swung Gilbert around and headed for the house, which was now dully lit upstairs. As they floated toward the front door, the man hollered for the kids to get back inside, and Gilbert could see miniature, shadowy figures scatter from the porch like mice. He felt panic, clear and hot in his throat. At first he allowed himself to be drawn along, the vision of his left eye obscured by the stout gun barrel. He told himself he would bide his time, engender trust within a few paces. Then he would move. So they walked over the lawn, all of Gilbert's energy going into the effort of moving his feet along, keeping himself afloat. Then, in a burst of panic, he thrust himself from the arm. He felt a stunning crack against his face. The gun burst before his eyes, the yellow flash of burning powder rupturing like a single flare from a roman candle.

He hit the ground and lay there for a second to discern whether he was alive or dead, dreaming or awake. Then he rose in one spastic motion and found himself running across the lawn, through the darkness while behind and seemingly all around him, the gun cracked in the night. He could hear the bullets popping to his left and right. When he came to the fence, he simply flopped over the sagging wire and again found himself running. His wounded eardrums rang in his head, then gradually, very gradually at first, he could hear his own labored breathing, his whimpering voice, his feet against the moist dirt. He could no longer feel his legs beneath him—invisible, ghostly, churning away at the earth, propelling him toward the edge of the field. He tumbled down the grassy slope into the hollow, slammed the truck's tailgate shut, and jumped into the cab. When he turned the key in the ignition, the yellow dome light came on, and he caught a glimpse of himself in the rearview mirror.

He saw the face—the bloody maw at the bridge of his nose, where the bullet had passed laterally, just under the eyes. He saw the flash and the clap in his imagination, the assault on the senses that contained the wound. The tip of his nose was gone, the cartilage that shaped the nostrils exposed so that it resembled a pig's snout. His cheeks were marred by tiny powder burns that extended radially, like the spokes of a bicycle wheel. He didn't yet know how badly he was hurt; the tiny rectangular picture in the mirror was but a patch of black and red blood.

Gilbert pulled out of the bushes onto the road, flicked off the headlights, then raced the engine out of the river bottom. He drove around the circumference of town before entering by way of a side road. When he finally got to Kate's house, it was nearly dawn, the birds noisy in the tree-lined streets. He pulled the truck into the driveway, then continued over the lawn to the back of the house, next to the pool. With his black shirt pressed to his face, he entered the house through the sunporch and staggered directly to the bathroom, where he stood before the broad reflective surface above the sink and saw clearly for the first time what had been done to him.

When Kate awoke she felt with her foot for Gilbert's leg. But all she found was the cool sheet beside her. She sat up and looked about the still room, then sauntered through the house. It wasn't until she came to the locked bathroom door that she found him. After calling his name again and again and trying the brass handle, she finally felt the tumblers of the lock shift.

At first she was mute. The walls of the tiled room were smeared pink, Gilbert's hair sticky and wiry like cotton candy. He held a pillow of bloody gauze to his nose as he tried to stand, but slumped to the floor, into a shallow black pool of blood. It's happening all over again, she thought. It's never going to end. Showing no emotion, she took his bloodied skull into her hands.

"Go away," he tried to say.

She peeled his hands from the saturated bandage and saw the grotesque wound, the skin and cartilage torn away, the flimsy right nostril hanging like a ragged pennant from his face. Across both cheeks spanned the radial powder burns.

"You were caught," she said, her hands shaking.

"My nose is gone, Kate." His eyes were closed. "My nose was shot off."

Kate looked around the room with its terrible new black and pink color, then down at Gilbert's pug face. When she finally screamed, it was abrupt and shrill. In the din of the echo, she asked herself if she was going to survive this. It's all over now, she thought. It can't just go on and on. . . .

Meanwhile, Gilbert took a fresh strip of gauze from the roll resting on the lid of the toilet seat and dressed the wound again while Kate squatted before him, her face in her hands. His ears no longer hurt. Behind all sound was a constant ringing—the musical note of a nine-millimeter bullet leaving the barrel of a gun. When Kate recovered, she went to the sink and washed her face and hands. Then she gazed at Gilbert where he sat slouched in his own blood.

"We've got to get to a hospital," she muttered. "Oh Gilbert, *what did you do?*"

"I didn't shoot myself, Kate," he said. His voice had changed, as though he had a bad cold.

"We've got to get to the hospital."

"I can't go to the hospital."

She stared at him, her pupils dilated with shock. Then, as her composure began to return, she stood and took a washcloth from the cabinet. She held it under a thin stream of hot water and applied it tenderly to his face, wiping away the blood from his cheeks and forehead before moving it against the wound itself. She dabbed at the wound with the thick hot cloth, yet Gilbert did not wince, would not acknowledge the touch. At this proximity, she noticed that his eyes were glazed and wild. Little green pools of despair. As she cleansed the wound, tears rose up in her eyes from time to time and spilled onto his face. When she finished washing his face, she took cotton balls, saturated them with hydrogen peroxide, then held them, one by one, to his missing nose. She watched the tiny bubbles fizz like pink champagne against the cartilage. She could see that half an inch or more of Gilbert's nose had been torn away.

"You need a doctor," she said, now calmly, as they stood together before the mirror. "A surgeon."

"Not in this town."

"Where then?"

"Anywhere. Just not here."

eighteen

The dressing covered his face like a muzzle—strips of tape under the eyes, over the nose, across the upper lip and either cheek. He spent the afternoon in the gloomy quiet of the sunporch, sipping scotch from a snifter that sat in his upturned palm as he watched squirrels race through shady new leaves. As the sun set, Kate walked up to his side and touched the pink arm.

"I'm going to call the doctor," she said.

Gilbert didn't say anything. His eyes fluttered above the grid of bandages.

"The doctor who did this," she said as she brought a fingertip to the tiny scar on her shoulder. "I think we should call him."

Gilbert nodded his uneasy approval.

Kate turned and went inside to make the phone call to Dr. Milo in St. Louis. Offering no explanation, she asked if he could come to Fayette; she needed him. He politely refused. He didn't go anywhere without a reason. She hesitated, and for a moment neither spoke.

"My fiancé hurt himself," she finally said.

The doctor exhaled in exasperation. "Well *how?*"

"His nose was shot off."

The doctor was silent. Kate could hear him flipping through a book of some sort. A daytimer, maybe.

"By a gun?"

"That's right."

"When?"

"Early yesterday morning. Before dawn."

"He needs to go to an emergency room, Kate."

"That's not possible."

There was another long pause, a moment for Kate to reconsider. When it was clear that she wouldn't, Milo asked some particular questions about the nature of the wound, all of which Kate answered with a word or two.

"Keep it clean. It's important that the sinus doesn't become infected," he began his instructions. "Keep the mucus out with an eyedropper." The earliest he could be there was the following night around seven or eight, he said. Then he hung up.

Gilbert spent the evening on the front porch. Kate turned in early, well before the sun went down, as schools of mosquitoes swarmed around them. But Gilbert seemed immune to their maddening buzz and tiny stings. He sat there deep into the evening while a family of bats slowly scoured the cool night air. She didn't recall him coming to bed. In the morning, she saw him by the pool, rubbing calamine lotion into the mosquito bites scattered over his arms. She watched him through the storm windows of the sunporch. Even from there she could see how the white patch over his face covered only a nub of flesh. The nose beneath it did not exist. She could see his eyes were glassy not from pain or discomfort but from despair. He applied the calamine as if in a trance, a witness to the porous action of skin, a blind man reading the Braille of mosquito wounds. Once he'd finished with the lotion, once the exposed skin was painted in this lifeless pink, he reclined deep into a canvas chair and let the sun strike him. He lay like that as the shadow of hemlocks drifted over his body. In the afternoon Kate walked through the steamy sunshine to join him. She sat quietly at his side, glancing surreptitiously at his diminished profile. An arm's length away, she could see how painful the wound must be. All around him was a charged air, a static violence, the presence of some formless menace.

Late that evening, Dr. Milo's German car pulled up in front of the house. Kate watched him approach the side porch, apelike, his black bag swinging from his long arm nearly to the sidewalk. He looked so different outside the bright walls of the hospital, Kate thought. Now he was a real human being, recognizable on her own scale. She swept open the door just as he was about to knock, and invited him in. He smiled down on her. The crown of his polished bald head shone in the kitchen light. Ill at ease, he didn't say much, only grunted with polite apprehension. Out of habit he stooped as he passed through the door, bringing into the house his own medicinal odor, an antiseptic smell this house had never known. Without a word he walked to the kitchen table and lowered himself into a mule-ear chair. He set his gleaming black bag on the floor alongside his wingtips. Looking across the broad surface of the table, he smiled.

"How is he?" Milo asked.

"Not so well," she stammered, lowering her eyes. "I don't think there's an infection, but . . ."

"Good. That's very important," he said. "Wounds near the brain carry their own special risks."

"But his nose is gone," she mumbled.

Suddenly she felt tears rise up in her eyes. She looked at her pale thin arms on the table and noted how they quivered so finely. She stared at them for a long, silent while, then saw the doctor's large white hands descend upon her own.

"This isn't the end of the world," he said in a calm, hopeful voice. "We have tricks up our sleeve. Lots and lots of tricks."

The room was quiet.

"Where's your mother, Kate?"

"She passed on."

Another silence. Milo looked around the room as if the walls could answer his questions.

A short while later, they began to share a few details of their lives, warding off any more of Kate's tears with a commerce of trivial history. School, small-town life, college. Kate found herself lying about everything. She was amazed and relieved that he never asked anything more about her mother. Eventually he asked if she thought it was time to see Gilbert. She said she should go upstairs first.

Gilbert was sitting on the edge of the bed, staring out the window at a raccoon in the trees when Kate came into the room. All was utterly silent and still but for a twig tapping against the pane as the raccoon shifted its weight across the branch. As she came up to Gilbert's side, he said quite flatly, "He can come up now." At that, Kate touched his shoulder and went back downstairs.

The doctor followed Kate up the dark, narrow staircase, her yellow ponytail swinging like a metronome before his eyes. At the bedroom door, he hesitated. Gilbert didn't turn to address the doctor but continued to stare out the window.

"Well, here he is," Kate said, kneeling at Gilbert's side, then moving to a corner of the room as the doctor drew up a chair to the bedside and began by pulling away the homemade mask of athletic tape and bloody gauze. He asked no questions. To him, it seemed a kind of archaeology. He merely stated his observations as if regaling Gilbert with an outline of what had happened that night. An apparent gunshot wound, powder burns. A mutilated septum, a fractured maxillary sinus. Extensive cartilage damage. The doctor's odorless breath fell on Gilbert's face while Gilbert's glassy eyes fixed on the tidy knot of the doctor's tie. Kate stood in the corner, her arms folded before her, both doctor and patient clearly within her field of view.

"I'm an oncologist, a cancer specialist," the doctor said, gently shoving his chair away from his patient. "You need a plastic surgeon. Someone who can reconstruct those nasal passages and give some form to the nose. Psychologically . . . well, you need a nose."

Gilbert said nothing. His eyes clung to the doctor's knotted tie.

"This must be hard. I can't imagine," he continued. "The emotional impact alone must be . . . overwhelming."

"Who can we go to?" Kate asked from across the room.

"Referral shouldn't be a problem."

"We need somebody who understands."

"That narrows the field down," the doctor said, showing irritation with Kate's wariness. "But I have someone in mind."

"Somebody who understands?" she said quickly.

"Look. I'm not asking questions, Kate," he said, standing up, his long body unfolding vertically, seemingly to the very ceiling. "So you have to decide whether or not you trust me."

Kate's eyes filled with tears. Gilbert rose and took her into his arms. The cool tone of the doctor's voice stunned her, the impatience. As she began to whimper, Gilbert answered for them both in his strange new voice: "Just give us a goddamn name."

A bloody handprint lay across the chrome latch. At first the door wouldn't open, as blood had pooled in the door frame and glued it shut. But after Kate gave it a good tug, the door finally creaked open.

The fleshy leather interior was smeared with tacky crimson-black. Kate could see the trail of Gilbert's movements—how he had fumbled with the keys, how he had positioned the rearview to see himself, how he had adjusted the dome light to fall on the fresh wound.

Kate wiped down the upholstery, then drove the truck over the lawn to the cellar doors, where she unloaded the stereo, the television, everything Gilbert had stolen that night. Each time she came into the basement, she asked herself if she felt guilty, if she was now somehow an accessory to Gilbert's crimes. Was she responsible in any way? Or was their predicament ultimately a product of impermissible blood? This, she thought, might be Uncle Charlie's explanation. She was not only reliving her own recent past; somehow, the outline of her family's greater history lay in this. But she told herself she didn't need an explanation. What she needed was guidance. What she craved was a stern voice telling her what she could and could not do. Gilbert just bred trouble. So far, life with him had been many months of regret and exile. She missed her former life. She missed having friends, and she missed her mother.

In the morning they packed heavy, as though planning never to return. They took Bedford out to the Penny Farm, then they were gone. In the beginning, the roads and highways were those they'd taken down to New Orleans a few months earlier, and traveling through the same terrain, there was a joyless familiarity to ponder. What was and what had been appeared so incongruous, irreconcilable. Kate once read that history was an angel with her back to the future. In a flash, an epiphany, Kate saw how this was so.

They crossed the Mississippi at Alton, then drove through St. Louis, moving south alongside the swollen river for an hour or so until the city faded to cornfields and pasture. When they came to a small town in the valley with a hotel, a few restaurants, and churches, they pulled over and took a room with a kitchenette. The French Colonial–style hotel was old and built of wood. Its vast porch and windows faced the river, and a clay bluff stood against its back.

Their room looked out over the dense green canopy of trees along the river so that the barge traffic could be plainly seen as it floated around a gentle bend to the north. From the beginning Gilbert took to opening the French doors and sitting out on the small balcony to watch the ceaseless flow of ships churning up and down the river. Kate bought bottles of scotch and bags of crushed ice. Gilbert kept a bowl of the ice next to the spindle legs of his chair as he sat all day long, more or less in silence, watching the river flow, drinking. Kate kept him company until she found she could no longer endure the spells of quiet. At that point, she would run extended errands, make arrangements at the hospital in St. Louis, buy groceries, go to the bank. Gilbert didn't seem to mind her absence. When she returned in the late afternoon, she inevitably found him sitting just as she'd left him several hours before. Only now he was shirtless, sunburned, and happily drunk.

A few days after their arrival in this town called Clemente, Kate drove up to the city alone for a preliminary appointment with the doctor. His name was Dr. Laskow, a plastic surgeon originally from Warsaw, Poland—an Orthodox Christian whose family had left the country in 1938. He was supposed to be very good as a surgeon and sympathetic to cases that clearly originated outside the realm of the law or discretion. The law in any form, he told Kate in his motley, slightly British accent, was an institution he did not trust. Since he had come to America, he felt most comfortable operating at the margins. Of course he would take their case. This was nothing. He wanted to meet Gilbert as soon as possible.

So the following morning Kate and Gilbert prepared for their first meeting together with the plastic surgeon. As Kate drove deep into the city, Gilbert drank from a stainless steel flask. By the time they arrived, he was mildly drunk.

They found Laskow drawing charcoal sketches of a woman's cheek on a large sketchpad when they came into his office. When he stood, they could see how short this man really was. The intro-

ductions were brief and curiously warm. The doctor folded his
sketchpad, tucked it away in his hopelessly cluttered desk, then offered them both a seat. He began the meeting by telling them about
life in Poland before the war, the story of his immigration to America via Britain, how he came to settle in St. Louis—the same story
Kate had heard the day before. She listened patiently. As she sat between this doctor and her cousin, she could see Gilbert felt safe
here, unashamed. She could smell liquor on his breath and wondered if the doctor could as well. Then she thought how it didn't
matter. At least to Laskow it didn't matter. After nearly an hour of
narration, the doctor finally mentioned Gilbert's bandage.

"Injuries to the nose are painful," he said, smiling.

"But it won't always hurt, right?" Kate said.

"Let's take a look."

He brought his small gray hands to the bandage and began to
peel it tenderly from the skin. As he revealed the wound, Kate observed the doctor's expression carefully, trying to discern his true
opinion. But his face did not change. She could detect nothing.

"This will take some time, a series of procedures," the doctor
said. "But I've had more difficult cases."

He went on to describe what would be done—the theory and
practice of reconstructive surgery. Two things were needed: bone
and skin. The skin was easy, as it could simply be grafted. Giving it
a certain rigidity and consistent shape was another matter. But
there were lots of options at their disposal. The doctor was at once
noncommittal and confident.

"Can you make it, you know, like it was," Kate asked as the
doctor began dressing the wound with fresh gauze and tape.

The doctor chuckled into his small fist. "It's a matter of de-
grees. These things take time. Hopefully we can bring back most of
what's missing."

"And someday no one will know."

"The nose is a complicated organ. There's bone, cartilage, skin," he said, twisting his own with a thumb and forefinger.

Gilbert shifted in his seat. He said nothing. Just a face behind a grid of bandages, a noseless face.

"And such a prominent organ. It's right there between the eyes and mouth. If there's something the slightest bit uncanny about someone's nose, we notice it. It's all so very delicate."

"We understand," Gilbert said, his glassy eyes smiling over the crest of white tape. "We won't expect much."

"Oftentimes patients are disheartened in the beginning," the doctor went on. "Progress is incremental, always incomplete. Some find the novelty difficult to bear."

"So long as it heals," Kate said.

"We can begin next week, I think," the doctor said. "But I need to explain a few things first. Oh, remind me to give you something for the pain before you go."

They spent the afternoon with Laskow showing them cross sections of the nose and face, the peculiar anatomy and interrelation of the ears, nose, and throat. Gilbert sat between Kate and the doctor, his eyes peering over the dressing at the glossy diagrams in the medical text, at once keenly interested in the pictures and silent. He saw the complexities involved, how the nose was a gracefully shaped and magical organ. Form followed function. Repairing the injury would take a peculiar skill and a lot of money. And even then there would be a phony shape and an iridescent luster to the skin. He would never again be regarded with the same approval by strangers. As he listened, he told himself he would not miss his looks. He'd been handsome his entire life, and this might be good for him in some nebulous, spiritual way.

On the way back to Clemente, Gilbert's mood lightened. At times he seemed downright cheerful. He pulled out the magnetized steel flask from the frame of the bench seat and drank all the way back to the hotel. He seemed to become drunk so quickly, Kate thought. Perhaps it was his voice, only vaguely familiar with the silly distortion of clogged nostrils, the fettered passage of breath. The nose softened the voice, made it more fluid and languorous. What had once been so versatile and rich was now tinny.

They eased through the city, then sped into the endless green countryside with its new crops, overgrown forest, and grassy ditches, when Gilbert's voice came forth, telling her of his cautious new hope, the inconvenience of not having a nose, the constant pang, the joy of pharmaceutical pain relievers. She knew it wasn't the sudden presence of this voice after several days of silence, nor the alteration in its character, that made him seem so drunk.

"Adam would've handled this better," he said.

Kate wiped away a suntear and then brought a hand down upon his knee. "Let's don't talk about Adam right now."

Gilbert raised the metal flask to his lips. "Kate, I'd laugh if the pain wouldn't overwhelm these painkillers."

Melancholy and concern mixed with ridiculous laughter rushed out of Kate in a single torrent. All around them a thick green fled past the windows.

"Sometimes I can't believe what's happened," she said, her tears clearing. "It doesn't seem real. And it's a secret. I can't believe Isabelle and Hap don't know. Nobody knows. All this has happened and nobody knows."

"You must miss your mother, don't you?" Gilbert said solemnly. "Your father too. There's no adult in your world telling you what you should do next. Nobody with only your interests in mind. I've pulled you into this trouble. . . ."

"Come on, Gilbert," Kate moaned. "Don't let the conversation go this way."

"You can't be in love with me. You can't. Too much has happened."

"Without a doubt, too much has happened."

"You're so young, and all this has happened," he repeated. "How old are you, anyway?"

She turned and glared at him. "What do you mean, *how old am I?*" she said, her face suddenly reddening. "I'm nineteen!"

Gilbert shook his head as if thoroughly disappointed in himself. "I'm sorry, Kate," he whispered. "I'm kind of stupid right now."

Kate felt an onslaught of tears, but tried to suppress them by returning her attention to the road. If she started to cry, she would have to pull the truck over, and there would be a scene.

"We'll get through this," she said. She reached for the metal flask, and Gilbert watched her take a drink. She could feel his eyes on her as the scotch pooled against the back of her throat. Its antiseptic touch smarted. But somehow the pain felt good, soothing.

"This is going to cost a lot of money," Gilbert said, his voice tame, cool.

"But that's not one of our problems."

"For me it is."

"I have access to a whole bankful."

"This is a funny situation I've gotten us into."

"We should call Hap and Isabelle. Tell them what's going on."

"Let's wait on that," Gilbert said. "They're in Wyoming. I don't want to ruin their vacation."

Kate shrugged. "I'm sure they'd want to know."

"We'll wait until the end of the month. Then I'll give them a call."

"Fine."

Gilbert fidgeted in his seat for a moment. Then he said again, "This is a funny situation I got us into."

"Definitely an unusual situation," Kate said, returning her attention to the road. "But somehow it seems inevitable."

The glow of lights passed laterally beyond the open doors. Kate could hear Gilbert sucking on a Demerol as they lay in bed, could hear it clicking against his teeth. The capillaries of the gum and lips absorbed the medicine, then drew it to the center of the face. His eyes were glassy, glittering in the reflected light of river traffic.

"There's something you should know."

Kate didn't respond.

"Of course it's top-secret knowledge," he said, as if he hadn't yet made up his mind whether or not to tell her.

"What is it?" Kate said. She felt her face chill.

"Ready?"

"Yeah."

"Hap . . ."

"Yes."

"He's my brother."

"Yes."

"He's really my brother. My half-brother."

At first, nothing made sense. Then it descended. The knowledge came down, settling out of the darkness over the bed. Then the darkness was altered, lit by comprehension. Hubris, she thought. Hubris and horseplay . . .

She wasn't aware of Gilbert's voice carrying on and on through the darkness until she heard Isabelle's name. Isabelle . . .

"Her too."

"Isabelle."

"My half-sister."

Kate stroked her chin.

"Their mothers were nannies. *My* mothers, in a way. Isn't the kind of thing you talk about. Even within the family. Just isn't mentioned."

When Kate spoke, her voice sounded tinny like Gilbert's.

"Do they know?"

"Of course. But I'm sure they don't care to have the subject brought up either. Nothing anyone can do."

"What if they had children?"

Kate heard her breathing cease. She listened to the clock on the nightstand.

"Isabelle had herself fixed when she was nineteen. Uncle Charlie paid for it. Drove her to a doctor he knew in Memphis, just like in the olden days. She and Hap were already in love. Uncle Charlie told me once that all history begins as genetic history. Twenty-three chromosomes pairing with twenty-three chromosomes, splitting and pairing down through the generations of all mankind. Chicken and egg, chicken and egg. All history's genetic. The idea of free will is lost on him. I think it's an unhealthy fascination with antebellum times. Needs that all-important reference to the past."

Kate was stunned. There was too much to absorb. Meanwhile, Gilbert's voice carried on and on.

"And there's one more thing," she heard him say. "This may make you feel a little better about your own lineage."

"Don't tell me," she interrupted. "I can't put it all together at once. Just let me think about what you've said."

nineteen

For a week they lingered in Clemente, strolling along the river-front, where an old steamboat rested against a dock, rotted hemp ropes permanently coiled next to the wooden gangplanks. They walked through town with Kate's bare brown arm looped through Gilbert's elbow, like tourists, lovers. People gawked at Gilbert's face, imagining the wound that lay beneath the gauze. But he seemed not to mind. The physical discomfort and shame dissolved in a tide of narcotics, and so they made their way on a cushion of etherized grace, strangely hopeful and content with the progress of events. Kate had no idea where all of this would lead as the days passed in this town of strangers. The sense of threat was dampened by the idea that Gilbert was being treated and would soon be get-ting better. This provided a very necessary reprieve from the over-whelming certainty that disaster was finally at hand. Little was at stake, and she could only relax. In the meantime, they shopped, ate at one of the two restaurants in town, had drinks out on the deck of a bar, then came home in the early evening, locusts and tree frogs creaking all around them.

Toward the end of the week, Kate again drove Gilbert to the hospital, where she delivered him to Dr. Laskow's office. The diminutive man appeared pleased to see them, as though they were family or celebrities. He invited them to sit beside him at his desk so they could go over in greater detail what this first procedure would involve. Only a tiny bit of bone would be smoothed, so they shouldn't expect any grand transformation. Think of it as laying down a foundation. Skin would be grafted from the hip, more narcotics prescribed. When the doctor rather sternly asked Gilbert if he understood the modest scale of the operation, he nodded like a small boy.

Gilbert was led by a nurse to a shower, then down the elevators to the OR. Kate walked at his side as they drifted over the polished concrete to the post-op room, where Gilbert sat on a guerney. They waited in the cool, dank silence for Dr. Laskow, and watched the lethargic business of surgeons and nurses and patients as they moved beneath the fluorescent lights, their eyes drawn against the brightness. By the time Dr. Laskow arrived, Gilbert was chilled in his blue surgical gown. Laskow offered him a thin cotton blanket and gestured down the hall toward the surgical suite.

"Take your time," he said to both Kate and Gilbert. "We'll be in suite number three." Then he walked off.

Kate turned to Gilbert and looked up into his masked face. He held the small blanket about his shoulders. She swept her hands up and down his cold arms, smoothing the pimpled skin.

"Well, this is it," he said. "Gilbert will once again have a nose." Kate took his head in her hands and gently kissed his cheek. "I'll see you upstairs."

She kissed him on the mouth—something she hadn't done for some time now—careful of the bandage, both of them so aware of the phantom presence below the eyes. Then Gilbert walked off, his pale ass peeking through the parted blue gown as he floated down the hall.

Kate's face hung against a swirled plaster ceiling within Gilbert's oval field of vision. Form seemed to arise from formlessness. Empty space, then the world . . . Gilbert contemplated this idea as his mind emerged from anesthesia. Then there was again nothing. He slept for another hour or so before she reappeared, her face clearer, more defined.

Kate slept beside him on the hospital bed that night, and in the morning Dr. Laskow came in to inspect the dressing and sign the papers that would discharge Gilbert. Kate and Gilbert returned to the hotel along the familiar back roads, Gilbert holding a tall, translucent bottle of Demerol in one hand and the flask of scotch in the other. Every now and then he would twist off the plastic cap and swallow a few of the pink pills. The third time he did this, Kate took the bottle and read the instructions. Gilbert's mouth smiled below the bandage.

"This says you're only supposed to take two every four hours."

"Narcotics never work as advertised."

When they got to their room, Gilbert fell into bed and slept until dusk. Then, as the room darkened, he rose and joined Kate where she sat out on the balcony, drinking a beer. She saw immediately that his eyes were clearer, his mind sharper now that the influence of painkillers had faded, leaving a throbbing pang in its wake. Gilbert said he could feel a pulse at the center of his face.

"Does it hurt?" she asked, straightening her posture.

"Imagine every heartbeat as a fist to the nose. That's what it's like."

"You'll run out of Demerol."

"Twelve a day won't do."

"Maybe we should call the doctor."

"Try a couple," he said, taking a seat beside her. "They enhance beer."

Gilbert plucked the bottle from the breast pocket of his shirt, twisted it open with some difficulty, then handed Kate two pink tablets.

"Laskow has got to realize how painful reconstructive facial surgery actually is. I mean, this just won't do," he said, indicating the directions.

Kate's eyes shifted from Gilbert to the Mississippi river valley spread out beneath them in the purple shadows of dusk to the little pink pills. She tossed them into her mouth, feeling the bitter chalky disks against the back of her throat before flooding it with a canful of American beer. They talked for a while, watching the sun ease behind the curve of the earth, then the conversation faded as the drugs swept Kate's thoughts. So they spent the early evening watching the river, the colors of dusk muted by wave after wave of Demerol-laced beer. The valley faded from purple to blue as the sky gave up its fantastic colors. The incandescent lights of farms scattered over Illinois burned across the plains. Kate and Gilbert observed it all, their minds supple and pliant. From this vantage, a few dozen feet above the valley floor, the world appeared so lovely and manageable, laid out before them like the mock landscape of a train set.

Twice a day Kate irrigated the wound with saline solution and re-dressed it. Each time Gilbert begged for the mirror so that he might see his nose in profile, and each time she wouldn't allow it. Gilbert couldn't insist, stoned as he was. There was nothing to see anyway. Just a mutilated mass of skin and bone. Privately Kate grew worried, as she couldn't make out the doctor's grand design. His work looked so ragged and arbitrary. Toward the end of the week, Kate called Laskow for a new prescription, which he granted easily.

Kate asked if he would double it so that they wouldn't have to refill it in another week. Again he complied. Once the conversation ended, she left for the pharmacy and returned an hour later with a bottle of scotch and Demerol—all set up for another pleasant evening of watching the day come to an end.

Daily life wasn't a problem. The operations were expensive but entirely within Kate's means, considering the money she had at her disposal in Fayette. She wrote checks to the hospital and kept in a satchel a brick of hundred-dollar bills held together by a rubber band with which she bought groceries and paid for the hotel room. After a month, however, they'd spent nearly five thousand dollars, half of which had gone to the hospital and Dr. Laskow. As time passed and money was spent, Gilbert began to feel uneasy. One night as they sat out on the balcony, he looked at Kate and ran a finger over the soft white down of her upper lip. "I'm worried things are going to change," he whispered.

"How do you mean?"

"I don't see this lasting forever," he said.

"I still don't understand."

"We were going to get married, weren't we?"

"When was that?"

"Seems like years ago." His gaze swept the distance. "Time gets distorted beyond all recognition."

"I don't even know what day or week it is anymore," she said.

"Maybe it's the Demerol."

"Maybe," she said, giving truly serious consideration to her own conception of time.

"Maybe things will quiet down some."

There was a long silence. Gilbert felt so high he couldn't keep his train of thought.

"So you want to get married?" he finally said.

Kate smiled. She seemed about to say something but unable to fix it in words. Gilbert placed a hand on her bare knee. He understood.

"We should do it soon," he said, taking her hand.

She wagged her head. "I don't know, Gilbert," she said, afraid of contemplating the idea. "I just don't know anymore."

"Kate, what else is there left to do?" he said. "Just live together? For the rest of our lives?"

Kate felt incapable of thinking about her life beyond the scope of a day. She didn't know how to respond, so simply repeated herself. "I don't know, Gilbert."

"Let's just sit here and think about it."

Kate sat quietly beside him. After a few minutes the subject seemed to have drifted from his hazy mind, and she felt a huge relief. She gazed at his profile as he studied the progress of river traffic. He's just too high, she thought.

But the following morning Gilbert quietly got up and left the hotel room with Kate lying facedown in the sheets. When he returned a couple of hours later, Kate was cooking a western omelet on the stovetop. Gilbert carried a small bag of groceries in one arm, in the other a modest yellow dress in a clear plastic garment bag. In his pocket were two thin gold bands. Kate appeared puzzled as he came into the kitchenette.

"That for anything in particular?" she asked, pointing at the dress.

"For the ceremony."

Kate set the metal spatula down. She watched the eggs harden against the skillet.

"I have it all figured," Gilbert said, spreading the dress out on the unmade bed. "I thought we'd do it today. We'll call the courthouse, get me a suit, and so on and so forth." He quietly approached her as she stood before the noisy black skillet. He pulled out the two wedding bands.

"Let's have some breakfast, then go get married," he whispered.

A heavy tear rolled from Kate's cheek onto the hot iron. Kate looked down and saw the puddle fussing about the surface like a bead of mercury.

"Sure we should do this, Gilbert?"

He pulled her head under his chin.

"We have to," he muttered.

"We'll be Mr. and Mrs. Willoughby," she said, taking one of the gold bands. "Just like we are now. Nothing will change."

"But we'll be married."

"I don't know about this," she said, not knowing how to refuse.

Because they couldn't find a tailor who could alter a suit that very afternoon, they rented a black pin-stripe that came with a red bow tie and cummerbund. Kate thought Gilbert looked silly in it. From the rental shop they drove directly to the courthouse, where they purchased an application for a marriage license from a leery secretary in the county clerk's office who didn't seem to like the fact that they had the same last name. As she studied their driver's licenses, Gilbert said sorrowfully that there wasn't much they could do about it. The secretary carefully set both licenses down on the counter. As if unwilling to tolerate the insolence of a noseless man, she announced that they had to wait twenty-four hours before they could marry, claiming it to be Missouri law.

"Fine with us," Gilbert said. "We have all the time in the world."

So the following day, they strode up three stories of marbled steps to the dark courtroom, where a very old, withered judge sat waiting to marry Gilbert and Kate Willoughby. He sat behind a tall mahogany bench, raised upon a dais, his gavel resting on its side, perusing their driver's licenses and the marriage document with the matching last names. Then he lifted his eyes to the young woman in a yellow dress and the man in a black pin-stripe suit, bow tie, and a white patch over his noseless face.

"Both last names are Willoughby," the judge announced from above. "This isn't a clerical error, is it?"

"No, sir," they answered in unison.

"You have the same last name."

"Yes, sir."

"You ever been married to each other before?"

"No, sir."

"You related?"

"No, sir,"

"You just have the same last name."

"Correct, sir—Your Honor," Gilbert said, suddenly uncertain of the manner in which to address a judge.

"I see," he said. There was a long silence. "What happened to the nose?"

"It was an accident, Your Honor."

The judge appeared puzzled.

"You been in trouble with the law?"

"My nose was shot off during a robbery."

The judge appeared to think the matter over.

"Looks painful. Hope it heals properly."

Another pause.

"You're mighty young to be getting married, miss."

"We've been dating for some time," Kate said.

"Nineteen. That's awful young these days. Your parents know about this?"

"They've both passed on, Your Honor."

The judge nodded as though this explained everything.

The wood paneling creaked all around them and dust motes passed laterally through the slanting light. Kate and Gilbert stood there, side by side, for several minutes, then the judge abruptly rose and commenced the ceremony. Thirty seconds later they exchanged rings, and they were husband and wife. They walked through the glass courthouse doors and into the windy sunshine holding hands, the marriage license flapping from Gilbert's hand.

They drove along the river for several hours until they came to a state park, where they lay on the grass on the riverbank and watched a group of Boy Scouts construct a raft of logs and rope. Once the Scouts had lashed the craft together, two of the older boys shoved their yellow-skinned poles into the soft riverbottom and were soon drifting with the gentle current. Within a few seconds, a corner of the raft began to list into the dark brown water, then suddenly it was entirely submerged. Gilbert and Kate watched as the boys swam to shore, towing the raft, each with a cotton rope in his small fist. They rose up out of the water, their uniforms now dark against the bright day. As Kate and Gilbert lay there, they each downed a couple of Demerols with beer.

As the sun began its descent, they drove slowly back toward Clemente with the windows open, a current of warm, moist air rushing through the cab, the pollen and milkweed seeds swirling all about them. When they came into their room they made love on the cotton sheets, the French doors to the balcony parted, allowing in the ruckus of traffic on the road below. Afterward they showered together and strolled out to the balcony in their bathrobes. There they downed a few more Demerols and some scotch while they watched the dagger-shaped islands of the Mississippi fade to silhouettes and become lost beneath the moonless sky. Kate found herself floating toward the Big Easy in her mind. Sometime deep in the night they wandered back to the tousled bed and fell asleep as husband and wife.

twenty

They dressed and re-dressed the wound with gauze and tape as the sun settled into the bluff. Gilbert sat on the toilet seat in the bathroom. Kate listened as he told her of his secret life, the mechanics and motives.

"Of course there was the money," he said. "Money becomes a funny thing when you're raised in an affluent household. Greater things are expected. When the poor succeed in the tiniest way, it's the result of heroics. Nothing heroic in being an heir."

He talked about his undistinguished high school career, the brief and bawdy life he led at Tulane, the ugly necessity of staying out of the army's reach, her brother's death, the comparative spectacle he made in his father's eyes as an unrepentant layabout.

Gilbert had a theory. The harder you worked, the harder you tried in life, the more you eventually had to lose. Wealth and high position were gained by the sweat of your brow, yet any day you could lose everything. Always this terrible knowledge. An ill-informed decision, bad weather, a turn in the futures market. He knew this feeling vicariously. He'd seen it in his father time and again. Uncle Charlie was a nervous man, a chronic worrier. Gilbert had decided while still in high school that he would never take life as seriously.

Then he was quiet.

"It's been a shoddy life, Kate. I'm thirty-two and tell people I play the piano for a living, that I'm an artist."

Another pause.

"I've always been a thief. For more than a decade, I've been a thief."

When she finished with the dressing, they crawled into bed, where Gilbert held her as they slept. A cool breeze blew through the balcony doors and over the cotton sheets. An hour before dawn, Kate awoke. She lay in bed, staring at the ceiling for a time. Eventually she turned to Gilbert and saw he was still asleep. She lifted his arm, which lay slung about her naked waist, waking him.

"Gilbert," she whispered.

He answered as though never having been asleep.

"Yes?"

"What else did you have to tell me?"

"Are you sure you're ready?"

"I think so. Pretty sure, I guess."

"You need to be sure."

"Okay. I'm sure."

"I have reason to believe we aren't related. At least not in any meaningful way."

"What do you mean?"

"It's hard to describe, but . . ." Kate waited patiently as Gilbert struggled for words. She lay quiet at his side in the darkness, her heart pounding in her ears with the anticipation of what she was about to learn. Then it came with a succinctness that she wasn't quite prepared for:

"Uncle Charlie fabricated our relations with your family."

"I still don't know what you mean."

"He made it all up, how my family's related to yours."

Kate felt her throat become dry.

"When I was five or six, he came up to Fayette on business for the first time, purely by chance. He brought me along on the trip because we were between nannies, so I know exactly what happened. He happened to see the sign for the law office as we drove by. The sign had the same name as our own, so he stopped. It was a long time ago, but I remember that he went inside while I waited in the car. And that was when he introduced himself to your father. Then he came back outside and we drove to the hotel where we were staying, out by the highway. The next day he let it slip that he was a Willoughby, a relation to Cecil and Addy. It didn't take long for him to come to like the instant respect it elicited. Suddenly people were all impressed. By pure chance, he'd come into this fantastic heritage, this colorful history that made his world a whole lot more bearable."

"Gilbert, you can't be serious," Kate breathed. "You can't be."

"I am absolutely serious." Gilbert shifted onto his side and faced her so that she could see him speak. He didn't want there to be any misunderstanding.

"Dad would go meet with farmers, try to sell them a combine, a tractor, a plow. But it was clear that the sale wasn't going to happen until they heard he was related to the Fayette Willoughbys. They'd be standing out on the edge of a rolling spread of bottomland and Uncle Charlie would be telling the farmer how a new eighty-thousand-dollar International Harvester could increase yields by thirty percent. Pay for itself in two years, make the man rich. The farmer wouldn't be buying the line until Uncle Charlie mentioned his relation to your family. If they didn't believe he was really a Willoughby, he'd show them his business card, and then *bam!* People were all impressed that a Willoughby had gone into farming. Suddenly Uncle Charlie wasn't some bullshitting salesman but a goddamn Willoughby, you know. So they'd head on down to the bank and take out some mammoth loan."

"Gilbert, I can't believe this. I still just can't . . . How does he know all about our family then? How does he know everything about us?"

"That's the part you might find a little creepy," Gilbert said, smiling vaguely with embarrassment. "He learned a lot of it from your dad. Also, there were the journals your family had left behind. Uncle Charlie'd milk people around town for the outrageous Willoughby legends. The stories aren't so hard to find because people love telling them. Uncle Charlie himself suggested that the house was haunted, and some people seemed to buy into the idea. In that flowery language of his, he'd tell people how the house was 'so rife with history that the chaos of the family's past lived within the walls.'"

"Stop right there," Kate said, feeling her breath suddenly leave her. "Uncle Charlie started that rumor?"

"Oh, I don't think he started it," Gilbert said. "It was probably already floating around town. I mean, that house is a haunted-looking thing. He just enhanced the rumor. He wanted the family's past to be not only historic but colorful. And there's nothing more colorful than a haunted house. If history is a set of lies agreed upon, then Uncle Charlie wanted the Willoughby house to be the most historic one in the county. He's a romantic son of a bitch. I think it's fair to say it became something of an obsession with him. Anymore, I think he truly believes he's part of the family. He's immersed himself in the stories so completely. And after all these years, they couldn't be more real to him. I believe them myself sometimes."

"Why?" Kate whispered. "Why would you want to believe something you know isn't true?"

"I think Uncle Charlie's a good man. But he came from nothing. You know how he says you aren't human if you don't have a story to tell? Well, he had no story. His father was a guard at a maximum-security penitentiary down in Texas, and his mother the daughter of some wheat farmer who had about twenty kids. His parents died when he was sixteen or seventeen, then he came to Missouri with a tiny bit of money and absolutely no past whatsoever. He hated that so much. Couldn't stand being another fella moving through the world. I know he took some odd jobs here and there. Then he started work at the farm implement dealership back when it was owned by a grumpy old man in Caruthersville who hated everyone he knew. When he died, he left it to Uncle Charlie. The business struggled for a while—nobody knew who Uncle Charlie was, and they didn't want to buy from somebody who wasn't, you know, one of their own, someone without a past. Sometime around then he met my mother. Not long after I was born, she died when her car stalled on some railroad tracks, and he had to hire a nanny to take care of me while he was away at work during the day. There was a whole string of nannies—every one of them left after a few weeks of being chased around the house. Uncle Charlie would be pawing at them night and day, and he couldn't pay them regularly. You have to remember, he was a young man. A young widower, all charged up, struggling to make ends meet. Then along comes a Mexican nanny, and then along comes Hap. His mom dies a few years later and is replaced by a young Haitian nanny. . . . So you see where I'm going with all this?"

Kate climbed out of bed and paced about the room. Her mind reeled. Gilbert lay in bed, naked to the waist, watching Kate move through the darkness, her mind struggling to sift through what she had just learned. Finally she stopped.

"So you and I are definitely not related," she said.

"We share the same last name. That's about it."

"Gilbert, why didn't you tell me this a long time ago? Why didn't you tell me this before we got married? Why didn't you say something?"

He sat up.

"What could I say? And why would I say it? There wasn't any reason to bring it up and every reason to just forget it. I knew what the truth was. And besides . . ."

The darkness between them fell silent.

"Kate, my whole life's been a lie. From the ground up. Where would I begin telling the truth? I'm not a pianist. I'm not even who my father says I am; my brother and sister aren't who I say they are. . . . Where would you have me start telling the truth, Kate?"

From the other side of the room she could see the glitter of tears forming in his eyes. She stood for a moment, then started across the floor.

"So how did he do it? How do you make yourself a part of another family?"

"You start by telling stories. And in some discreet way you merge yourself into them," Gilbert said. "You very carefully blend the fiction in with the fact. After he learned some of the family history—who parented which generation of Willoughbys—he drove up to the house and simply told your dad that he had just discovered they were cousins, that he was a great-great-grandson of a particular Thomas or Cecil Willoughby from way back when. I'm sure the names were vaguely familiar to your dad. And Uncle Charlie must have mentioned a few stories about ancestral duals with mother-of-pearl-handled pistols, death by consumption. He knew that Cecil was probably familiar with the tales as well. So what could your folks do about it? Deny it? Insist there was no way? Of course not. They accepted it as a happy fact."

"Only it was a lie," Kate said, holding his head.

"A myth, Uncle Charlie would say."

Kate felt something stirring in her. For a moment she thought she might fall down.

"He wanted to have a story to tell," Gilbert said. "Before he introduced himself to your parents and Adam as their long-lost cousin, he was just Charlie Willoughby. But after that he was *Uncle Charlie*."

"Is that true?" Kate asked. "That's when he started calling himself Uncle Charlie?"

Gilbert nodded. "Absolutely."

Kate could hear herself breathing. Standing there in the darkness, naked before Gilbert, she viewed him for the first time in her life as an utter stranger. She had no idea who Gilbert Willoughby really was. He stood and took her into his arms.

"I guess it's pretty strange," he said.

"I feel like everything's so screwed up." Kate wiped away a few little tears, he kissed her forehead, and together they crawled back into bed. The sky beyond the balcony began to brighten. As Kate lay beside Gilbert, her mind tumbled on and on. Finally something occurred to her that leavened any self-pity she felt.

"What about Hap and Isabelle?" she said.

"What do you mean?"

"Where do they tell people they came from?"

"They don't," was all Gilbert could say.

"It seems kind of cruel, doesn't it? They have no past."

"I wouldn't know," Gilbert said. "I really couldn't say."

Kate thought she couldn't say either. Slowly it occurred to her that Hap and Isabelle had been cheated. They had stories to tell; only their father didn't want them to be told.

The stars burned without warmth in the black sky. The next night Kate took a seat in Gilbert's chair, propped her feet against the balustrade, and watched the barges churn up and down the river. As she followed the ruby necklace of lights, she felt herself overcome as if by mild hypnosis—lights forever and ever, streaming into either horizon, toward the ends of the earth.

She could recall the pictures, the stories, and her own faded memories of her brother as a boy. The last, she knew, were authentic. In the afternoon Adam would come home from school, charging through the kitchen door with a baseball cap pulled over his brow, the red crescent of the bill concealing his green eyes. His hair was straight and Indian-black, which gave him even as a boy an air of gloomy preoccupation. A miniature portrait of her father. Adam barely got by in his classes, oblivious to his books, immersed in his own world of adolescent shadows and baseball. At thirteen he had a poetic fascination for the game. He loved how it progressed in bursts of action separated by stretches of calm and order. That's what he loved: the procedure, the progress of order conducted in the vacuum of play. Like his father, Adam needed an environment of quiet through his day. And like Cecil he tended to keep to himself—the only exception to his solitude being his mother, whom he embraced and kissed even in adolescence. When he grew into a young man, this behavior never really changed, except that he also took to his baby sister.

Yet a distance was always maintained between Adam and their father. When Cecil returned home from work, his son would watch his outline approach through the black night air from where he sat upon the front porch steps, sipping vodka. As Cecil neared, Adam tucked the tin flask into a pocket and greeted his father with nothing more than a casual nod. Cecil responded precisely in kind as he mounted the steps and stepped into the bright, warm indoors. After a late dinner, Cecil typically retired to his study with a glass of ice water in one hand and a cigarette in the other, not having spoken ten words throughout the meal. He was in his late forties then, his hair streaked with gray at the temples, his voice lower, suggestive of a man worn down by time. He appeared weary but distinguished, with crowsfeet laying siege to his scalp at the receding hairline.

On fall weekends Cecil and Adam shared time with each other

in the only activity that both loved. In a Ford station wagon, they drove down to the Mississippi floodplain with shotguns, pine duck decoys, and an old army-issue ammo box filled with twelve- and twenty-gauge shells. In the evening, they came home smelling of game and spent gunpowder, their wool and flannel coats smeared with bloody feathers and mud. They cleaned the fowl in the basement, sitting shoulder-to-shoulder on upturned buckets, then brought the plucked carcasses up to the kitchen, where Addy wrapped them in paper and lodged them deep in the ice-caked freezer. In this way they conducted their stoic relationship, never fighting and rarely even arguing. The coolness between them was more a product of innocent discomfort, like that of being in the company of someone whose manner and expression are too much like your own. A percussion and repercussion, a thunderclap and its echo, Cecil and Adam.

Cecil never knew of his son's fondness for alcohol and downers until the fall of Adam's junior year, when he found the flask and bottle in the boy's wool hunting jacket. One evening after dinner while Kate lay in her father's lap, Cecil called his son into his study to show him what he had found. He slipped Kate out of his lap, and asked her to go find her mother. Kate left the study and stepped out into the narrow hall, leaving the door ajar. She sat behind it with her arms wrapped around her knees, and listened as her father asked Adam to explain.

"They settle me down," he said, not with the tone of apology but that of unabashed ingenuousness. He could not have been more nonchalant had his father held up a ukulele and said, "Son, please explain."

"They can be dangerous," Cecil said in an equally benign tone. "Especially mixing the two."

"I'm careful."

"Where'd you get them?"

"Medicine cabinets, here and there."

"You stole them."

Defiant silence.

"Perhaps we could get a prescription. Dr. Lutz is a client. . . ."

"I get by fine."

"I don't like it, son."

And the conversation ended. Adam said he would be careful, then left the study, unaware of his sister crouching in the lee of the door.

Addy never understood why Cecil condoned Adam's drug use, but she later told Kate that he probably sympathized with his son's need to seek relief from the same obscure anxiety which he himself suffered. Though Cecil didn't drink, his friends and colleagues did. He held no taboos, and intellectually he saw no difference in the means of getting relief, apart from the legal issue of theft and the ethics of taking drugs prescribed to someone else.

So in the beginning there was a measure of understanding and empathy, a rapport that gradually eroded as the times got complicated: in the early spring of 1972 Adam announced at the dinner table his plans to quit school and work as an apprentice for a local contractor who built tract housing on the outskirts of town. School, he casually pointed out, wasn't his thing. He felt that in two years he could be a foreman, that there was nothing holding him back. "There *is* something that will hold you back," Cecil said, gravely weighing his words.

Adam didn't care to hear what that was, simply because he knew, and promptly left the table. From that night on, he generally kept to his room, where he listened to old doo-wop records, cleaned his shotguns, his deer rifle, or fooled with the sights. From the window of his room he watched his friends' cars round the square. The hindquarters of the chassis jacked up, the noses lowered, poised like house cats about to pounce on field mice. The cars were louder than anything else in town. From time to time, he took up the newspaper and read stories concerning the grim progress of the war, the accounts of Tet, My Lai, op-ed pieces, stories of campus protests, which only hardened his resolve not to attend college.

Each day bled into the next, never varying, never surprising, subdued by tranquilizers and Everclear, so that when his draft notice arrived early that summer, it brought with it a measure of anticipation, relief from the routine. Addy and Cecil were beside themselves. Addy quietly went hysterical, muttering in a pleading voice for Adam to leave for Canada, hide in the basement, anything, while Cecil merely brooded over his son's decision to participate in a dirty civil war twelve thousand miles away simply because he had nothing else to do. This was the product of adolescent fatalism. This was what he had wanted all along, Cecil thought, and now he was about to get it. A lottery designed for young men like his son.

Outwardly, Cecil wasn't concerned. The war was clearly winding down, and it wasn't World War II. Fewer than thirty thousand American combat troops remained in Vietnam, and for the last week there hadn't been a single American casualty—a first in nearly eight years. And Adam would be going there, technically, as a "military advisor" to the South Vietnamese army, as many of the American soldiers there at the time were called. Because the title sounded so ridiculous to Cecil, he shared it with Addy, thinking it might make her feel better. But it didn't. To her, Vietnam was still a war, and the boys who went there soldiers.

In July of 1972, Adam took a bus to St. Louis, then headed for Camp Lejeune, in North Carolina. There he became a Marine, while at home his mother would thoroughly go out of her mind with dread. The following month, Kate spent her mornings at kindergarten, while Addy withdrew to the bedroom, sitting in the heat and silence through the afternoon, her mind turning over scenarios of her son's return. She imagined seeing him for the first time under various circumstances—in different parts of the house, with various sensations of surprise. She kept her fingertips to her mouth, her small white teeth gnawing at the bloodied crescent-moons of the nails. When Cecil returned from the office late in the evening he found her upstairs, sitting in the unvarnished oak chair beside their bed, whispering to herself. She had done nothing all day. He knew there was no dinner getting cold in the kitchen because the house held no smell. In the dying August light, he quietly approached her hunched figure and placed a hand on her rounded shoulder. She lifted her face, her mind having been miles away. Eventually, Cecil would take her hand, and together they descended the stairs.

They spent each evening with this quiet tension underpinning everything that was said and done. Even Kate sensed the spirit of gloom. After every dinner, she followed her father into the den and climbed into his lap, clinging to his warmth and scent, while Addy slowly and carelessly washed the dishes.

Not for a full month did they receive a letter from Adam. The first was written while he was still stateside, followed by another month of silence. The second was sent from Vietnam and, like the first, was addressed to Addy. In his swooping boyish script, he told his mother of the heat, a new tattoo, the eeriness of the rich green landscapes he flew over by helicopter, the sense he got that in the end only the flora would prevail. Cecil carefully read each letter twice, as was his habit, then surrendered it to Addy, who read them again and again, carrying the collection about the house in the pocket of her apron. But as winter settled in, the letters all but stopped, with one of the last arriving between Christmas and New Year's. Again, Adam addressed the letter to his mother and wrote of matters other than what he was doing. The unmistakable strain of his daily routine weighed on the prose, or so Cecil claimed. He told Addy this, handing her the small blue envelope.

"He doesn't mention how scared he is," Cecil said, his brow pinched with worry, his voice perfunctory.

"Maybe he has nothing to be scared of," Addy said. She snatched the letter and tucked it into her apron pocket with the others, then returned to her work at the stove.

But Cecil was right. And he discovered he was right three weeks later when he found in the mailbox an envelope from the United States Marine Corps. When he opened it he saw the letter was printed on onion-skin paper, and he instantly knew what it was. So thin and smooth against his fingers. Beyond the door he could hear his wife in the kitchen, the sound of a pan floating in dishwater, bobbing against the porcelain walls of the sink. Cecil thought they delivered such letters in person, or that they were at least accompanied by a phone call. Then he thought that Addy might have already been paid a visit. But when he came inside, the stiff paper jutting from his hand, his forehead crimped in horrified wonder, she said, "What is it?" and he knew that she hadn't. Someone in the military had made a terrible mistake. Her eyes fell to the letter in his hand.

From then on, time would always be measured in Addy's mind relative to the moment she first set eyes on the letter in her husband's hand. Henceforth she would live in two worlds: the one in which Adam was alive, the other in which he was not. And one seemed to lie superimposed, or impaled, upon the other. She moved through her day lost in a maze of conflicting images and voices, her eyes fixed on stationary objects, a hand to her mouth, often holding her breath. It seemed that this was the result of some unconscious effort to slow, then stop, and ultimately reverse the flow of time. Kate came to understand that her mother could never fully divorce herself from this unconscious effort. That's what she would try to do for the rest of her life: wish herself back through time.

It was an obsession with the past—the immutable past, Uncle Charlie would say. Kate would see her mother standing before the window over the kitchen sink, gazing out at the trunk of a maple, her lungs fully inflated. Here was the by-product of that superstitious effort to suspend the malicious progress of time. The expression her face held was that of someone who was about to say something, as though she was about to say, Wait, this must be done again, and the world might halt upon its axis with these words, freeze the day, then return to the morning of November 28, 1972, the date of her son's death, and begin again.

twenty-one

Early one morning, Gilbert found Kate out on the balcony in her bathrobe. Her feet were still propped on the balustrade, her eyes on the horizon. Gilbert came up behind her and kissed an ear.

"You're awake early," she said as she slowly emerged from thought.

Gilbert stepped to the balustrade and began petting Kate's feet. "It's getting hard to sleep. I think I need to switch over to a new narcotic."

Kate studied his glassy eyes, his wobbly figure.

"Sweetheart, you're too high," she murmured. "You're too high for six in the morning."

"Not as high as I'm gonna be," Gilbert said. "What are you thinking about?"

Kate tried to redirect her train of thought. "Do you think any of those stories Uncle Charlie tells of the family are true?"

"They're true but for the parts where he introduces himself as a character."

"But he never does. None of the stories he tells are about himself."

"He likes revealing other people's secrets," Gilbert said, smiling too happily for Kate's mood. "Like most people, he doesn't care to have his own aired."

"And he likes being a part of a colorful past."

"He likes the idea of having a heritage," Gilbert said. Then the smile washed from his face. "He especially likes the idea of having a military tradition in the family. I think it's a Southern thing, Miss Kate."

"He talks about Adam as if he died fifty years ago. As if he was in World War II."

"Maybe it's because Adam's history runs too close to my own. I imagine that isn't something he wants brought up. He's fascinated by your past, humiliated by his own. When I didn't go to Vietnam, he probably saw it as hard evidence for . . ."

"For what?"

"For our family not measuring up to yours," he said, his voice slurred, his stoned face smiling, almost laughing. "Reality came rolling back, *hauling ass!*"

Gilbert stared down on Kate as she gazed out over the Mississippi river valley. Her brow crimped. Gilbert saw that she was about to cry. In his altered state of mind, he felt he could somehow read her thoughts.

"What happened to my dad and . . ." she began.

"Adam," Gilbert said.

". . . what happened to them ruined our family."

"I know."

"So how can that be fascinating? Don't you think there's something—I don't know—*perverse* about that kind of fascination?"

"Your husband couldn't say," Gilbert whispered. Then he knelt before Kate. "All your noseless husband can say is that he is sorry. That he is sorry for absolutely everything."

"I always hated that rumor about our house being haunted," Kate said.

She looked away from Gilbert, back out over the river valley. He kept talking, but she was no longer listening. She had had enough of this brooding and romanticism. She was through with it.

For a time, there was a vague serenity. Then it faded as the drugs abandoned the bloodstream. Mornings and evenings left un-buffered.

Surgeries were scheduled all through the summer, but by early August it seemed little had been accomplished. All that remained was the wound, which Dr. Laskow brutally reopened every few weeks without bringing about any visible improvement. The sum-mer itself seemed to be capriciously assaulted by this little man who spoke so cautiously of hope.

It was Kate who began to see the lack of progress most clearly. She was the one who dressed the wound each day and measured the improvement after each surgery on a mental yardstick influenced equally by optimism and despair. She observed each of her opinions from different angles, but gradually lost sight of the doctor's ulti-mate design. The wound began to fold in on itself, the sutures tug-ging at the lustrous skin, drawn down into the center of the face where they were anchored to a root cartilage. Beneath the rag-ged seam stood the two blunted nostrils like the twin muzzles of a double-barreled shotgun.

Gilbert didn't recognize the horror. Only the phantom sensa-tion of a complete face. Kate thought perhaps the drugs created the illusion. She observed the evolution of his mood from hopelessness to this weird confidence. After the second surgery she gave him the oval hand mirror when he asked for it, and as he raised the reflec-tive surface he saw for the first time in weeks the two bloody holes

at the center of his face, the diminished profile. Kate was momentarily terrified as he viewed himself. But she didn't need to be;
Gilbert saw nothing horrific. All he perceived was a lovely nose
budding within the circle of destruction.

At times Kate's mood ebbed into self-pity. One morning she
went to the liquor store, where she stood behind a young woman
and her boyfriend at the checkout counter. As they waited, they
talked about their college classes in the fall, the girl's major, the
boy's part-time job at an Italian restaurant in Rolla, Missouri. They
looked so happy and carefree as they stood there, a six-pack of beer
cradled in his arms. They looked so collegiate. Kate wondered
what Gilbert would say if she came back with a six-pack, the nervous confusion it would create. What's going on? Where's the
scotch? So little seemed at stake with this couple. The sun came
through the store's plate-glass window and fell on the girl's long,
auburn ponytail. They looked so healthy. Kate wondered whether
either of them was old enough to be buying beer. The three of
them were probably the same age.

As Kate stood in line she imagined how she would find Gilbert
when she returned to the room. A bloody bandage on the bathroom sink, his face a nub of gristle. He might be rifling through the
closet for another bottle of scotch, his voice senselessly carrying on
and on. She felt a rush of dread come over her. She wondered what
would happen if she simply didn't return to the room. Gilbert
would get along. He was an adult. What if she just followed this
couple to their dormitory in Rolla? Kate thought these thoughts as
she carried the bottles of scotch out to the truck and drove back to
the hotel. But when she came through the door she found Gilbert
sitting up in bed, sipping water, downing Demerol, reading *The Adventures of Huckleberry Finn,* smiling so wildly and boyishly, pleased
beyond all words that his young wife was home. She didn't say anything but merely returned the silly smile as she crawled across the
unmade bed and into his arms.

In the weeks that followed, Gilbert grew accustomed to the surgeries. Once he emerged from the anesthesia, he seemed remarkably sober, ready to rise from the hospital bed and head home. The doctor was amazed at his recuperative powers, while Kate secretly attributed them to his burgeoning tolerance for pain relievers. Anesthesia, she thought, couldn't be so different. When they returned from the third surgery, he spent the afternoon on the balcony, downing pills and talking constantly while Kate stood before the blender, churning strawberries, liquor, and ice into daiquiris. He was so ridiculously cheerful, mindlessly yammering away, his fresh wound packed with gauze, which was strapped to his face with athletic tape.

"Soon as I'm presentable, we'll move to St. Louis or Kansas City. I'll start up the piano again," he said as she brought out two large glasses on a metal tray. "I can play lounges, restaurants. Anywhere."

Kate handed him one of the massive glasses and took her seat beside him.

"Maybe in the fall."

Kate didn't know what to say. Then she saw that it didn't matter. Gilbert was lost in some dreamy world, the world of his father, where the past existed only as an apparition, void of all consequence. He was just so damn high.

From time to time, Kate thought everything would work out—that Gilbert's nose might regenerate like the severed appendage of a starfish, that he would one day find legitimate and gainful employment, that they might settle down together and just be. But eventually, usually late at night as she lay awake beside his stoned and sleeping head, her sense returned, her cool abject vision and the limits of rational hope came back in a rush. As the familiar pattern of stars burned between the parted doors across the room, the reality of their situation came to her with terrible clarity.

One night she went to the bathroom and looked at her face in the mirror. She wanted to see if she looked nineteen, if she looked as young as the girl in the checkout line. But in the glaring white light she appeared haggard, the lines on her face drawn by the ghosts of her mind. She went back to bed and lay awake for several hours, tight-chested with worry, overwhelmed by the certainty that the future held some unspeakable doom. A little later she got up again, stepped outside, and breathed the cold night air, then returned to bed thinking she had driven anxiety from her thoughts. But it crept back across the sheets, from where it dwelled deep within the sleeping mind beside her. As she lay in the uneasy darkness, she thought of how Gilbert and Uncle Charlie were reflections of each other. Both took things that did not belong to them.

A few days after the third surgery, Kate secretly drove to St. Louis by herself to talk with Laskow. She sat at his cluttered desk while he darted about the room looking for the charts to another case, the keys to his car, an old phone bill he needed for tax purposes. As he wandered, Kate asked simple and direct questions, such as, How much of Gilbert's nose could ever be brought back? How long would it take? How many surgical procedures would it require? But the doctor seemed unable or unwilling to answer. After half an hour, Kate simply left while the doctor stood over his desk, his mind lost upon the pool of paperwork under his small, hairy hands.

On the drive back to Clemente, Kate thought about Laskow's manner, slowly convincing herself that he did not in fact expect much progress and that this was a racket. Gilbert could endure any number of procedures and he would still have no nose—and what could someone like Gilbert, clearly a criminal, do about it? By the time she got back to the room, she had hopelessly convinced herself of this.

A few weeks later, the fourth surgery was undertaken. Again there seemed to be little or no improvement. When the doctor emerged from the OR and approached Kate in the hallway outside the broad swinging doors, he was smiling and optimistic as usual, full of some airy hope. Gilbert, he said, had come through the surgery fine, all had gone well. In no time, he would have a new face.

"How long's that?" Kate asked curtly.

"Soon," was all the doctor would say. Then he walked off.

Even if it would have taken years, Kate would later remember, she was prepared. She would have managed. Money wasn't a problem, and she still felt devotion to, if no longer love for, Gilbert.

Kate could mark the beginning of the end. It was the day Dr. Laskow urged Gilbert to go without his bandage so that the wound might heal more quickly. At night he should dress it for protection, but otherwise expose it to fresh air. Sunlight, the doctor said, quoting a surgeon general whose name escaped him, was the best antiseptic. Gilbert thought this strangely poignant. Before they left, Kate asked Laskow for another prescription of Demerol, but he would only agree to write one for half the usual amount. He rather sternly told Gilbert he was concerned about his growing habit. He didn't want to foster one problem while solving another. Kate saw how this made Gilbert momentarily anxious. But only momentarily. The doctor concluded the meeting with instructions for Gilbert to lay off the pills correspondingly, and in three or four days, once the wound was nicely closed, to remove the bandage and allow in the sun. Kate left the office utterly terrified. To Gilbert this all seemed so auspicious, the instructions a sign of progress. The drugs, he must have already concluded, were available from other sources.

A few days after the operation, Kate removed the bandage, and Gilbert began to drift through his limited world with his nose exposed. In the beginning he kept to the hotel room, every now and then glancing at his face in the hand mirror. Kate saw the full extent of her husband's delusion, how his perception was warped by something more than mere Demerol. When he saw his reflection he tenderly passed a cupped hand along his cheek, down to the chin, up the other cheek, as if in love with himself. For some reason, he was sure the nose was growing before his very eyes, as if it were a plant, a mushroom button after a warm summer rain. She watched him as he did this, his eyes narrowly focused on the center of the preposterous face.

When his Demerol ran out, the pain didn't return as Gilbert had predicted. Instead, he came down with full-blown flu, which aggravated his healing sinuses. For two days he lay in bed, sweating in the late-summer heat, his temperature hovering in a mild fever. Once the fever broke, he went out into the night and burglarized a pharmacy on the outskirts of town. Kate read about the incident in the local paper, and after a bit of looking around the room, found the vast collection of pills in a brown paper bag he had stowed in a compartment of the closet. She didn't say anything. Wasn't angry. Everything was coming to an end.

One afternoon Gilbert insisted they go out for dinner, and against Kate's better judgment, she agreed. This would be the first time they'd gone out together in public without covering the wound. As he dressed before the mirror in a button-down shirt and tie, Gilbert told Kate this would be his coming-out party. It was a kind of celebration, he said, carefully placing the bridge of a pair of dark sunglasses upon the truncated nose.

They walked the familiar path to the restaurant, passing strangers who tried their best to conceal their horror at the sight of Gilbert. Yet he seemed oblivious. Demerol and alcohol together made his head spin rather pleasantly, he said. Kate saw how necessary they were. But she sensed that Gilbert really did understand everything going on around him. His awareness was a secret he had been keeping to himself. This was a frightening thought. It was then, as they approached the little French restaurant where they had eaten lunch on the shaded porch many times before, that Kate felt the trepidation, the terrible inevitability of what was about to happen.

"Gilbert," she said confidentially as she tugged on his shirt-sleeve. "We shouldn't be doing this."

He turned to her, the smoked lenses of his sunglasses looking down from where they sat precariously upon the trunk of the half-nose. "Why?" he said. "I'm fine with it."

Kate couldn't speak to this face.

As they came up the short gray wooden stairs, the maitre d', in his immaculate white shirt, stared as if trying to attach a name to a vague acquaintance. Kate looked at Gilbert and saw him smiling serenely, full of understated confidence, certain everyone in this quaint riverside setting would look with approval on his ragged nose glistening with blood and peculiar clear mucus about the root of white bone in the center of the otherwise exquisite face. Then she turned to the maitre d' and saw the panicked blue eyes, the sense that an abomination had set foot in his restaurant. Kate's heart trilled. Her gaze flickered between the maitre d' and her husband. The maitre d' appeared to contemplate asking them to leave, then as pleasantly as he could he said, "Hello, Mr. Willoughby, Kate."

They were led between round tabletops, while all about them mouths hung ajar, aghast at the smiling face of destruction that floated by as they sat before their dinners. Kate followed Gilbert, her hand in his, her pretty flesh pink with hurt. In the next half hour, she chugged two glasses of Chardonnay, one right after the other, and picked at her food. All the while, heads turned, straining for a glimpse of this cheerful face of death.

"It's too early to be going out like this," Kate whispered, almost crying. She felt sick and drunk.

"We'll never see any of these people again," Gilbert said, smiling at anyone who might be staring at him.

He turned to Kate. She saw her reflection in the smoked lenses covering his eyes and felt a sudden and powerful wave of nausea race up her throat. It was a wave of heat, an actual change in the temperature of her body. He didn't love her, she thought. This wasn't how you treated someone you loved. She wanted to ask him again how old she was because she knew he wouldn't remember, and then she could point out how he loved only himself. She wanted to hold up a mirror to that horrible face. She sat there, feeling something inside herself harden. She could feel the future in the instant.

"Gilbert," she whispered. "You know that old man, Robert P. Lester?"

"Yeah," Gilbert said, still smiling behind the glasses.

Kate felt her face go warm. She paused to reconsider what she was about to say, and then she said it: "He died."

To Kate's astonishment, Gilbert kept smiling.

"When?" was all he said.

"A few days before we left for New Orleans."

Kate looked around to see that her voice was adequately hushed.

"I killed him," he said flatly.

"That's right. There was a story in the paper. You're wanted for his murder."

Kate watched Gilbert bring a cloth napkin to his mouth. He made a face, and she was certain he was about to vomit wine and salad. But he didn't. Once he had recovered, he started to eat again, his shaded eyes on his plate. But after taking another bite of food, he thrust his chair back and said to Kate, "You know, I'm really not at all hungry." Then he stood and left the restaurant.

Kate watched his figure pass behind the screen of lilac and trellised bougainvillea. Once she could stand, Kate went up to the maitre d' and calmly told him she would also be leaving now. She forced a smile and said, "Everything was fine." Then she unrolled a hundred-dollar bill, placed it under a water glass on their table, and walked from the porch toward the hotel.

The evening was cool, and lazy townspeople milled around her. All the while, the image of Gilbert's ragged face filled her mind as the streets bobbed in her vision, convulsing with each step. When she reached the hotel she ran up the stairs, stumbled into the room, and tore off her dress. Then she climbed into the shower. For most of the next hour, a stream of hot water was focused on her naked spine and gradually quelled her thoughts until she felt she could leave the watery sanctuary. She emerged from the bank of steam, pulled on her bathrobe, and saw at once that Gilbert had come and gone, as his sunglasses and a pile of small bills lay within the cone of yellow light cast by the lamp on the nightstand.

Instead of feeling any sort of dread or foreboding, she felt a kind of relief. She didn't care anymore, couldn't care anymore. When she looked at their situation, it was as though she were viewing it from a zeppelin. She had become invulnerable, incapable of being touched by what was going on around her. Unpleasantness was unnecessary, so avoidable. Gilbert was less the product of flawed genetics than of abysmal parenting. In Kate's mind, the two were inextricably tangled, yet Gilbert should have known. Uncle Charlie should have done better by his children, and Gilbert should have known. For most of the night, she lay awake, feeling more anger than dread, expecting any moment the slow click of Gilbert's boots on the wooden floor beyond the door. Then the day's first sunlight came streaming in through the glass doors, and she realized she would never again hear that sound.

twenty-two

For the next two days Kate kept to the room. She lay about with the windows open, listening to the brittle racket of a late-summer day, her mind relentlessly occupied with things that did not matter. She made no phone calls, rarely ventured beyond the domain of the bed. Every few hours she summoned room service, and every morning a pair of black maids carried away dirty dishes and cleaned the room. Then something finally happened.

She was lying on the short sofa, reading a mystery novel, when there was a knock at the door. She hollered for whoever it was to come in, and when they did, she lay looking down at the book where she had put it on the floor. She noticed the shoes, the gleaming seamless leather at the edge of her vision. But she could only lie there.

"Mrs. Willoughby?" a voice asked.

She wouldn't answer promptly. Then: "Kate Willoughby," she replied.

She was quietly escorted down the stairs, through the lobby, and out into the bright sunshine, toward a squad car. As they passed the hotel concierge, whom she had come to know during the past few months, he stared in amazement at the sight of this familiar young woman suddenly being taken away by two police officers.

She was driven south out of town to the county coroner's office, in Langford, Missouri. Kate sat behind the wire mesh that separated the front from the back of the car while the officer on the passenger's side told her about Gilbert.

"Some kids found him," he said. "He was tangled up in the branches of a fallen willow along the riverbank. . . ."

Kate closed her eyes. When she opened them again, she saw the green of the landscape rushing by.

"Your husband had a serious wound to the nose," the officer was saying. "It looks like it'd had some medical attention. But to be perfectly frank, Mrs. Willoughby, it seems kinda peculiar to us. We need to ask you about that. And we need to know what he was doing in the river in the first place."

Kate closed her eyes again. She slumped against the window and told herself she would try to rest. Eventually the voice ceased—whether she had fallen asleep or it had stopped of its own volition, she could not say. After a while, Kate heard traffic thickening all around her. The car paused at a few traffic lights, then the engine died.

"We're here, Mrs. Willoughby," the officer said.

When she stepped from the car she recognized Uncle Charlie's Suburban parked a few spaces away. The officers led her into a small gray-brick building, down a short hall to a small waiting room. The place smelled strange, Kate thought. Like her high school biology room. Once she was seated in a vinyl-upholstered chair, Uncle Charlie appeared in the doorway. His eyes were dry but very red. As he came up to her, he murmured, "Oh, Kate." Then he parted his hands and gathered her up in his long arms.

"Is he really gone, Uncle Charlie?" she said, tears coming for the first time.

"M'honey, I could hardly recognize him," he whimpered. "Somethin' happened to his face. Somethin' terrible."

Kate's feet gently touched down on the tiled floor, and she stood, still swaddled in Uncle Charlie's immense arms. After a short, vigorous cry, her tears began to fade, and as soon as they did, the two officers came into the waiting room. When Uncle Charlie noticed them, he separated Kate from himself and smiled at her.

"Kate, these two sheriff's deputies want to ask a few questions," he said warmly. "But if you feel you don't want to answer them right now, then you just don't."

"But Mrs. Willoughby," one of them interrupted. "It would help us out immeasurably if you would."

Kate said nothing. She gazed at the officer for a moment, then up at Uncle Charlie. He seemed somehow different, less imposing—almost vulnerable. In his eyes she could plainly see that Uncle Charlie would prefer that she kept quiet. She could see that he sensed the answers to these questions would only breed more ugly questions. So she turned to the pair of officers. "I don't think I can talk right now," she said. As the words left her mouth, Kate felt Uncle Charlie's giant hand upon her head, stroking her hair.

"But Mrs. Willoughby," the other officer said. "We should know what happened—if only for your husband's sake."

"Listen, boys," Uncle Charlie interrupted. "My little niece here has been through a lot."

"She's your niece?" the officer said, incredulous. "Your niece was married to your son?"

Kate shrugged. She looked up at Uncle Charlie as if she were asking the same question.

"You weren't biologically related to your husband, were you, ma'am?" the officer asked.

Uncle Charlie gazed down into Kate's eyes. "Gilbert probably told you, didn't he?"

Kate nodded.

"You must take me for some stupid ol' fool," he whispered, the tears welling in his eyes.

Kate gently shook her head.

"They weren't related, boys," Uncle Charlie said, looking down apologetically at Kate. "They weren't really related."

"Okay," the officer said impatiently. "So we got that cleared up. Now what about the nose, Mrs. Willoughby? What happened to your husband's nose?"

"Boys, boys, boys," Uncle Charlie said with angry impatience. "Is Jimmy Jenkins still sheriff of Langford County?"

"Yep," they answered in unison.

"Well, can I please use your phone and give him a call? We're a couple a ol' buddies, and for some reason I suddenly feel like saying hello."

The older officer shook his head and pointed toward the door, and then Uncle Charlie and the officers left the room. Kate waited in the murky silence, wondering exactly what Uncle Charlie was about to do. She asked herself how much she should tell the police. Maybe she should keep quiet until Uncle Charlie returned. Yes, that's what she would do, she told herself. She would let him do the talking. She was too tired, and she probably wasn't thinking straight. As she sat in the vinyl chair, her head resting against the wall, she felt herself suddenly twitching in a dream. She pulled her arms about herself for warmth and tried to return to that blissful realm, but then the door swung open and the three men came barreling in.

"Kate, we can head on home now," Uncle Charlie said, touching her on the shoulder. "You don't need to go in there and view him either," he said, his words meant for the cops. "It's my son, and that's all there is to it." He offered Kate a hand. Without another word, the younger officer nodded contemptuously as she and Uncle Charlie passed. Once they were alone out in the bright sunshine and walking toward Uncle Charlie's Suburban, Kate looped her hands around his thick elbow.

"What did you talk to the sheriff about?" she said.

"Told him how my son had just died," he said, petting her hand, his voice breaking as he spoke, "and how his boys weren't being very sensitive to our great loss."

"He's a friend of yours?"

"He is," he said, smiling. "He's an old friend who from time to time must run a very expensive campaign in order to keep his god-damn job."

"So they won't be asking any more questions?" Kate said.

"No they won't, m'honey."

They climbed into the Suburban, and headed south out of town, toward Caruthersville. Kate situated herself against the door and laid her head against the glass as they drove, a current of cool air pouring against her forehead and bare shins. Neither spoke much. As they eased along the riverside, Kate could see Uncle Charlie glancing over at the brown stream that had held his son a few days earlier. Then he began to cry silently. Kate turned to him every now and then, and seeing this, could forget herself for a time.

Half an hour later, they were at Uncle Charlie's. Isabelle was sitting in a wicker chair on the porch when the Suburban came wobbling up the long gravel drive. As it slowed to a stop, she rose and descended the wide brick steps. She and Kate came together on a corner of the lawn, holding each other while Uncle Charlie watched. Hap stood within the doorway, gazing from the narrow refuge of darkness at the sight of his wife and cousin. When Kate and Isabelle finally turned toward the house—Isabelle's eyes marred with red, Kate eerily composed—they saw him standing there with his hands sunk into his pockets, looking down at his boots. Everyone's grief, it seemed to Kate, was mixed with a trace of guilt. And it was a guilt that touched herself.

That night Kate sat with Hap, Isabelle, and Uncle Charlie at the dinner table. She wasn't hungry and didn't eat. Her eyes were drawn to the feathery grain submerged in gleaming lacquer. After dinner Isabelle showed her where they would be sleeping. It was a small building that had once been slave quarters. The cabin stood within a tangled thicket and looked out secretively at the immense plantation house at the crest of the horizon. As they sat on the cabin's stoop that night, drinking tea and wrapped in blankets, Isabelle shared with Kate her memories of this place as home.

"My bedroom was at that end," she said, pointing toward a glowing buttress of light a few feet away. "Hap would crawl through the window and we'd go swimming in the pond late at night."

They listened to the wind passing through the trees for a while. Isabelle looked over and saw the flatness of Kate's eyes. A moment later, Isabelle continued her narrative of memories. As her voice carried on and on in the darkness, Kate felt herself growing tired. She yawned and told Isabelle that it was time for her to turn in. Isabelle smiled and said good night.

Tired as she was, Kate couldn't recall falling asleep that night. She had no memory of dreams, no memory of awaking in a strange room. But as the window at the foot of the bed began to brighten, she found herself alert. She slipped out of bed and stepped out onto the porch to watch the morning break. While Isabelle slept, she witnessed the sky above the house fade from velvety black to purple violet. The birds were noisy in the surrounding pines as the sun rose, then they suddenly hushed, as if foretelling a storm.

Later that day, the family prepared for the wake. They gathered in the living room of the house, and drove in a solemn caravan of a truck and the Suburban for the Presbyterian church in town. More people came than Kate expected. Somehow, she'd always imagined the life Gilbert led before he moved to Fayette as existing in a vacuum, divorced from the world at large. But at the church, people streamed endlessly before them, their faces swollen with sorrow as they greeted each member of the family.

That evening, Uncle Charlie made proud references to the size of the crowd at the visitation. Kate, Hap, and Isabelle could see that such talk was meant to stifle any expression of grief on Uncle Charlie's part. The following morning, the family dressed again, this time for the funeral. After a brief ceremony at the church, the parade of cars commenced toward the grave site. In the late summer heat, Gilbert's body was lowered into the earth. Kate watched on, her tears thickening as the ratchet clicked and the wooden coffin descended lower and lower until it was gone. Slowly, in tiny increments marked by the metallic clicking of the mechanism, it occurred to her that he was gone. Gilbert was dead, and now he was buried.

The family drove back home and spent a quiet afternoon within the splendor of Uncle Charlie's estate. In the early evening, as the family sat out on the front porch between the thick stone columns, sipping beer, the headlights of a truck came bobbing up the drive. Kate stood abruptly, her eyes on the shifting beams of light. Everyone watched her as she rose. She kept her fingers to her mouth, as though catching her breath. The engine died, and an anonymous voice addressed everyone on the porch. For a moment, the recent past flickered with doubt. Perhaps it was all a dream. A resurrection . . . Then the figure drifted into the gauzy light, and Kate saw that it was a stranger, an employee of Uncle Charlie's who'd been sent to retrieve Gilbert's truck from the hotel parking lot in Clemente.

"The keys are under the driver's seat, Uncle Charlie," the man announced before turning and fading into the darkness.

"Thanks, Edward," Uncle Charlie said.

Kate lay awake that night, listening to Isabelle's rhythmic breath and thinking. Her mind wouldn't still itself but kept tumbling on and on, deep into the morning. Finally she arose and packed a few things into a brown paper grocery sack, and carried them out to Gilbert's truck. Without really knowing what she was doing, or why she was doing it, she stashed the bag in the passenger's seat, climbed in, and turned the engine over. She wanted to go home. She didn't know why, but she wanted to get away from Uncle Charlie.

She drove north, reaching Clemente in an hour or so, then she kept driving north, a warm wind pouring through the lowered window, the lights of the Mississippi river valley all around her. Stopping only for gas and something sugary to eat, she kept driving, watching the landscape wheeze by, seeing how the towns thickened as she pushed on. Then the highway descended for an impossible distance, until she thought the earth had no bottom to it.

The gaunt ruin teetered against the town. The mailbox was clogged with envelopes. Everywhere lay newspapers, familiar little gray batons. Kate entered the kitchen, made coffee for no one, then sat at the kitchen table and listened to the labor of the percolator. The air hung still and sour, the mellow ripeness of a condemned house. Late in the morning she walked out to the pool and spread herself on a chaise lounge. Dried maple leaves rattled as they were thrust over the surface of flagstone. She slept for a while, the sun warming her. The phone rang. Her eyes opened as it prattled on and on, then she fell asleep again.

When the noon whistle carried over town, Kate walked back into the kitchen. A sharp hunger bit at her side. She went to the cupboard, opened a can of tomato soup, and heated it on the stovetop. She stood before the star-shaped iron grates, hypnotized by the steady blue jets, the pale flames curling around the pot's copper bottom. Suddenly the red soup was fizzing over the brim and spilling onto the stovetop. She turned off the gas and ladled some soup into a bowl, then sat at the table and watched the wind push at the trees. The soup felt hot and tart in her stomach. Once she had finished, she set the dish in the sink and went outside by the pool and slept some more. She lay there until the sun was down and the evening air cooled. She then came inside, the house standing around her still and empty.

Late in the night, a rainless wind picked up. Brittle tree branches snapped and blew against the sunporch, shattering the pretty grid of French windows. The dust on the surfaces of the room shifted, fogging the air. Kate didn't know what to do, so she did nothing. Just sat on the sofa and watched the dust stir all around her. As she sat, elbows cupped in her hands, storm sirens wailed over the town. A few minutes after they started, they ceased.

Eventually she lay down. She seemed to lie awake for only an instant before being overcome by a severe fatigue. In her dreams, the lights throughout the house flickered as though conscious. Then softly, hardly audible at first, Uncle Charlie's voice came to bear, telling her of his faith in primogeniture, his belief that history lends coherence to the chaos of experience, that past forms present, that past implies the future, that hauntedness is merely history in the process of consuming itself.

Not until deep in the morning did she emerge from the uneasy sleep. She slowly sat up and gazed about her dank surroundings and tried to recall how she came to be at home. But her memory was vague. Her legs felt weak when she tried to stand. She needed to eat something, she told herself, but she didn't have the energy go to the kitchen. Only to lie down and rest, to sleep. Time passed un-noticed. The phone rang. Kate thrust herself to her feet, staggered to the kitchen, and picked it up. It was Isabelle, telling her how worried they were, how they figured she was in Fayette, and was she all right.

Kate's voice was weary and calm. "Sorry I left without saying anything," she said. "But I need to be by myself for a little while."

"Are you sure you're going to be okay, Kate?" Isabelle asked. Kate could hear Uncle Charlie's whining voice in the background asking the same question.

"I'm fine. I really am. I just need to rest and be alone. Can I call you back, Isabelle? I'm really tired right now."

Isabelle made Kate promise again that she was fine, that she was only tired. Once Kate had reassured her of this, she was allowed to hang up. Kate went to the cupboard. She opened and ate a can of peaches, and soon her energy returned as the sugars of the syrup and fruit crept into her bloodstream. She decided to take advantage of this new vitality by calling the grocery store and ordering a few dozen things for stew and bread, and spent the rest of the day in the kitchen. In the evening she slept while smells ebbed and flowed from the kitchen. The house was still and quiet. When she awoke, she walked into the kitchen, where loaves of bread lay in neat rows, rising on a bed of sifted flour. A pot simmered on the stovetop. That night she dusted the house, vacuumed, then sat down at the kitchen table and ate a bowl of her own stew. When she went to bed she immediately slipped into a deep sleep and didn't wake up until long after her room had brightened.

The first thing she did was drive her mother's car out to the Penny Farm to pick up her dog. When she arrived, the lady was wearing the same overalls, and in fact looked precisely as she had the last time Kate saw her. As Kate got out of the car, Bedford came galloping out of the barn and into her arms. "He was fine," the lady said. "No trouble at all. And this time I ain't taking none of your money, young lady." But Kate insisted. She rolled up the cash left over from her time in Clemente and tucked it into the lady's bibs as she had done before. Then she loaded Bedford into the car, thanked the woman, leaving her standing there, dumbfounded, counting eleven or twelve hundred-dollar bills.

For the next three days she stayed at home, apart from one foray downtown for cleaning supplies. She baked and cleaned and had a lawn boy come over and cut the impossibly long grass. With a rake and pruning shears she prepared the tea and shrub roses for winter. As the days passed, she began to feel more settled. She felt like being alone; she felt healthy. Then, one warm autumn day after the house and yard had been tended to, she went out to the pool with Bedford and lay in a chaise lounge to read. She had been reading for an hour or so when she heard a car pull up to the house and a small group of voices approach. She didn't want it to be Uncle Charlie and his children. But when she got up to see who it was, she couldn't quite believe her eyes. There at the front door was Martha Duncan—at least Kate thought it was her old friend—along with three girls Kate didn't recognize. All were very made up, all were smoking long, thin cigarettes. A blond, a redhead, a brunette—all with the same hairstyle. Martha herself looked emaciated.

"Martha?" Kate said from the corner of the house. "Is that you?"

Martha scurried down the steps, the ash of her cigarette breaking away and scattering over the lawn as she ran.

"Oh, *Kate!*" she screamed. "I can't believe you're here!" She ran right up and took Kate in her skinny arms, and then very carefully kissed her cheek so as not to mar her own makeup.

"What are you doing in town?" Kate asked excitedly, invigorated by her friend's giddiness. "Aren't you supposed to be at school?"

"These, Kate, are my friends," Martha said, gesturing toward the three young girls smoking on the porch.

The girls stared through slitted eyes and smiled disingenuously. Then, one by one, each drew on her filtered cigarette. They exhaled, expelling thin streams of smoke at every angle. Kate raised a hand. "Hi," she said.

"They're in my calc class," Martha said. "A lotta people have trouble with it if they didn't take very much math in high school. So I'm sorta their tutor."

"Didn't school start a few weeks ago?" Kate asked.

"Yeah, but I wanted to show everybody my hometown," she explained. "Later in the semester they get too busy."

Kate smiled. "Martha, you look so, well, slim."

"I've been dieting," Martha said, her voice deeper and gruffer.

"You look hungry. I've been cooking——"

"We aren't hungry," Martha said abruptly. "I wanted these guys to see the house. Can I show them around?"

"Well, sure," Kate said, surprised. "It's a little musty, but sure."

Martha took Kate by the wrist and led her up the steps to where her schoolmates stood on the front porch, wearing petulant expressions. None of them spoke when Martha introduced everyone. Kate walked by them and opened the front door. As Martha's friends entered, their large, painted eyes swept the high ceiling, the broad arc of the hanging staircase, the piano. Their dull expressions momentarily gave way to curiosity as they looked about this house so unlike any they had ever seen. One of Martha's friends turned to Kate, and as if speaking for the three of them, said, "You live here?"

"Well, yeah," she said, not knowing whether to be proud or ashamed.

The girl looked down at her hand. "With your husband?"

Kate quickly covered her wedding band with her right hand. She saw the ash from Martha's regenerated cigarette fall to the floor. Suddenly Martha was holding Kate's hand up to her own eyes.

"Oh my god . . . Kate. You're *married?* I do *not* believe what I'm seeing. I do *not* believe this." Then her eyes shifted from Kate's hand to her face. Martha saw Kate's blush and instantly knew it was legitimate. *"You're married."*

"Not anymore," Kate said.

"You're divorced?" one of the girls asked.

"No, not really." It hadn't occurred to Kate what her marital status was. She told herself for the first time that she was probably a widow. Yes, that's what she would be. She was a widow. In the midst of this awkwardness, she decided that she should simply tell the girls and then prod them along to another subject. So she smiled and said, "I'm a widow."

Martha's friends brought their cigarettes to their mouths and drew on them simultaneously. Kate could see that they clearly did not know what to think.

"She's pulling our chain," the blond said.

"I don't know," the redhead answered. Martha stared into Kate's eyes, utterly bewildered herself.

"Let me show you the rest of the house," Kate finally said. And with that she led them through the broad oak doors and into the dining room, where the table gleamed beneath the candelabra. Martha shrugged, trying to assimilate what had just taken place. Then she attempted to assume the role of museum curator, moving around the table as if it were her own. As she led the girls, she explained that this was where she and Kate had done their homework together as children. She told them of the dinners she had had with Kate and her mother, how it had been just the three of them in this terrifically long room, how Kate's mother would tell them stories about her family while they ate. Kate could see that Martha was actually proud of their shared past. Eventually, they made something of a circle and came back to the front door, where the tour had started. Martha announced in a hushed voice, "Well, that's the house." She looked at Kate. "This is where we grew up," she said.

Kate's eyes moistened as she stared at Martha's drawn face. "When are you going back to New Hampshire?" she asked.

"The day after tomorrow," Martha said.

"Martha's got to be there for sure on Wednesday," the blond announced. "She's taking the mid-term for us, so she better be."

Martha smiled wanly. "I'm sort of their tutor," she repeated.

"You're sorta our test-taker," the blond said, and the three girls began giggling. Martha just stood with her extinguished cigarette pinched between her bony fingers.

Kate felt the sudden urge to slap each girl. But even in the face of this humiliation, she could see why Martha would want to have herself counted among them. Kate believed that she too would want to know what they were like, how they had been brought up. Perhaps they could teach her something about being nineteen years old. Yet she felt the enormously incongruous desires of wanting to be a part of their group and wanting to slap each of them silly. Finally Martha opened the door. A faint breeze spilled in and whirled the cigarette smoke as the five of them stepped out onto the front porch.

"We need to catch up," Kate said, closing the broad oak doors behind her.

Martha turned as she descended the steps. "Maybe I'll come by tomorrow," she said.

Kate shifted her posture and leaned against a pillar.

"So what are you doing now?" Martha asked, licking her glossy lips.

"I really have no idea," Kate said.

"Ever think about going to school?"

Kate looked at her feet. I could, she thought; but she only shrugged in answer.

The three girls quickly grew bored as Martha and Kate spoke. Soon they turned and walked down the sidewalk toward Martha's car. They mouthed good-bye and waved to Kate with the shells of their tiny hands but made no sound. A moment later they were climbing into the car, their doors slamming shut. Martha turned as if actually afraid that they might drive off without her.

"Kate, I'll come by tomorrow," she said quickly and began walking backward. "I'll definitely see you, okay?"

"I'll be here," Kate said. She watched Martha hop into the car with her friends and vanish into the town.

Once they were gone, she walked behind the house to the pool. She spread herself over a chaise lounge and picked up her book. But she couldn't read.

I have a bankful of money, she thought. I can do whatever I want. She looked at the pool. The shrunken water stood black and green, thick with chlorophyll. She could smell the decay of algae. In her mind, the pool matched the house; both appeared to have been formed by the earth itself. The grass had grown ragged around the house again, the shrubbery stood over the windows. The poppies were withered, the terra cotta pots split and leaking soil and fuzzy pale roots. The dark green moss had taken to the fissures in the limestone with a fury. The place seemed to be on the verge of being reclaimed by the very thing that had created it.

Start over, she thought, mentally waving her hand at the house, as if it represented the whole of her recent and ancient pasts, as if the two were one and the same.

Kate looked up at the house again. The green copper roof sagged against the skyline. The guttering hung limp, choked with leaves and branches of hemlock. The wretched pool.

This isn't the home of a nineteen-year-old girl, she told herself. It's a museum. A museum inhabited by an orphan and a widow. But she would be neither, and so she would simply say good-bye to it all. As she lay there, the cool air washing over her face, her mind began to wander with fantastic ease, like a child's, borne on a flying carpet. Begin again, she told herself. Within seconds she was miles and miles away.

Dwight Williams was raised in Princeton, Illinois, and now lives in Steamboat Springs, Colorado, with his wife, Jennifer. He graduated from the University of Colorado at Boulder. Williams is a coauthor, with Dr. Robert Pensack, of *Raising Lazarus,* and with Dr. Edgar Mitchell, *The Way of the Explorer.*